Also by Patrick Dennis

3-D

Paradise

How Firm a Foundation

Tony

The Joyous Season

First Lady
by Martha Dinwiddie Butterfield,
as told to Patrick Dennis

Genius

Around the World with Auntie Mame

The Pink Hotel
by Dorothy Erskine
and Patrick Dennis

Guestward Ho!
by Barbara C. Hooton,
as indiscreetly confided to Patrick Dennis

Auntie Mame

As Virginia Rowans

House Party

Oh, What a Wonderful Wedding!

The Loving Couple

Love and Mrs. Sargent

Little Me

The Intimate Memoirs of That Great Star
of Stage, Screen and Television

BELLE POITRINE

as told to

PATRICK DENNIS

Little Me

With Photographs and a New Preface by

CRIS ALEXANDER

and a Foreword by

CHARLES BUSCH

BROADWAY BOOKS
NEW YORK

To

Agnes, Arlene, Bette, Billie, Billie, Brigitte, Cobina, Cornelia, Diana, Diana, Elsie, Ethel, Ethel, Ethel, Eva, Fanny, Frances, Gertrude, Gertrude, Grace, Gracie, Gladys, Gypsy, Hedda, Helen, Ilka, Ingrid, Irene, Jeanette, Joan, June, Kate, Katherine, Laurette, Lillian, Loretta, Louella, Mae, Marilyn, Marlene, Mary, Mary, Mary, Natasha, Norma, Olivia, Osa, Pauline, Pearl, Ruth, Ruth, Sheilah, Shirley, Sophie, Tallulah, Wendy, Yvonne, Zsa Zsa and those whose life stories will follow

Little Me was originally published in 1961 by E. P. Dutton and Company, Inc.

Broadway Books titles may be purchased for business or promotional use or for special sales. For information, please write to: Special Markets Department, Random House, Inc., 1540 Broadway, New York, NY 10036.

BROADWAY BOOKS and its logo, a letter B bisected on the diagonal, are trademarks of Broadway Books, a division of Random House, Inc.

Visit our website at www.broadwaybooks.com

First Broadway Books edition published 2002

Book design by Ralph L. Fowler
Photographs by Cris Alexander
Photos printed by Steven Kafcsak/Diane Sasaki

Cataloging-in-Publication Data is on file at the Library of Congress.

ISBN 0-7679-1347-7

CONTENTS

WHAT IS THIS? A book filled with old photographs? Who is this blonde lady on the cover? Is it one of the Gabors? Belle Poitrine? Who is that? Could this possibly be the autobiography of a movie star that I somehow never heard of?

These are some of the questions that many of us pondered when we first laid eyes on *Little Me*, Patrick Dennis's brilliant literary parody of self-reverential celebrity autobiographies. I stumbled across this sacred volume during my childhood in the early sixties. One day, like a magic talisman, it appeared on the nightstand in my parents' bedroom. It came into my life around the same time that my father brought home the recordings of Lenny Bruce and Vaughan Meader's parody album of the Kennedys, *The First Family*. It was during this period that I also discovered, to my eternal fascination, that the twitchy but strangely beautiful lady singing and wrestling with the microphone cord on television was actually Dorothy grown up.

All of the artists above set a deliciously perverse tone during the early sixties, a worldly sophistication and wit that were an enemy to sham but self-mocking as well. Perhaps as a reaction to the irreverent glamour of the new presidency, anarchic comedy found its commercial voice. Among the forms of humor that flourished was that queer, bastard child known as "camp." Volumes have been written analyzing this cultural phenomenon. Purveyor that I am of this frequently abused and misunderstood form of artistic expression,

I'd present *Little Me* in court as exhibit A. It defines camp at its most delirious and finely tuned.

If Patrick Dennis's best-known novel, *Auntie Mame*, had provided Eisenhower America with a crash course in camp humor, then *Little Me* was its master's degree. To my way of thinking, camp is both a celebration and a satiric comment on the mad excesses of popular culture, particularly those involving feminine images. And with that last sentence, I've already betrayed one of camp's chief dictums: Any statement that smacks of pretension must immediately be followed by a cheap laugh, preferably at one's own expense. Much camp humor derives from the dropping of a mask, the revelation that what was thought to be grand is, underneath, really rather lowdown and dirty. The literary voice of *Little Me*, Belle Poitrine, is always that of a great lady. But reading between the lines and scanning the photographs illustrating her memoir, we see that she's still Belle Schlumpfert at heart, a denizen of Drifters' Row. Like Auntie Mame, who escaped from Buffalo to be the belle of avant-garde New York, this Belle also continually reinvents herself as she climbs the ladder of success wrong by wrong. However, Belle Poitrine is the anti–Auntie Mame. She is not above the most unscrupulous of methods of achieving her goals—murder among them. She may share Mame's "Live! Live! Live!" philosophy, but adds to it "and be damn sure nobody gets in your way."

Little Me is a Chinese box of reinvention and disguise. Even its author's identity is a complex one. This is the autobiography of a fictional star as told to Patrick Dennis, who also never existed—he was himself the *nom de plume* of Edward Everett Tanner III. "Pat," as Tanner was known to his friends, was the author of sixteen books, many of them bestsellers. Some of them were published under yet another *nom de plume*, that of Virginia Rowans. Rabid Patrick Dennis fans can debate till the next millennium which of his books was his masterpiece. For some it's *Genius*, for others it's *The Joyous Season*. For little me it's *Little Me*.

This faux memoir of a deluded but determinedly optimistic grade-Z movie star is a forerunner of the "mockumentary" that is more and more becoming a staple of American film comedy. *This Is Spinal Tap* and the films of Christopher Guest such as *Waiting for Guffman* and *Best in Show* owe much of their deadpan and meticulously accurate tone to this seminal work by Patrick Dennis and his brilliant collaborator, the photographer Cris Alexander. *Little Me* can be enjoyed as an outrageous comic novel but also as a history of Broadway and Hollywood through the first half of the twentieth century.

Patrick Dennis and Cris Alexander never falter in creating the illusion that Belle Poitrine is a real person in a very real world. This is one of the few works of fiction that would satisfy the nitpickings of the most finicky theater and film historians. The line between fact and fiction is so deftly blurred in *Little Me* that it's easy to think of the characters as real show-biz figures. Belle Poitrine and Jeri Archer, the remarkable actress/model who plays her in the book, are forever one.

It's been my privilege to get to know a number of the friends of Patrick Dennis who posed for the photographs in the book. I met my first *Little Me* alumnus about fifteen years ago. I was attending a very grand transvestite ball at the Waldorf-Astoria, "Night of a Thousand Gowns," and, leaning across the bar in a spectacular white crepe Adrian knock-off originally created for Katharine Hepburn, I began chatting with a handsome, white-haired gentleman named Kurt Bieber. Having a bit of Belle Poitrine's delusions of grandeur myself, I sought to impress Mr. Bieber with my status as a self-described drag legend. Rather shyly, he confessed that he had once been something of a cult figure himself. As soon as he mentioned the novel *Little Me*, I recognized him at once. I was conversing with the one and only Mr. Letch Feeley, Belle Poitrine's leading man in such fictional movieland epics as *Papaya Paradise*, *Tarzan's Other Wife*, and *Nights on the Nile*! I was as speechless as if I had bumped into George Brent or Cesar Romero.

Years later, my partner Eric Myers wrote a biography of Patrick Dennis entitled *Uncle Mame*. During the two years that he worked on the book, Eric and I got to know so many members of Patrick Dennis's circle. His late wife, the scintillating Louise Tanner, who was photographed in *Little Me* as Pixie Portnoy, and his two children, Michael and Betsy, all became friends. We've dined at the home of adorable Elaine Adam, the model for Belle's arch-rival Magdalena Montezuma, and have enjoyed the divine compay of nonagenarian Hervey Jolin, who played, among other rôles, Mrs. Palmer Potter. No book on Patrick Dennis could have been written without the participation of his dear friends Shaun O'Brien and Cris Alexander. Shaun, the great character dancer of the New York City Ballet, was the stunningly handsome Mr. George Musgrove. Cris not only took the photographs for *Little Me* but played Belle's first husband, Fred Poitrine, and the Dowager Countess of Baughdie. (In Groucho Marx nose and glasses, he was also the Elated Nurse who announces the birth of Belle's child.) When Eric and I spent the night at Cris and Shaun's beautiful, eccentric Victorian home in Saratoga Springs, they put us in the

Russian-themed "Prince Yussupov Room." Fans of this book will understand our heart-stopping thrill at sleeping in the very bed shared by Belle Poitrine and her third husband, Morris Buchsbaum.

Flipping through the pages of this book, I always imagined that the making of it must have been so much fun. Apparently it was indeed a hoot. For all of us, *Little Me* is a bit like looking through a scrapbook of photographs of the greatest house party of all time. One of the major achievements of this madcap tome is that it doesn't make us feel excluded—instead, we're deliciously in on the joke. For far too long, we fans of Belle Poitrine have had to nervously lend our precious copies of her memoirs to our closest friends with the most severe warnings to return them unharmed. How divine that this new edition is now available to be given as gifts to those we love—and to corrupt a new generation of children who will stumble across *Little Me* on their parents' bookshelves. As Belle herself would exclaim, "Youth will be served!"

HOW DID ALL THIS COME ABOUT? Welllllllll, better go back to 1954.... If, as an actor, I hadn't been in *Wonderful Town* at the Winter Garden Theatre with the even more wonderful Rosalind Russell, I wouldn't have been in *Auntie Mame* (the 1956 play based on the 1955 novel) and most probably would never have met up with Patrick Dennis—outside of hardcovers.

My first vision of this bearded dandy was at the read-through of *Auntie Mame* on the bare stage of the Broadhurst Theatre where he appeared, uninvited, to the dismay of the entire cast, the producers (Fryer and Carr), the playwright/adapters (Lawrence and Lee), and especially Miss Russell. He had come to give us his blessing, after which he just disappeared, "brolly" furled, as suddenly as Mary Poppins—but out the stage door, not straight up into the wings.

It wasn't until he took to materializing at the Philadelphia tryouts that I began to know and marvel at this amazingly sensitive and kind man. We would gravitate to the same bar after performances and soon found that we shared enthusiasms for many more things than vodka. So by the time his fabulous Auntie hit Broadway, we'd gotten to know each other pretty well and he had also become interested in my being a professional photographer, which he thought very sensible. When I boasted that I had shot a number of no-slouch authors such as Christopher Isherwood, William Styron, and Georges

Simenon, he was relieved that I didn't just snap animals or weddings. It wasn't long after the gala opening of *Auntie Mame* that he began popping in at my Fifty-seventh Street studio.

Whereas my studio walls were formally adorned with such clangers as Vivien Leigh, Ethel Merman, Judy Holliday, Gloria Vanderbilt, Martha Graham, Lenny Bernstein, etc., the powder room was hung helter-skelter with various greeting cards, stills from semiridiculous 8mm movies I had made, and altered Hollywood stills (my favorite was a dreamy close-up of Garbo in the embrace of not John Gilbert but Marlene Dietrich). There were a few cut-outs from magazines too irresistible not to include, such as Wanda Landowska tenderly stroking a crocodile on her lap, or Mary, the world's fattest mouse. Sitters often took a long time washing their hands.

So, back to the question: How did all this come about? Ah, Patrick's first visit to my studio turned out to be the trigger. The master had insightful observations on all the famous faces—except Gladys Cooper, about which he said, "What a beautiful picture of Danny Kaye!" It took a beat for my leg to realize it was being pulled. Spotting a likely door, he shyly asked, "Is that it?" This was my first indicaton that this unusual person ever urinated. Even before the flush I could hear him chuckling. The door flew open. "Get in here and explain all this, if you can!"

One photo had particularly tickled him: Grand old Queen Mary strolling proudly out of Whitehall accompanied by two dowdy duchesses and being ogled by a pair of Liverpool librarians.

"Oh, that was a Christmas card. The message inside was 'Greetings, You Buggers!'"

"Hmm, I see." Patrick lowered the toilet lid, sat down, crossed his legs, and bade me make myself comfortable on the wash basin. "A notion has been rolling round up here about an autobiography . . ."

"Why ever not?" I ventured. "You're famous enough already and . . ."

"An autobiography of this famous movie actress—not like Bette or Katie or Pola—but a really rotten one, on screen and off. And now I'm beginning to see it!"

So it *could* be said that *Little Me*'s conception took place in my studio loo!

Well, a merry three years rolled by before that notion resurfaced. Five novels had been published: *Guestward Ho!*, *The Loving Couple*, *The Pink Hotel*, *Around the World with Auntie Mame*, and *Love and Mrs. Sargent*. During

From left to right, Carl Reynolds, Herbey Jolin, Mrs. Geo. Windsor, Shaun O'Brien, and Yours Truly. Circa 1952. We had all been in London together that summer. One of these Christmas cards got passed along by an English friend of ours to Ernest Thesiger (Dr. Pretorious in "The Bride of Frankenstein") who was a long-time tatting companion and gossip monger to the Queen Mother. Unlike Victoria Regina, she was much amused and acquisitively propped it upon her wig stand. That document may still be in the Royal Archives.

those years a lasting friendship developed. He also met and admired my mate, Shaun O'Brien, who was then on his way to becoming a highlight of the New York City Ballet. I met and adored his equally witty wife, Louise, a successful author in her own right. And *they* soon became super simpatico.

When it came to light that I was a painter as well as a photographer, they put me to all sorts of projects. Portrait of her, portrait of him. Murals in the baroque dining room of their posh Ninety-first Street townhouse. On such occasions I got referred to as "Fra Lippo Lipschitz." I especially relished doing a study of their two young children sheltered under an umbrella with their formidable and funny governess and "general everything," Corry Salley.

Michael and Betsy were the only children I have ever been crazy about. I have been accused of pedaphobia, but they were the exception. The first time I met Michael he was standing at the top of the two-story flight of stairs in their apartment. Forty years ago it was my habit to zoom up two stairs at a time. As Pat introduced us, Michael extended a hand and said in one breath:

"My, Mr. Alexander, you came up those stairs with the speed of light. I understand you don't like children." He was all of four years old at the time.

We were all enjoying those rarefied times in Manhattan, and somehow the idea of writing the confessions of a movie star was rekindled. Patrick may have chanced upon one of the many Hollywood memoirs that proliferated in the late fifties, but whatever the reason, we were back on track. "If I write you a bunch of pictures, would you take them?" "Are Johnny Ray's feet wet?" We agreed to give it a try.

"Firstly, dear boy," he said, "we need a beautiful blonde model who would be willing to do anything . . ."

"Have I got the babe for you! A beautiful actress who is often blonde and not only would, but *does* do practically anything." He cocked a large ear.

Now, here we go back again . . . 1938. Picture this. As a stage-struck teenager going up in an elevator with a fellow hopeful to the "prestigious" Feagin School of Dramatic Art in the newly risen Rockefeller Center, I was introduced to the most stunning (I think is the word) creature I had ever seen off the silver screen—statuesque to parody, in full slap at nine A.M., draped and turbanned in purple jersey. My companion, with as straight a face as he could make, introduced this creature as "My chum, Herman Beulahfield." Herman seared me with rolling eyes and, in a foggy baritone, purred, "I just know we're going to be special friends, darling." She had obviously been bitten by Tallulah Bankhead. In fact, she claimed to actually have been. But as she'd predicted, we did soon become good friends. She was more fun than a barrel full of Thelma Todds and, surprisingly, not a drag queen. "Herman," by the way, was her camp name, Gladys Tinfow was her real name, and Jeri Archer was her stage name, God bless her.

Now, Patrick had recently been advised by his accountant, honest Abe Badian, to incorporate—which just wasn't the sort of thing he could manage too solemnly, so he designed a logo for the newly formed "Lancelot Leopard" to satirize the procedure. I was to make a line drawing of a nude, helmetted Patrick holding a quill and sitting astride (what else?) a leopard. Abe was never quite comfortable with this, but it definitely left an impression.

It just so happened that Herman (Jeri) had been posing for a nude I was painting that Hugh Hefner might be interested in acquiring, or so she claimed. So I scheduled a meeting between her and Patrick just after my next session with her. It worked like magic. He came. He saw. He chortled and offered my odalisque a generous contract on the spot. We were off!

Jeri Archer and Patrick Dennis during the making of "Little Me"

Before I could finish reading Giuseppe Tomasi di Lampedusa's *The Leopard*, Pat tossed a detailed list of fifty pictures in my lap. These were to chronicle our heroine's rise and fall and rise, and were scrupulously limited to those occasions that would conceivably have been photographed—this would remain our criterion (stretched a little, maybe). An adamant censor, in that respect at least, Pat vetoed several tantalizing comeuppances where a photographer could not possibly have been lurking.

Pat had surrounded our star with so many other fascinating characters that I feared we might end up with a cast of thousands. Where were we going to find all these people? When we actually sorted it out, we realized there would be no need to pamper professional models; between us, we numbered more than enough highly photogenic friends to people a production of Max Reinhardt's *The Eternal Road*.

So we began in our backyards, so to speak. Louise would make the perkiest Pixie Portnoy—she had great legs and wouldn't flinch at hanging by her teeth from a trapeze. Michael and Betsy were to be stripped of their dignity and encouraged to let go in "Steerage" (page 105), for which "Honest Abe" Badian consented to display his stomach. Corry Salley could Hattie McDaniel it as Mademoiselle. Elaine Adam, to whom (along with Vivian Kardaris) *Auntie Mame* was dedicated, had all the fiery spunk to ignite the vicious Magdalena Montezuma.

Shaun O'Brien not only cavorted as wily George Jerome Musgrove but contributed many a choice idea and brought along a number of worthies from the New York City Ballet—Deni Lamont, Sara Letton, Col. Edward Bigelow, Roland Vazquez, Ducky Copeland (the wardrobe master), and Vincent Warren as Lance Leopard. Now, Ross Hunter may have discovered Rock Hudson, but I discovered Kurt Bieber during a summer package of *On the Town* (Pittsburgh, '58). These two gentlemen, Shaun and Kurt, generated an unprecedented amount of fan mail, all sent to the publisher's office.

Hervey Jolin and Carl Reynolds, who were the Duchesses in the Christmas card in my studio loo, became, respectively, Morris Buchsbaum and the seducer, Mr. Hopper. All five of my best pals from shows past rallied. The divine Alice Pearce braved jail as Winnie. Dody Goodman became Belle's gorgeous stand-in, Helen Highwater. Peggy Cass distributed donuts to our boys as part of the war effort. Kaye Ballard and Jan Sterling starred at Metronome, and Kaye even let us misuse her grandmother. Dickie Morris, whose *Unsinkable Molly Brown* was enjoying mega-hit status, was also under contract. Edgar Daniels, from *Finian's Rainbow,* was monumentally helpful as Carstairs Bagley. And Wally Mohr put his stamp on many stills; he and I had become such silly cohorts during *Auntie Mame* that Rosalind Russell sometimes referred to us as Bunny Bixler and Muriel Puce. Even Patrick himself lowered his uppers as Cedie. As for myself, I turned into his wizened mother *and* Fred Poitrine *and* the Happy Nurse. We didn't have to search for Momma. Our star accommodatingly spread herself out over all four generations.

When we first thought about costuming all these characters, the prospect didn't seem too daunting. Many of the movie stills would be of scantily clad people anyway, and between us all we had quite a stash of finery. Pat owned every known article of male attire, Jeri Archer claimed to have thrown away nothing since kindergarten, and my studio closets were overloaded with thrift-shop treasures. Pat came to refer to this mess of costumes as "Central Drag." Useful as all this was, we realized we fell far short of authentic couture spanning the decades from 1900 to 1960.

Salvation came with an introduction to Bob Reilly, then curator of the fabulous collection of designer dresses at the Brooklyn Museum. Luckily, he was intrigued with our project and let us set up shop there for the duration. We could have our pick of creations by the likes of the Boué Soeurs, Natasha Rambova, Erté, Schiaparelli, and Valentina. Some of them fit, but most were either clothes-pinned or open in the back.

Many of the pictures were taken against a blank wall and then superimposed onto an appropriate background. The images I used for these backgrounds mostly came from a remarkable and friendly shop, now closed, called Brown Bros., where one could climb a ladder and find, stacked deep on dusty shelves, photographs of nearly anything taken since the invention of the camera. I miss them.

Of course we did still need to go on location all over town. Much use was made of the Tanner townhouse, as well as of our top-floor apartment on East Sixty-first Street. One particularly "Feydeau" afternoon there was especially productive. First we staged "J'Accuse!" which involved Jeri, Shaun, Pat, and me—so Hervey Jolin, who on the previous day had been Mrs. Palmer Potter at a colleague's belter showplace on Gramercy Park, obligingly clicked my shutter. Now, as Mr. Buchsbaum, he ripped off his shirt and jumped into bed with Belle as soon as Mr. Musgrove (Shaun) had leaped out, and we shot "An Evening with Morris." Then we worked our way up front to wrap up pages 75 and 77. There I broke in the Baughdie Diamonds for the first time.

Those priceless jewels were the icing on the whole affair. Diamonds had often been literally close to Pat's heart. Every year he was in the habit of wearing Louise's magnificent heirloom necklace down to Gimbel's for its scheduled cleaning by their expert. "Safer than carrying it in a paper bag!" he always said. But this time, when we took a jaunt, it wasn't to Gimbel's or to Forty-seventh Street, but to Forty-second.

Now, at a store called Nate's, as we were being bedazzled by pounds of glittering rings, bracelets, brooches, necklaces, earrings, even tiaras (but no stomachers), Pat began softly humming "Diamonds Are a Girl's Best Friend." None of the other browsers seemed to notice, so I began to harmonize with him. Soon a few lyrics would slip out as we succumbed to trying on a few baubles:

PAT: "A kiss on the —— may be quite continental."
CRIS: "But a dildo is a girl's best friend."

I'd like to say we were greeted with a round of applause but everybody just straggled out. We came away with a sackful of sparklers that would have chagrined even Peggy Hopkins Joyce. (I shall not reveal their current repository lest some unprincipled person mistake them for real and slit my throat.)

That afternoon in the Times Square diamond mines was probably the beginning of an act that we would be doing at forthcoming booksellers' conventions after we had put all the pieces together and gone to press. Dressed all

Savile Row, we would mount a piano top, Pat playing himself and me playing a reporter asking the author about his formula for turning out bestsellers. We would toss in a few appropriate songs and make fools of ourselves altogether. Pat's voice was surprisingly musical and the act was a smash on the book circuit. Our farewell performance was at the Waldorf-Astoria, where young Michael was in the audience, aglow with pride.

How long was *Little Me* in the making? Well, a bit longer than it takes to make a baby yet not as long as it takes to make a camel. Given the choice, I'd still settle for Belle. Our pace was leisurely. A week would go by and everybody concerned would be elsewhere. Remember, those were the days before computers had taken over—before your mouse could sink the *Titanic*—so I spent much of that time in the darkroom. Before we staged the first pictures, the whole scenario was complete, but as soon as we actually got into gear, the fifty photos we'd originally planned on soon doubled and eventually tripled. A voice from Dutton, *Little Me*'s original publisher, suggested that 150 would certainly suffice, but nonetheless we wound up with 165. Only two of these were rejected: one of Belle and Letch sharing a pair of pajamas and one of a filmstrip of Belle with the Hoolighan brothers (which was returned with this simple comment: "Taste?").

Patrick did indeed "write" every photograph, save one—I sneaked in "Luncheoning with Roz." He was right there for almost every session (they weren't called "shoots" yet) and was the most cheerful and efficient assistant/grip/prop-man imaginable. Just occasionally he would toss in a subtle suggestion to our actors, such as "Belle, you're looking too intelligent!" or "No method, please, Letch. Your motivation is just *What the fuck*?" All very helpful.

Making *Little Me* didn't seem to take nearly as long as it actually did. Often when creative people have too jolly a time collaborating, the "oeuvre" seems apt to sag. But, I do believe, in spite of a prevailing party atmosphere, we did manage to pull this one off. Reviews were great. We enjoyed nine months on the *New York Times* bestseller list, an unlikely serialization in *Sports Illustrated*, and got snatched up by Neil Simon for Broadway. However, our most rewarding accolade came from a real live movie star of the silent era—Anita Loos gave a first edition of *Little Me* to Mae Murray (the bee-stung seductress of D. W. Griffith's *Intolerance*), who said she remembered Belle well but confessed that she never liked her!

Opposite: Belle and Letch sharing a pair of pajamas
Overleaf: Editorially rejected with one comment: "Taste?"

Little Me

A STAR IS BORN

1900-1914

THE SUN WAS JUST SMILING its first shy gleam over the Illinois River when
I made my debut into the world—a red, wrinkled, writhing baby girl.

"What day is it?" Momma murmured.

"Why, it's May Day, Miss Schlumpfert," the midwife said. "The first
of May."

"Then we'll call her Maybelle," Momma said and drifted off to sleep.

I was a rosy, happy, healthy little thing with bobbing curls and an insa-
tiable curiosity. Everyone who saw me toddling along the dusty streets of
Venezuela, Illinois (population—then—9,000) stopped to admire me and it
was evident to even the most obtuse that I was going to be a great beauty. But
beauty wasn't enough in a hidebound little provincial backwash like
Venezuela. "Family" mattered a great deal in the town and, alas, of family I
had only dear Momma. I never knew my father. When I was old enough to ask
about him, Momma would become very vague and, looking off in the distance, she would answer simply, "He was a traveling man, Belle." Perhaps it
was from him that I inherited my lifelong *wanderlust*.

And, oh! how I longed to wander away from narrow-minded little
Venezuela, never to return again. Or—even better—to return as a rich and

famous woman, to buy the biggest, finest house on "The Bluff," overlooking the river, and to snub the *haute bourgeoisie* of Venezuela just as they had once snubbed little Belle Schlumpfert. For tiny Venezuela was divided into three classes. First there were the rich old families who lived in big, beautiful houses with stained-glass windows, *portes cochères*, turrets and towers and ornamental iron statues up on "The Bluff." They were the rulers of the town—the Hobans, the Kerrs, the Hollisters, the Williamses with their seven talented daughters. They were the families with "hired girls" and their own buggies, the cream of Venezuela who thought nothing of going to Peoria, or even to Chicago, to do their shopping! Mary Elizabeth Hoban had even visited New York and travelled to Staten Island! Little Belle Schlumpfert was beneath *their* haughty gaze!

In the lower town were the businessmen and shopkeepers—the clannish middle classes of the community who formed the second stratum of so-

ciety. They noticed me, all right, but always with contempt. For I lived beyond the Rock Island tracks in Drifters' Row and, even worse, Momma was a career woman—something unheard of in those days.

Drifters' Row was the "shanty town" of Venezuela, peopled by railway men, by the foreign element, by the poor, by those whom life had treated more harshly than the denizens of "The Bluff." Those who lived there had not been in Venezuela for long and presumably did not intend to stay. Hence the name. All of us were looked down upon by the older families of Venezuela. We were the "dregs."

I resented this. I wanted to say "My family is as good as yours—even better. Come and see how we live! Although our house is humble from without, the interior is a thing of beauty." And it was. Momma had exquisite taste and a natural knack for making any place homey, attractive and inviting. In fact, it is from her side of the family that I inherit my own taste—often remarked upon—and my artistic flair. Although our tiny little house had but two small rooms, Momma had made the most of them. She had turned the sitting room into a veritable conversation piece by bringing together her large collection of seashells, the gay Kewpie dolls and souvenirs from her many travels. Almost every inch of wall space was hung with artistic reproductions, pictures of her lovely southern friends and of the distinguished-looking gentlemen she had received. On the center table stood a huge bouquet of bead flowers which Momma had fashioned herself during slow periods at her place of business. A lovely bead and bamboo curtain separated this room from Momma's bedroom. A lamp with a big red silk shade in the front window cast its rosy glow over the entire room.

Nor would Momma ever allow herself to be seen in house dress and apron like the other women of Venezuela. True, in the mornings Momma lolled about in the Morris chair in *deshabille*—a Japanese kimono, a pink velveteen wrapper trimmed with maribou or her lovely mauve satin with bead fringe (another product of Momma's busy needle). But every day at noon Momma put on one of her beautiful evening gowns and went off to pursue her career as breadwinner for herself and little me. "It's a tradition in our family, Belle," she used to say proudly.

True, Momma was a newcomer to Venezuela, but she had come from something far finer. Momma was a southern aristocrat whose family had been ruined by the Civil War and the depredations of the "carpetbaggers." She never liked to talk much about the past. She told me only that she had come to

Venezuela from the finest house in New Orleans. When I asked her why, she said simply, "New Orleans was unhealthy for me. Now run along." Although Momma always seemed a pillar of strength to me, I guess she was just a delicate southern flower underneath.

Although it was on Drifters' Row, Momma's place of employment was one of the most beautiful establishments in Venezuela. Momma had accepted a position with Madam Louise, another New Orleans belle, who had opened a sort of gentlemen's hotel and social club near the depot. Madam Louise catered mostly to lonely travelling salesmen who needed cheering up in a strange town, and even a few gentlemen from the families on "The Bluff" would drop in for a glass of wine, a bit of music and some stimulating conversation after their tasks of the day were done. Evenings, Saturday afternoons and Sundays were especially busy. In order to keep her thriving establishment going, Madam Louise employed Momma and three or four of the better conversationalists among the ladies of Drifters' Row. Although Madam Louise did not often permit me to enter her place of business, the few times I was permitted into the parlor were to little me like visits to a veritable fairy land. It was an intimate room with red damask walls, deep red sofas, potted palms, a statue of Venus and a magnificent gas chandelier with rose shades. On a draped table were plush-bound albums containing photographs of Madam Louise's hostesses, which Momma never permitted me to see. In an alcove there was a "Turkish corner" with a divan covered by a red Oriental rug and many "whatnots" filled with the most amazing collection of curios. Against some exquisite Spanish shawls stood a lovely black and gold upright piano where Madam Louise's distinguished friend the Professor played such grand old songs as "In the Good Old Summertime," "Meet Me in St. Louis, Louis" and "There's No Place Like Home." If it was from Momma and Madam Louise that I first learned about visual beauty, it was from the Professor—that kindly old gentleman strumming the keyboard in Madam Louise's stunning parlor— that I acquired my lifelong appreciation of music.

I am told that the bedrooms upstairs were every bit as tasteful and luxuriously furnished, but I was never privileged to see them.

Because she was French and not of Venezuela, Madam Louise was not "received" by the *grandes dames* who lived up on "The Bluff," nor by the housewives in the lower town. But you could easily tell that the women of the town felt a great respect for her as she was the only woman in Venezeula to be called Madam.

Madam Louise's girls

Of course there was a school in Venezuela and of course I was sent to it. Naturally quick and bright, I paid little attention to what the teachers were saying. True, I had a God-given gift for literature and the arts, but I was prone to daydreams and although little Belle Schlumpfert's body may have been in that musty, drab schoolroom, her heart was not. Because of my attitude, several teachers were prejudiced against me and I was often held back to repeat a grade. But I didn't mind. Madam Louise had once said to me, "Belle, honey" (she always called me "Honey"), "as soon as you've developed, you can come to work here." I didn't quite understand what she meant. Knowing that the ladies who worked for Madam Louise were all brilliant conversationalists, I practiced talking quite a lot at school, which, I am afraid, the teachers did not

Madonna and child and "Rowdy"

appreciate. But that made no difference to me. I dreamed only of the day when I would be "developed" enough to leave school forever and work with Momma in Madam Louise's beautiful, beautiful establishment.

In my spare time I was very much the lonely dreamer, disdaining the childish games of my classmates (who, by the time I was twelve, were all much younger than I was) to revel in my make-believe world of fantasy. Much of the time was spent in Momma's gracious little drawing room daydreaming over the well-thumbed pages of mail order catalogues from Sears, Roebuck and Montgomery Ward or surreptitiously trying on Momma's many dazzling evening gowns and posing as a grown-up lady in front of the cheval glass. Although I was only twelve, I noticed that I was different from the other girls in school for already I was becoming endowed with tantalizing curves and swellings which Momma's *décolleté* creations did nothing to conceal. With a bit of cochineal on my lips and cheeks, with my langorous eyes outlined by a burnt match and my face liberally dusted with *poudre de riz*, I felt that I could pass as a young woman of eighteen or so. And this must have been true, because even in my prim little school dresses visiting "drummers" would give me the "onceover" as I walked along the quiet streets of the town.

But what really opened my eyes was the opening of the Argosy Nickelodeon right in the heart of Venezuela in 1911. There for the first time I witnessed the magic of what was locally known as "shifting pictures." Every time I came into a nickel—and I am afraid that I will have to admit that sometimes I even "raided" Momma's purse—I would run down to the nickelodeon and sit spellbound at such grand films as *The Great Train Robbery, The Reception, Uncle Tom's Cabin* and other "thrillers" of that ilk. I knew right then and there what Fate had intended me to be—a great dramatic actress. From that moment on I had but one aim in life—to perform, to bring joy and laughter, heartache and tears to the American public. But I knew that some sort of training in the art of the drama would be essential to bring out my natural endowments as an actress, and where, oh where, would I find the necessary money for my training?

Then, as if by magic, it came to me, right in the Argosy Nickelodeon. Sitting there in the darkened auditorium one evening I suddenly felt a hand on my knee. Out of the corner of my eye I caught a glimpse of my neighbor. To my surprise it was none other than kindly old Mr. Caruthers, *the* leading citizen of Venezuela. Mr. Caruthers owned not only the box factory and the pickle bottling works, but also much Venezuela real estate, including all of Drifters'

Joy

Row. He was chairman of the board of the local bank and had vast holdings in farmland throughout Marshall, Woodford, La Salle and Putnam counties. Not only the richest man in town, Mr. Caruthers was also the most respectable—a true civic leader. He was a deacon of the church and an outspoken crusader against any form of vice. (He had even gone so far as to hint that Madam Louise's lovely home was a "blot on the escutcheon" of Venezuela!) In fact, he had been so vehement against the very existence of the Argosy Nickelodeon that I was amazed to find him sitting next to me.

In addition to his many good works on behalf of the underprivileged, Mr. Caruthers was widely known for his interest in young people. Only the year before he had been most active in organizing the town's first Boy Scout troop and a group of Campfire Girls (into which, by some oversight, I had not been invited), and on almost any balmy afternoon he could be found at the abandoned quarry watching the young blades of the town disporting themselves in the "ole swimmin' hole." I could sense now that Mr. Caruthers was beginning to take a deep interest in little me. "Perhaps," I thought, "just perhaps . . ."

At the end of the reel a sign was flashed on the screen. "Ladies," it read,

Sorrow

"If Annoyed While Here, Please Inform the Management." Screwing up my courage, I turned to my neighbor and said, "Please, Mr. Caruthers, would you read that to me? I'm only eleven." (In point of fact I was thirteen, but I have never had a "head for figures.") I have never seen a gentleman quite so excited. Over a strawberry soda in Guernsey's Ice Cream Emporium, I poured out my little heart to kindly old Mr. Caruthers. I told him of my hopes and dreams, my desire to receive dramatic coaching, and mentioned once or twice how very surprised I had been to find him sitting right next to little me at a place like the Argosy. By the end of the evening we had worked out an arrangement concerning my future that was to bring profit and pleasure to both of us. As Mr. Caruthers found it necessary to journey to nearby Ottawa on business twice each week, it was agreed that I would accompany him to take instruction in elocution and dramatical attitudes from a Miss Neida Anderson who taught there, returning on the late train to Venezuela with Mr. Caruthers.

Thus it was that Mr. Caruthers became a sort of "patron of the arts," and for the next year that affectionate old gentleman and I travelled to and fro on the Rock Island Line. I was on my way to fame and fortune in the theatre!

CHAPTER TWO

MY ALL FOR MY ART

1915

I meet Mr. Musgrove, the new photographer in Venezuela · Mr. Musgrove is interested
in my career · My introduction to the cinema · Making my first film with the Houlighan
brothers · My first personal appearance at the Pharaohs' Smoker · A rude shock · Mr. Hooper
A Peoria interlude · Mr. Hooper learns the facts · My first folding money. · Flight!

THE STORY OF MY LIFE would not be complete—nay, could not even begin—without mention of Mr. George Jerome Musgrove and his "little black
box." For it was he who introduced me not only to artistic photography but
also to the mysteries of the cinematograph.

In all of its history, Venezuela, Illinois, had never had a photographic studio of its own. From time to time various itinerant camera *artistes* would ride
over from nearby towns such as La Salle, Peru, Streator or Ottawa to take cabinet photographs, wedding pictures and group "shots" of graduating classes
and so on. When the people from "The Bluff" wished to be immortalized on
film, they usually entrained to expensive studios in Chicago or Peoria. But
never before had our town had its own resident photographer. Therefore, you
can imagine the excitement when Mr. George Musgrove "set up shop" in the
Caruthers Arcade.

As usual, the citizens of Venezuela were highly suspicious of Mr. Musgrove, as they were of all newcomers. I, however, remained free of prejudice. I
had already been photographed many times in my dramatical attitudes while
studying under Mr. Caruthers' patronage in nearby Ottawa. I had been told so
many times that I was possessed of a beautiful face and a comely figure that I
took this information quite for granted, as one accepts having blue or brown
eyes. I also understood that actresses were accustomed to "sitting" for their

portraits. Thus, I determined to meet Mr. Musgrove and perhaps work out some arrangement whereby I might acquire some artistic "stills" of myself to use in furthering my career on the "boards."

So one afternoon, when Momma had left for Madam Louise's place, I took the liberty of borrowing her red duvetyn *tailleur* with the soutache embroidery, her "Merry Widow" hat and her burunduki muff—the gift of an admirer who travelled in furs—applied a touch of color to my face and, feeling very grown up, made my way down Main Street to the studios of Mr. Musgrove, mindful always of the admiring glances that came my way.

I found Mr. Musgrove all alone in his "digs" behind the studio. (Indeed, Venezuela, always wary of strangers, had not yet "accepted" him.) What shall I say of the man Musgrove who was to play such a vital role in my turbulent life? He was a bachelor of thirty summers or so, neither tall nor short, trim of waist and—I could not avoid noticing—of muscular build. His clothes were dapper and "citified" in the extreme, his hair glistened with a sweet-scented brilliantine and he wore sweeping moustaches in the manner of former president William Howard Taft. To an unspoiled country girl such as I, Mr. Musgrove exuded all the glamour I had always connected with the "big city."

Feeling nervous and extremely shy, I hesitantly inquired as to Mr. Musgrove's rates and I was horrified to learn that he charged a dollar per study. I knew then that I would never be financially able to avail myself of Mr. Musgrove's professional services. Murmuring a hasty, almost inaudible, apology, I prepared to take my leave of his studio when Mr. Musgrove made a counter offer. In addition to cabinet studies, Mr. Musgrove explained, he was also a specialist in "artistic" poses and had not been able to secure the services of a suitable model in Venezuela. Would I, perhaps, be interested? He had, he explained, a flourishing mail order business in such studies which he supplied to professional artists and others and acquired therefrom a major part of his income. He then proceeded to show me a part of his large collection. There were beautiful young ladies clad only in filmy garments in a series of most tasteful classical attitudes. In some of the studies Mr. Musgrove had, himself, appeared as Atlas, Hercules, Mercury and other pagan "deities." I was immediately impressed by his splendid physique and the superior quality of his work. Diffident at first, I was of two minds about posing in a state of semi-nudity. (In my childish dreams I had always fancied that actresses were photographed in pearls and chinchilla and large feathered hats.) When displaying my dramatical attitudes before the camera, I had always worn veilings of theatrical gauze that were modest in the extreme. However, Mr. Caruthers, who was a "pillar" of the church, had told me on many occasions that God had given me my body—that I was a "masterpiece" of the "Great Sculptor's"—and that it was nothing to be ashamed of. Mr. Musgrove was *most* persuasive.

Thus began my career before the camera. The afternoons when I was not with Mr. Caruthers in Ottawa studying for my career were spent posing for Mr. Musgrove—usually alone, sometimes with an older lady from nearby Utica who was named Rowena and, on certain memorable occasions, with Mr. Musgrove himself.

George Jerome Musgrove

Pygmalion and Galatea

I felt that I was learning a great deal about my best camera "angles," and Mr. Musgrove was a most stimulating companion—worldly, sophisticated, urbane but also tender and kind, or so I thought at the time.

Knowing my all-absorbing interest in the cinema, Mr. Musgrove said to me one day, "Belle, my mail order business has been so good that I have been able to invest in a moving picture camera. Would you be interested in doing a one-reeler?" Would I be interested! I was so thrilled to think of being at last in a motion picture that my heart almost stopped beating.

"Ooo, I'd love to, Mr. Musgrove!" I cried. "Tell me, what is the story about?"

Mr. Musgrove explained that his was to be an artistic film—a "*pastorale*," he called it. The plot concerned a young girl who is taking a stroll in the country. It begins to rain. She runs to the shelter of a barn where she removes her dress to let it dry. There she meets two young farm boys who are also seeking sanctuary from the storm. She is mortified at being seen in her shift but they soon overcome her shyness. The sun comes out again and the girl goes on her way. It didn't seem a very exciting story to me, but at least Mr. Musgrove's film would provide a suitable background for my talents. When I asked about the costumes I would need, Mr. Musgrove explained that they would be furnished to me. He explained that he had engaged a "studio" out in the country where there would be plenty of privacy and light and that we would "shoot" the very next afternoon. Would any aspiring young actress have refused?

All that night I dreamed of being a motion picture star like Mae Murray, Lillian Gish or Clara Kimball Young. But the next day—what a shock! Mr. Musgrove drove his camera equipment and little me out into the country in an old wagon. His studio proved to be a deserted corncrib, and my fellow players were none other than the notorious Houlighan brothers!

The Houlighan boys were simply *not* in my set. They were brawny, boisterous troublemakers, constantly in "hot water" with the local constabulary. Drunken and vile-mouthed, they came into Venezuela every Saturday night doing their best to create disturbances. Madam Louise had once refused to admit them to her social club, and they retaliated by throwing a live skunk into her lovely parlor! I have never understood why she did not summon the police immediately. At any rate I found them both coarse and uncouth and I was loath to appear with them even on the silver screen. However, Mr. Musgrove reasoned with me and told me that all great *artistes* must make sacrifices in the name of art.

The film began very quietly. Clad in a sweet white dimity dress and sunbonnet, I tripped prettily along a winding road. Following Mr. Musgrove's direction, I held out one hand, palm upward, feeling for rain. I looked toward the heavens and arranged my features in an expression of anxious concern. Then I ran in the direction of a deserted barn (the corncrib) where I removed my dress very artistically. Suddenly the Houlighan brothers appeared and from then on all direction ceased. Never have I been so humiliated! Needless to say, neither brother had had any dramatic training, and they didn't seem to be in the least concerned with the artistic qualities of the film—although Kevin, the younger Houlighan boy, was a far more accomplished performer than his older brother Rory. Oh! The liquor on their breaths!

When the ordeal was over and the Houlighans had dressed and departed, I told Mr. Musgrove in no uncertain terms how extremely annoyed I was, and that if my artistic career depended on associating with such social inferiors as Kevin and Rory Houlighan, then I would prefer *not* to appear in the cinema. Strong words, indeed!

I was very angry with Mr. Musgrove and determined not to pose for him again. Say what one would about Mr. Caruthers, he was at least a gentleman and would not subject a young innocent girl to the distasteful pawings of two drunken louts.

However, dear old Momma found a splendid opportunity for me to make my *début* as an actress in the town of Streator, about twenty miles distant from Venezuela. The Pharaohs' Lodge there was celebrating its silver anniversary with a banquet and smoker. My role was to conceal myself in a large pasteboard "birthday cake" and then, at the evening's end, to leap out and dance down the length of the table. The work was easy, Momma said it would be "good experience" and it paid five dollars and round-trip fare. I was ever so excited and even helped Momma to fashion my costume—a modish two-piece affair of bugle beads and fringe. It showed me off to the best advantage.

At last the big night arrived. I travelled to the Pharaohs' Lodge, was shown to my dressing room, changed into my costume and was waiting in the wings for my appearance, which was to be the climax of that gala evening. While anticipating my grand entrance, I was a trifle concerned about the "tone" of this meeting. From what I could hear of the off-color stories and *risqué* songs issuing from the meeting room, I received the distinct impression that the Pharaohs were not the benevolent brotherhood I had always understood them to be. Suddenly the lights in the hall were extinguished. I could hear the whir of a motion picture projector and then clapping, stamping and hooting. Always a devotee of the cinematic art, I peered out to see what was being shown. And there, projected onto a sheet hastily tacked up on the wall, was little me with those odious Houlighan brothers, quite nude save for our shoes and stockings! What I had assumed to be a milestone in cinema artistry had turned out to be nothing but a revolting and obscene performance!

Seething with rage, I marched to the back of the hall and, exerting all of my strength, picked up the hot projector and flung it into the smirking face of my false friend George Jerome Musgrove. Then I burst into tears and dashed to my dressing room where I cried as though my little heart were broken.

How long I remained there, I do not know. I was interrupted only by the entrance of a Mr. Hooper, Corresponding Secretary of the Pharaohs' Lodge. He was angry at first that I had failed to emerge from the cake and called me horrid names for having ruined the evening. But when, racked by sobs, I explained to him how I had been duped by Mr. Musgrove and that it was little me who had appeared in that unspeakable film, his manner changed abruptly. He became most solicitous, affectionate and sympathetic. With a keen insight, he said that I was much too fine and virtuous a girl to be so reduced and that he would like to help me. I was in need and Mr. Hooper was a friend in-deed. He said that Mr. Musgrove was a bounder and that my shame was such that it would be wiser for me not to return to Venezuela at all but to go to a strange city and start out afresh under a new name. That very night we boarded the train for Peoria, where Mr. Hooper was kind enough to allow me to share his hotel room. He could be so comforting.

I had never been in a big city before and I adored everything about Peoria. The time passed ever so swiftly, shopping for pretty dresses and furbelows, attending that city's fine film "palace" (with Mr. Hooper I saw my first twelve-reel motion picture, *Quo Vadis?* What a thrill!) and having little suppers *à deux* in Mr. Hooper's room. I felt that Mr. Hooper and Peoria were all a beautiful dream and I never wanted to awaken.

But, alas, I was jolted back to earth when, at the end of our third day, Mr. Hooper imparted the information that he was not *of* Peoria but that he had a business and a *wife* in Springfield, the state capital. Almost speechless with shock, I was just able to blurt out my true age to Mr. Hooper. Then I burst into tears and said something barely coherent about wanting to telegraph Momma. Mr. Hooper seemed even more shaken than I had been. However, he arranged to cash a check, to buy me a one-way ticket to Chicago and to give me a small amount of money to get started in the "Windy City."

I never saw Mr. Hooper again, but I shall never forget him for, without our chance encounter at the Pharaohs' Smoker, who knows where I might have ended up? Boarding the sleeper for Chicago that night, I thought—as I have thought so many, many times since—"Life *is* strange."

THAT TODDLIN' TOWN

ONLY THE OTHER DAY Billie Divine, my great friend and constant companion, was playing a "bouncy" old record on her phonograph. (Billie is an unreconstructed jazz "buff.") Passing by her door, I could plainly hear that old lyric—"Chicago, Chicago, toddlin' town." I have never been able to think dispassionately about Chicago, for the very name of that metropolis on the lake evokes so many memories, happy and sad, gay and wistful. To little me, Chicago is a city of "firsts"—the first World War, my first husband, my first real trouble and my first job in that wonderful, wonderful world of show business.

It was a clear, crisp morning in early October when I set foot on the soil of Chicago. Oh, the hustle and bustle of that busy station, the acrid smells, the shouts of conductors and "Red Caps," the scurrying of passengers arriving at and departing from the Railroad Capital of the World! I was terrified. True, I had some pretty new frocks neatly folded in a dress box from an exclusive Peoria *modiste*. I had a hundred dollars in cash—a farewell gift from Mr. Hooper—and hope in my heart for the future. Yet I was frightened to be all by myself in the big city—just a *naïve* "green" kid from Venezuela, Illinois. A fatherly old "darky" offered to carry my box for me, but in my panic, I thought that he was trying to wrest my only worldly goods from me. I snatched the box from him and, in so doing, broke the string that held it. Horror of horrors, there were all of my new pretties strewn across the floor of the station, including even my *chemises* and similar "unmentionables" that were not made for other eyes to see!

"Oh!" I gasped and scrambled to pick up my few belongings.

"May I help you, dearie?" a cultivated voice said.

There, in front of me on the marble floor, I saw a pair of bronze kid shoes with beautiful beige gaiters. Then a brilliant peacock blue walking suit trimmed with red fox that billowed about an aristocratic face surrounded by the reddest hair I have ever seen. Topping it all off was a towering edifice of peacock feathers.

"Oh, no, mum," I blurted. "Thank you, mum. I can manage."

"Oh, but do let me help, dearie," this grand lady said. "Packing is such a nuisance and I can never get my personal maids to do it properly." In a twinkling she was beside me on the floor, scooping up my new finery. "These are very pretty garments," she said, "but a little out of style."

"Out of *style?*" I said. "They just yesterday were bought brand new in Peoria." Then I flushed at being so forward to such a fine lady.

"As I thought," the lady said. "You're just in from the country."

I admitted that I was.

Then, as this "walking fashion plate" neatly folded my poor possessions and packed them away in their box, she asked me all sorts of questions. Had I ever been to Chicago before? Had I any friends or relatives in the city? Had I a position waiting for me? Had I secured a place to live? To them all I answered "No." The lady then asked if I had eaten breakfast, and my reply was once again in the negative. "Then you must have it with me," this *grande dame* said, "in my stately mansion on Prairie Avenue. But first, let us go to the station buffet for a little cocktail."

I certainly understood the meaning of cock and the meaning of tail—rooster and appendage—but I hadn't the slightest notion of what this woman was talking about. Unwilling to show my *naïveté*, I followed her to the ladies parlor of the station saloon, where she order two sloe gin fizzes. It was my first taste of liquor and I thought it delicious.

The lady introduced herself as Mrs. Palmer Potter, leader of Chicago's

Mrs. Palmer Potter

haute monde. She then asked me all about myself: when and where I was born; what my mother was like; what I was interested in. I blurted everything out to this comforting older woman who seemed quite pleased. Mrs. Potter then told me that, as a hobby, she ran a "salon." I hadn't the dimmest idea of what she meant. But she explained that it was a sort of finishing school for girls of excellent family where they could meet eligible men and learn the social graces. She said that she just happened to have a vacancy that morning. In fact she had been at the station to bid *adieu* to one of her graduates who was sailing to Europe to marry a Spanish duke. I could, if I liked, have the lucky girl's room. If I *liked*! But I told Mrs. Potter that I had no money—neglecting to mention Mr. Hooper's gift—and that I would never be able to afford anything so nice. But Mrs. Potter would not take "No" for an answer. She quickly ordered another round of gin fizzes and before I knew it, I was seated in the *tonneau* of her beautiful new Pierce-Arrow limousine—my first ride in a "horseless carriage"—driving along the magnificent shore of Lake Michigan while Mrs. Potter told me of the lovely gowns I would soon own, of the dashing men I was to meet. And it would cost me nothing! It all seemed too good to be true.

Mrs. Palmer Potter's home on South Prairie Avenue was indeed a stately mansion, making even Madam Louise's house suffer by comparison. The *façade* was of pink marble and brownstone with large plate-glass windows, discreetly veiled by genuine Brussels lace curtains. A man whom I mistook for one of Mrs. Potter's eligible gentlemen opened the great oaken front doors to us. (I found out later that he was only the butler.) A trim mulatto maid showed me to my room—a beautiful circular chamber in a tower on the third floor. It was all decorated in pink and the huge brass bedstead had a canopy of *pointe de Venise* lace. I had never seen such luxury!

Refreshed, I went downstairs to the parlor to meet Mrs. Palmer Potter's other students. It was then that I realized that my simple dresses from Peoria—pretty though they had seemed in the store—would never do in Mrs. Palmer Potter's salon. Her other students were all lounging about the golden parlor in the most elaborate *négligées*—cloth-of-gold, brocade, velvet and trimmed with plumes, with seed pearls, even with sable! I felt like the proverbial "country mouse." But Mrs. Palmer Potter said to never mind, my wardrobe could be supplemented later. She introduced me to the rest of her student body and a merry lot they seemed—always ready for a lark and never at a loss for the pert rejoinder! Although it was not yet noon, champagne was served. I had eaten no breakfast and I confess to feeling quite "tipsy." But the girls were so pretty and gay that I soon lost my shyness and joined in the fun.

As I have said, never before had I seen such splendor. Unlike Madam Louise's comparatively modest social club, Mrs. Palmer Potter's mansion contained not one, but *three parlors*—"drawing rooms," as she referred to them in her aristocratic fashion. The front room was all done in gold damask with delicate gilded furnishings of the French persuasion. The second drawing room was a symphony in blue furnished entirely with deep, downy sofas. In the rear room—all done in plum velvet—was a low stage where, I soon learned, the girls put on amateur theatricals for Mrs. Palmer Potter's guests every evening at nine o'clock. Electric chandeliers, lovely handpainted oil pictures and marble statues of nymphs and satyrs were everywhere.

I was extremely interested in the theatricals and confided to the girls my ambition to become a great actress. They laughed delightedly and said that I would have many opportunities. As the "new girl" in Mrs. Palmer Potter's school I would enact a bride—it was a tradition. Others of the student body were cast more or less to type. Little Midge (the other girls called her, affectionately, "Midget"), who was only four-foot-eight, always played a child, wearing dainty white pinafores and her lovely golden hair arranged in "sausage" curls. "Big Jo" (an extremely tall girl named Josephine) was perpetually cast as a young military cadet, wearing high-heeled red boots (to increase her already considerable height, I imagine), a braided jacket, shako and a smart whip. Others of the girls were given more opportunities to display their histrionic versatility.

After a delicious luncheon, a few gentlemen callers began to arrive. I was anxious to meet them, but Mrs. Palmer Potter said that she was "saving" me for the evening and that I would make my *début* on the stage in the plum velvet drawing room. She escorted me to my lovely little bedchamber, told me to take a nap and locked the door so that I would not be disturbed.

Effie, the "high yaller" maid, brought me a tempting supper on a tray that evening and then Mrs. Palmer Potter appeared with my "costume," a lovely satin bridal gown in virginal white. I fell in love with it at first sight, and I have had a "weakness" for wedding dresses ever since.

Dressed in my nuptial finery, I was waiting impatiently on the stairs to make my first appearance. From the plum drawing room I could hear appreciative applause of the girls' efforts and I hoped that I, too, would please the gentlemen who called upon Mrs. Palmer Potter. The electric pianola was playing "School Days," and I was informed that Midge (or "Midget") was performing on the dais when there was a dreadful hammering in Mrs. Palmer Potter's lovely golden oak vestibule. The great doors burst open and swarms of policemen surged into the house. "The cops!" called Ruby, the girl who was to play my "bridegroom." "Run!" Ruby said. I ran, but in my bewilderment, I dashed straight into the arms of a policeman.

A "Black Maria" was waiting out on Prairie Avenue, and I, along with the students who had not been able to escape this unwarranted invasion of the sanctity of a private home, found myself being hauled off to jail. For the first time in my life, I "made" the front pages of all the newspapers. What an eventful day!

I was booked on charges so horrendous, so unfair and so patently false that I will not, even today, lend dignity to them by writing them down on paper. Along with Ruby, Midge and "Big Jo," I was thrust rudely into a large cell, occupied by two extremely common "streetwalkers." Terrified and bewildered, I languished in that draughty cell until the following Monday morning when I was unceremoniously shoved into a courtroom to be given a "fair" trial. Oh, the humiliation of that experience! Instead of admiring the delicate workmanship of my bridal costume, the spectators in the courtroom—a motley crowd of idlers, curiosity-seekers and uncouth "news-hawks"—burst into rude guffaws when I made my entrance. Called before the magistrate, I told, with as much dignity as possible, my simple true story: That I was a girl from out of town; that I had met Mrs. Palmer Potter in the station; that she had asked me to enroll in her school; and that I had been carried off against my will by the brutal Chicago police force. Although I saw nothing mirthful in my sorry tale, again laughter resounded through the courtroom with Homeric sonority. His "honor" the judge pounded for order and then said, with a vicious chuckle, that he was going to send me to a different "school"—a boarding establishment in a westerly *banlieu* of Chicago. He added that if it had not been for my extreme youth and the fact that this was my first offense in Chicago, he would have sent me to a women's prison! I was too stunned to reply.

Later, of course, I learned how tragically I had been duped. Mrs. Palmer Potter was not really named Mrs. Palmer Potter at all. In fact, she was not even married! Her establishment on Prairie Avenue was not a school at all but, rather, a den of the blackest iniquity, and her "students"—girls of "excellent family," as she had described them—were nothing but *filles de joie*! It had long been her custom, I learned, to "scout" the various railway stations of Chicago for innocent victims to press into bondage in her loathsome calling. I had been tragically victimized by this human vampire! How many other guileless young girls, I often wonder, have been so ill used by Fate simply because they are as friendly and trusting as little me? My detractors have often accused me of being "overly familiar" with strangers. Perhaps they are correct, but I doubt it. I have always had a sunny and outgoing nature, and who am I to try to curb the natural buoyancy with which I was endowed by the Almighty? Yet, because of my God-given warmth, I was forced to pay a terrible price—my name on the police "blotter" and my liberty forfeited for the next two years.

Of the boarding school the judge selected for me, I am still unable to speak rationally. It housed twelve hundred girls, two to a cubicle. We wore ugly gray uniforms. Pretty *coiffures* and harmless touches of artifice were strictly forbidden. We marched in silent lines, two by two, to meals, to recreation, to work, to chapel—even to the bathroom! The food was frightful, the discipline unbearable, the working hours long and arduous. Because my darling Momma had taught me to "sew a fine seam"—as every gentlewoman then could do—I was put to work in the dressmaking department of the school where we made uniforms, nightgowns and "undies." One can readily imagine how onerous a task it was for a young girl with my inordinate fondness for pretty things. Every time I attempted to add a little "friv" to the school's costume—a higher hemline, a lower neckline—I was sternly rebuked by the supervisor and forced to undo all that I had done to improve the lot of my hapless classmates. I have a natural bent for design; indeed, my own clothes have always attracted wide comment. Many have said that, if I cared to, I could become a *couturière* of the first rank. However, I have always been satisfied to take a "back seat" and design unusual creations only for my exclusive use.

The unfeeling magistrate had arranged to have me enrolled in the boarding school until I was eighteen years of age—an eternity to a young lass of my high spirits. However, I was fortunate in my choice of a roommate. My little cubicle was shared with a vivacious minx from Steubenville, Ohio, a Miss D. Winifred ("Winnie") Erskine. "Winnie" had been booked on charges as totally unfounded as my own—shoplifting in Mandel Brothers when she had simply been taking that fur coat out onto State Street to examine it by daylight. Like little me, "Winnie" rankled under the injustice of it all. But, unlike me, "Winnie" was less crushed and more frankly rebellious. And it was she

who engineered our thrilling escape on New Year's Eve of 1917. Because of the Yuletide holidays, we girls had been grudgingly allowed to have a little celebration to "see the New Year in." I had been commissioned by the headmistress to decorate the recreation hall, which I had done with tasteful streamers of pink, yellow and *eau de nil* crêpe paper. Just as our pathetic little "party" was in full swing, "Winnie" touched a match to the decorations and extinguished the lights. The conflagration was considerable, as was the hysteria which it created. In the "hubbub" of the fire, I felt someone grasp my arm and a gruff voice saying hoarsely, "C'mon, kid." I followed blindly. It was good old "Winnie." We dashed out past the guards and spent that memorable New Year's Eve in a dense nettle bed some miles away where we were still afforded an excellent view of our hated alma mater burning to the ground.

At dusk the next day we set out, hand in hand, for Chicago. "Winnie" explained to me that her closest friend, Lola, was "going with" a theatrical producer and that she was sure we could obtain positions as ladies of the ensemble in the theatre where Lola was employed. After all, reasoned "Winnie," would the juvenile detention officers ever think of looking for two "fugitives" right out on the stage of the Cameo Theatre? Time proved her to be correct.

It was nearly three o'clock in the morning when we sought refuge in Lola's little flat on Cottage Grove Avenue. As luck would have it, her friend, Mr. Flinchy, happened to be visiting her at the time. Seeing our uniforms, he was dubious at first, but "Winnie," Lola and I soon convinced him. Miraculously we were hired!

In one short day we found our freedom and I, at least, had found a lifelong career. I was on the stage at last!

At boarding school with "Winnie," 1916

My Patriot Tableaux

The Kaiser

Belgium Ravished by the Hun

Home Fires Burning

Gold Star Mother

Safe for Democracy

CHAPTER FOUR

WAR!

1917

Burlesque, the *commedia dell'arte* of America · On stage! · Backstage frolics
Doing my bit for our boys · The Colonel's Lady · My first taste of high life
Deceived, disgraced, destitute · Fred

THE VERY NEXT DAY, freed at last from our hated gray boarding school uniforms and preening ourselves in the "fine feathers" borrowed from Lola, "Winnie" and I were taken to the Cameo Theatre to watch the show in progress and to learn as much as we could about it. I had never attended the legitimate theatre before. (The only attractions that had found it "worthwhile" to stop at Venezuela were "tent" shows such as Black O'Brien's Mississippi Minstrels and the Herman Beulahfield Circus.) What a thrill it was! I sat there in the darkened auditorium clutching "Winnie's" hand in excitement as the ladies of the ensemble paraded down the runway garbed as snowflakes, saucy soldiers and dainty fairies. I gasped at the splendor of their costumes—the diamonds, the ermine, the sumptuous velvets. To think that such fine raiment would soon be mine! Even when I watched the last show of the day from the "wings" and I discovered that the "diamonds" were glass, the "ermine" cotton batting and the "velvet" but humble flannelette, the *léger de main* of the theatre still had me in its thrall.

When the midnight show was over (the Cameo did three shows a day, interspersed by an installment of *The Perils of Pauline*), Lola took "Winnie" and little me to the dressing rooms and introduced us to the ladies of the ensemble whose "co-troupers" we were soon to be. And a merry lot they were! When they inquired as to how old I was, I told them twenty-one, although I was little more than a child at the time. It is possible that I have this "little white lie" to thank for some of the wild speculations as to my true age. Although I have never made a secret of my years, many actresses who have been less successful than I are still ruled by the "green-eyed monster" of envy and have been spiteful enough to broadcast "vital statistics" about me too risible to be believed by anyone. This has always afforded me a certain amount of amusement.

Being pretty and high spirited, the girls of the Cameo had no shortage of attentive *beaux* or "stage-door Johnnies." Indeed, that very first evening Lola introduced us to two salesmen from a high-class St. Louis cloak and suit firm and told us not to hurry back to her little flat, as Mr. Flinchy would be calling upon her and she would not be lonely for company. The gentlemen took "Winnie" and me to their lovely suite in the Sherman House for a little supper of chicken à la king and sparkling burgundy and later that evening my particular escort presented me with a very modish green merino walking suit with coney collar and cuffs.

The very next morning rehearsals began for the new show at the Cameo. Although good-natured "Winnie" thought of "hoofing" in the chorus as just a "lark" and a way to make enough money to "skip town," as she put it, I was very serious about it, considering the experience at the Cameo the first step in my long career. And how right I was!

Burlesque has been called the "*commedia dell'arte*" of America" and rightly so. I would like to remind my readers that in the "good old days," burlesque was not the tawdry spectacle of strippers, "bumps" and "grinds" and lewd so-called comedians, equipped with "blue" material and off-color jokes. At that time burlesque was both wholesome and refined, the training ground for some of today's great, great performers, among whom I am proud and happy to include myself.

Born with an almost ethereal grace, a sure sense of rhythm and a true, sweet soprano voice, I was both hurt and surprised when the *maître de ballet* or dance director, as such a person is called today, kept singling me out for especial criticism. "No, no, Belle," he would shout, "with the *left* foot. Keep time, Belle, keep time! No, Belle, you're singing it in F, the others are in G. No, Belle, now try it again—left foot, right foot, brush, step, brush, step. No, no, *no!*"

My heart was in my mouth when he asked me to stay behind after the rehearsal "broke." I thought I would surely die if he fired me. However, I reasoned with him, promised to do better and suggested that I accompany him to his studio that evening for some intensive training. The following day, it was decided that I was too individualistic a performer to be relegated to the mere rank and file of chorines. Hence, I was promoted to a mannequin or "show girl," where I would not be called upon to sing or dance but would, instead, lead the mannequins' parade down the runway and pose as the central figure in the *tableaux vivants* and the artistic "living statues." This work involved more lavish costumes, a higher salary and a prestige value just the other side of stardom. I was very pleased. Thus I was billed simply as "La Belle" (owing to my misunderstanding with the Chicago police, I felt it wiser to keep my last name a mystery) and under that simple soubriquet I paraded and posed happily as Queen of the Night, the American Beauty Rose, Aphrodite, the Motor Girl, Pocahontas and other timeless symbols of beauty and grace. If the ladies of the ensemble were jealous of me, they concealed that emotion admirably. In fact, a number of them told me that they were *glad* I was no longer in the chorus. Such was the *camaraderie* of show "biz" in those dear, dead days.

Thus I worked through those blustery winter months of 1917. *Worked?* The term is laughable! Every moment of it was fun of the most unbelievable sort. Although the hours were long, what with doing three shows a day, often having to devote our mornings to rehearsals and always our evenings to the gallants who admired us from across the footlights, the winter flew by. A *régime* such as ours might have taken its toll of well-rounded figures and rosy complexions, but we were young and healthy and carefree, always ready for a fling. Ah, if the dressing room walls of the old Cameo Theatre could only talk and tell of the fun they've witnessed! There was always an air of excitement backstage—the hustle and bustle, the pungent odors of greasepaint and spirit gum, cold cream and hot hair tongs. Between shows we girls would visit back and forth, gossiping and joking, speculating as to the intentions of the many "stage-door Johnnies" who waited each night to "squire" us out to supper. We were forever attempting new experiments with our *coiffures*, stitching away on blouses or remodeling our old street clothes. Heedless of our waistlines, we would cook up great batches of fudge over the gas burners, order huge, fattening sandwiches and "crullers" from a nearby delicatessen. We would read aloud from romantic novels and love story magazines, and the fashion journals were always in great demand. I thought of nothing but clothes, clothes, clothes and—having started literally from "scratch"—I soon assembled a very stylish wardrobe, thanks to my frugal shopping habits, to my infallible sense of style and to the generosity of some of the gentlemen I met who were connected with the garment industry.

And our nights were one mad whirl, as well. As first mannequin, I had my pick of escorts each and every evening. "Winnie" and I usually "double dated." As soon as we could afford it, we moved out of Lola's tiny apartment and took a room together in a refined boarding house on West Congress Street, within easy walking distance of the Cameo. (Unless we had *beaux* to pay for cabs, we always walked, mentally applying the saved carefare to some long longed-for hat or pair of gloves. As our suppers were always paid for by our admirers, we saved a great deal, as well, on meals.) And soon, even our rent was taken care of. We had met two gentlemen who were travellers in hardware. They had a lovely bachelor apartment out west on Chicago Avenue. As they were rarely in town, they asked us to move into it to keep an eye on things. The arrangement worked out splendidly for all concerned until America's entrance into World War I took me quite unawares.

I have always been a dedicated student of global politics. Nary an issue of *Foreign Affairs, The Economist,* the *Bulletin of the Atomic Scientists* appears without my sacrificing my "beauty sleep" to burn the midnight oil over the vital issues of the day. But in that exciting winter of 1917, I was simply too busy to notice the first World War, until, that is, President Wilson's earth-shaking announcement of April 6. After that, what a difference!

The streets of Chicago were suddenly swarming with soldiers and sailors. We were all singing songs such as "Over There," "Keep the Home Fires Burning" and "Pack Up Your Troubles." And we girls at the Cameo were right in the thick of it! Patriotically we gave *four* shows a day instead of three. Instead of tatting lace trimmings or making *lingerie* in the dressing rooms between performances, all of us were busily knitting socks, mittens and mufflers. Overnight the spring show, *April Showers,* was "scrapped" to be replaced by a whole new patriotic spectacle—a concept revolutionary to the world of burlesque.

Where I had once posed as a classical statue, a flower or a famous beauty of history, I now did only rôles of deep martial significance—the *entente cordiale* with "Winnie" and one of the more mature *danseuses,* the Spirit of France (in which I wore a miniature Eiffel Tower, a *tricoleur* and *fleurs-de-lys*) or Fighting Uncle Sam. It was a challenge to my dramatic ability, but one which I accepted gladly. I was nervous and unsure at first, but from the shouts

and whistles and applause that greeted my patriotic *tableaux,* I knew that I had not failed to "do my bit."

Nor did we girls continue to go out with men in civilian clothes, as of yore. Every night now, after the show, the tiny alley behind the Cameo was choked with boys in olive drab and blue serge. And it was at the stage door of the dear old Cameo that romance first entered my life. It was an unseasonably

warm night in early spring. I was hot and tired, headachey and "out of sorts."
"Tonight," I said to myself, "I'm going straight home to get a good night's sleep.
I *won't* go out, no matter if General Pershing himself asks me." But when I
went out of the stage door, a dashing older gentleman stepped down from a
shining, dark red Packard touring car. He wore the uniform of a colonel with
burnished boots and spurs, Sam Browne belt and a swagger stick.

"Good evening, Mademoiselle," he said, touching his cap smartly, "you
are Miss Belle, are you not?"

"Yes," I said impatiently.

"Would it be expecting too much if I were to ask you to solace a lonely
soldier, just back from the front, by having a bite of supper this evening?"

How could I refuse? Colonel Smith—for that is the name by which he introduced himself—was an officer of the United States Army, a leader of men,
a war hero recently returned from No Man's Land. It was clearly my patriotic
duty to accept his kind invitation. He took me to Jacques' French Restaurant
(a very fashionable *rendezvous pour l'élite* of Chicago), and the more Colonel
Smith told me about himself the more my heart went out to this lonely bachelor, many times a millionaire, the owner of gold mines, oil wells, ranchlands
and Manhattan real estate, with no understanding female to share in his
many rich rewards. He smoked fine, long Cuban cigars, and I have always
loved the aroma of a good cigar. Before the evening was over, I had breathlessly accepted his proposal of marriage.

From Colonel Smith's suite in the old Auditorium Hotel, I telephoned
the Cameo Theatre early the next morning to give my notice and to say that
I was renouncing my career as of that moment. Mr. Flinchy was furious but I
felt that duty to my country came first. I next went to the Fair Store to purchase my bridal *ensemble*—a sweet white lace dress, a fetching hat, a sable
scarf and a few other oddments that caught my fancy. As ours had been a
whirlwind, wartime courtship, there was no time for the elaborate wedding of
the sort I (and every other girl) always dreamed about—white satin, a large
cathedral, "Winnie" as my maid of honor and the girls from the Cameo as
bridesmaids. Instead we were married by an Army chaplain in Colonel Smith's
suite. Because of his high rank, he explained, witnesses and a license would
not be necessary. He did, however, produce a lovely wedding band.

The next few days were like a dream. As "The Colonel's Lady," I went on
a mad round of shopping—diamonds and pearls from Peacock's, glossy furs

from John T. Shayne, dresses of every description from Field's and Carson, Pirie, Scott with shoes to match from O'Connor & Goldberg. All of these purchases and dozens of others I had sent C.O.D. to the front desk of the Auditorium Hotel. I hadn't intended to be extravagant but it seemed incumbent on me to dress and act the rôle of a multimillionaire's wife. My old clothes I sold to "Winnie" at a fraction of their value, as she was finally leaving town. The Colonel didn't seem to mind in the least, he merely puffed away on his costly cigars, nodded with approval at each new outfit and said, "Very pretty, baby, now let's see how fast you can take it off." He had a great sense of humor! In our week together, Colonel Smith refused me but one thing—he would not consent to pose for a wedding photograph, saying that he was "camera shy." I was very disappointed. I am a notoriously slipshod correspondent and had not written to Momma since I left Venezuela to entertain at the Pharaohs' Smoker in Streator. I wanted her now to see how I had grown and what a fine husband I had found. However, I went to Mr. Alexander (official photographer of the Cameo Theatre) and posed alone in my bridal attire.

Returning to the hotel, I seemed to sense a slight difference in the attitudes of the doorman, the desk clerk, the elevator operator (like all creative artists I am highly intuitive and sensitive to the attitudes and feelings of others), but I thought little of it until I let myself into our suite. I peered into the sitting room, but there was no Colonel Smith puffing on his cigar in the easy chair. "Kittycat," I called (my "pet" name for the Colonel), "it's Pussykins." There was no reply. Mystified, I decided that Colonel Smith might be waiting for me in the bedroom, as he sometimes did. The door was open and I walked in to find only the manager of the hotel ransacking my wardrobe.

"What," I demanded icily, "are you doing with my lovely creations? My jewels? My furs?"

"*Your* jewels? *Your* furs?" he said horridly. "Hah!"

Then in a vile torrent of abuse the awful truth tumbled out. Colonel Smith was not a colonel at all. Nor was he a millionaire. Instead he was a penniless buck private who had been absent without leave for weeks from Fort Leavenworth, Kansas. He had been apprehended that very afternoon charged with being "AWOL," impersonating an officer, stealing an automobile (the lovely Packard touring car) and leaving a fortune in unpaid bills and bad checks across the entire Middle West.

"Sir," I said with great *hauteur*, "you are speaking of my husband and you

lie!" The manager all but laughed in my face. The "marriage ceremony" he said had been performed by one of "Colonel" Smith's miscreant cronies. It had been nothing more than a sham, a mockery of the beautiful marriage sacrament, and I was but one of many "Mrs. Smiths" who had been used and abandoned by a monstrous *poseur*.

Before I could protest, I was thrust bodily out onto the pavement with nothing save the clothes I stood in. I had again been duped, once more the victim of a glib stranger and my own innocent, trusting nature. I had resigned my position at the Cameo Theatre. "Winnie" had bought my old clothes for a pittance, and even now she was on her way to an unknown destination. My new finery had been impounded by the Auditorium Hotel as its rightful property. Deceived, disgraced, destitute, that was the cruel destiny Fate had in store for little me.

A chill wind sprang up from the leaden gray lake. A cold rain started to fall. Dazed, heartbroken—even hungry—I made my unsteady way, somehow, from Michigan Avenue to the corner of Wabash and Van Buren. I paused at the entrance of a brightly lighted saloon whence issued the raucous cries of soldiers and sailors. Then that capricious lady, Dame Chance, once more took the prerogative of changing her mind and thrust a savior into my arms in the person of a very young, very drunken "doughboy." It was Fred!

39

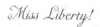

CHAPTER FIVE

THE LOVE OF MY LIFE

1917-1918

Mutual aid · I become Mrs. Fred Poitrine · Our little home · A lifetime of bliss in a fortnight's furlough · What the gypsy told me · Farewell, Fred. (Did I really know it was farewell forever?) The Armistice · The telegram · Fred's insurance policy · Good-by, Chicago, hello, New York!

SINCE THE DAWNING OF TIME, every fascinating woman has had one great love in her life. As Juliet had her Romeo, as Héloïse her Abélard, as Pola her Rudy, as Wallis her Edward, so had I my Fred.

He had lurched into me, quite intoxicated, at the lowest ebb of my life. Being young, "green" and not quite himself, he had mistaken me for a woman of loose habits and asked me to accompany him to his hotel room. Aghast, I was about to rebuff him. Then I thought better of it. Here was a poor, lonely "doughboy" at loose ends in a hostile city. I, too, was alone—penniless and pathetic—and it was beginning to rain quite hard. How could I allow this poor, simple soldier to wander the streets of the "Loop," a prey to heaven knows what sort of woman?

"Come along, soldier," I said. "I'll see you safely to your room."

"Surest thing you know, cutie," he kept muttering. "I'm the chicken inspector."

Fred's hotel was in a clean but humble *caravanserai* on Clark Street, not at all the sort of address I was accustomed to. But beggars can't be choosers, as the saying goes. As soon as I got the door of his room open, he stumbled in and collapsed on the bed. A second later he was dead to the world. Feeling sorry for the poor boy, I loosened his tight uniform, unwound his puttees and removed his heavy boots. There was still no response. Then, because I was both physically and emotionally exhausted, because I felt that this poor, lost lamb needed watching over and because it was by then raining in torrents, I removed everything save my corset cover and lay primly on the bed beside him.

The next morning I was rudely jarred into consciousness by Fred himself. "Gloriosky!" he said. "What are *you* doin' here?"

"Why, don't you remember?" I asked.

"Then are you one of . . . one of *those*?" queried Fred.

"One of those what?" I said.

"One of those hoor-girls?"

Outraged, I sprang to my feet, but not before he had found his wallet and counted the contents. I was furious until I saw that he had more than five thousand dollars in it. The poor darling had wandered into a "crap" game and, with proverbial beginner's luck, had "cleaned up." With a sigh of relief he said, "Well, at least you didn't get at that."

I was too angry to speak coherently. "Of all the insulting ingrates!" I said. "Here you come staggering out of a saloon, make an indecent proposal to a lady like me and, instead of calling the police, I bring you back to your room, put you to bed, watch over you like a mother and now—after all I did for you last night—you have the gall to accuse me of . . ." I couldn't continue. I burst into hysterical sobs and buried my head in the pillow. From the corner of my eye, I could see how abashed he was. In his clumsy way he tried to apologize and to comfort me, but I could know no solace. Seeing my abject grief, Fred spoke of himself as a cad and bounder, a rakehell, a devil with the ladies and a vile seducer of innocent girls. I had not the heart to contradict him. Through my racking sobs I could only repeat and repeat that I hadn't the slightest idea that he had had any money on him at all and that now he was accusing me of being a thief, as well as a wanton woman. When he told me that he had been inebriated and had not realized that I was a virtuous young girl, I cried all the harder. And when he offered me ten dollars, I emitted a high, piercing animal shriek of indignation that had him begging for my silence. That morning I became Mrs. Fred Poitrine at Cook County Court House with a license, a marriage certificate and two paid witnesses to prove it. At last I was a bride! That very afternoon I arranged with Mr. Alexander for new photographs.

As Fred had only five thousand dollars, I saw no need to squander it in that squalid hotel. Instead, we moved into a dear little two-room apartment, very prettily furnished, on West Lake Street, quite near the "El." Fred carried me across our own little threshold and, after a delicious chop suey dinner, I gave myself wholly to him. Far from being the vile seducer he had claimed to be, I discovered that I was Fred's first "conquest." As with all great loves, there was something so honest, innocent, childlike and pure about ours that it made all lesser *amours* seem sordid and tawdry. All that night Fred kept reiterating how glad he was that he had saved himself for a girl as worthy as little me and all I could do was reply that I, too, was glad.

Knowing literally nothing about one another's backgrounds, Fred and I had just a few days to "get acquainted." He was due to go overseas in two weeks' time, and who could know that those fourteen precious days were all we were to have together? But we made the most of them. As we bustled about our little honeymoon bower, tacking down gay oilcloth, placing fresh paper on the shelves, Fred told me the story of his life. He had been born in Eau Claire, Wisconsin, nineteen years earlier, the only son of poor, but proud, French-Canadian immigrants. His parents had passed away when Fred was but a babe and he had been reared in a foster home where he learned little of love and even less of the great world outside. He had taken a correspondence course in business procedure and was an accomplished typewriter. When Uncle Sam had "called his number," Fred was quite ready. In spite of being myopic and terribly underweight, he had passed his physical examination and had trained at Fort Sheridan, outside Chicago. I was the first girl he had ever really known and I am proud and happy in the knowledge that, as Mrs. Fred Poitrine, I gave the poor motherless boy all the love he was ever to have.

When Fred asked about my personal history, I was at a loss to know exactly what to tell him. How could a simple farm boy, sheltered from the seamier side of a cruel world as Fred was, comprehend the cruel pranks Fate had perpetrated on little me? What I told Fred about myself was true—every word of it—but am I to be blamed if there were certain omissions and *lacunae* in my personal history? I told him that I had come from a little Illinois town to seek my fortune in Chicago, that my few humble possessions had been stolen (as they certainly had by the hard-hearted management of the Auditorium Hotel) and that I had been alone in the world when I met him. Why tax the poor, trusting young bridegroom with unhappy information that would be neither pertinent nor beneficial to our relationship? Besides, that part of my life was now a discarded chapter, I felt sure.

Fred was not the handsomest man I have ever known. Only nineteen at the time of our marriage, he was thin to the point of emaciation with a slight tendency to stoop. He had been forced to walk at too early an age and conse-

My hero—Fred Poitrine—
the one great love of my life—1917

A modern Priscilla

quently his legs were a trifle bent. Having a delicate skin, the crude army meals of "slumgullion" had taken their toll of his fair complexion. He was so nearsighted that he had very nearly "flunked" his physical examination, and the Army Dental Corps had neglected his teeth shamefully. However, he had beautiful, artistic hands, a sweet, trusting nature and he was a "crackerjack" at shorthand stenography and typewriting.

Our fourteen days together—a lifetime of bliss in a fortnight's furlough—literally flew by. Fearing for the fate of Fred's five thousand dollars in a wicked city of cutpurses and pickpockets, I deposited the money in my name at a nearby savings bank except for a tiny amount which was needed to replenish my vanished wardrobe. Having a good head for practical matters, I saw to it that Fred changed his marital status with the army and named little me as beneficiary of his insurance. These mundane matters aside, sentiment reigned. I knew but little of the culinary arts and eagerly faced the challenge of cooking our own little dinners for two. Fred, however, saying that he didn't want me to spoil my soft, white hands, preferred to dine out.

Lamb for my lamb!

One night—our last together—while enjoying a meatless repast in a little gypsy tearoom, Fred excused himself to go to the gentlemen's convenience. While he was gone, a fortune teller came to our table. She looked at my palm and then said, "I see marriage."

"Yes, yes!" was my reply.

"Many marriages," the gypsy said. My heart fair stopped beating. "I see many husbands and many men. I see riches and poverty, fame and obscurity. But, above all, I see men." With that she was gone.

"What did that bohunk say, Honeybunch?" Fred asked.

"Only that . . . only that we would live happily forever and ever," I replied. But the magic of that evening was gone. I could hardly touch my tapioca. Later that night when Fred, quite spent, was snoring beside me (he was troubled by adenoids), I tried to dismiss the soothsayer's prophecy and its effect on me as superstitious "balderdash," but somehow I could not. Fred left from the old Polk Street Station the next morning. When I said farewell to him on the platform, did I know it was farewell forever? I wonder.

For a week I brooded alone in our little apartment, but I soon realized that solitude was not for me. Fred, I later learned, was in the very thick of it, doing important, confidential clerical work in the Insecticide and Fumigation Corps based just outside Glasgow. My heart was in my mouth every time I heard the doorbell ring. But after a few days of this bleak, agonizing despair I realized that I would achieve no positive good by torturing myself in lonely solitude. Besides, my little "nest egg" would dwindle to nothing if I did not seek some means of livelihood. There was a crying need for workers in the munitions factories, but I decided that it would not be fair to take a position away from a better-qualified employee. Besides, Our Lord had bestowed upon little me the great gift of bringing happiness to others. I would work where I could be the most useful in the all-out war effort. Hence, I accepted a rôle as combination entertainer and social hostess at Stanislaw Slutsky's Shamrock Cabaret, a popular mecca for lonely "gobs" and "doughboys." My duties were to appear as a mannequin in the thrice-nightly "floor show" and to mingle with the *clientele*. This latter duty I enjoyed especially because it gave me the opportunity to inquire, of each new serviceman, whether my Fred was in any danger in the Insecticide and Fumigation Corps in Scotland. Trying to put my tortured mind at rest, they all said—to a man—that I had nothing to worry about. How gallant those simple boys in uniform were!

Although I questioned the propriety of my actions, I decided that it was my duty to show these brave boys, whose very lives hung in the breach, as good a time as possible. After all, I reasoned, wouldn't I be grateful to some bonnie Scottish lassie for taking my poor Fred beneath her wing? Thus, of all the girls at the Shamrock, I became the gayest, the most madcap, the most devil-may-care—my painted smile concealing a breaking heart. And it was a rare evening, during those trying years of 1917–18, that I did not ask some shy, strapping boy home to our little apartment for a cup of cocoa and stimulating conversation, into the wee hours of the morn.

Somehow the days and weeks and months crept by and then it happened. On November 9 the Kaiser abdicated. On November 11, 1918, the Armistice was declared. Of all the merrymakers thronging State Street, in downtown Chicago, I was the merriest. I rode on the roof of a trolley, kissed every uniformed man in sight, drank beer and champagne and wine and whiskey, laughed and cried and sang and cheered with the rest of them. But the next morning, when I returned to the little home I had shared with Fred, I found a telegram slipped under the door. With my heart and temples pounding, I opened it. My husband, it said, had passed away at the very hour of the Armistice!

Two weeks later I numbly read a letter from poor Fred's commanding officer. Fred had died a hero's death. He had caught his thumb in the space bar of his typewriter, but had valiantly refused medical aid or relief from his duty. With a "buddy" he had gone off to Loch Ness for a few days' furlough from his exacting and exhausting work. Upon his return it was noticed that his whole right arm was seriously infected, swollen and painful to the touch. He had been hospitalized but by then it was too late. Life ebbed rapidly from my brave soldier-husband. As the ghastly war faded from being, so did dear Fred.

I had barely the strength to apply for Fred's insurance money or my widow's pension. I did so only in the knowledge that Fred would have wanted me to. Added to my paltry bank account, these last mementoes of dashing Fred Poitrine would enable his little widow to get a new start in life. But where? Certainly not in Chicago. After all, what had Chicago brought me other than two weeks of ecstasy with Fred? The rest of it had all been heartache, disappointment and disillusionment. If I were to work for my living—and as a poor widow it was essential to earn my daily bread—I would have to do the one thing I knew how to do, perform on the stage. And what better place to seek employment than the theatre capital of the world—New York?

I knew that a position would be hard to secure if I were in widow's weeds and that Fred, who had loved me in gay colors, would be unhappy could he but see me in sable hues. So I invested a bit of my capital in a smart travelling suit à la Irene Castle and, as a touch of somber mourning, a large black and white fox muff.

In Fred's absence the landlord had been so persistent in his unwelcome attentions to a helpless lone woman that I chose not to inform him of my impending departure. Instead, I waited until he had gone to East St. Louis to spend Christmas week with his married daughter, then I called in a second-hand furniture dealer, sold off the entire contents of what had been our honeymoon bower and slipped quietly away from the "Windy City" on the evening train.

Seated in the dining car, I toyed with the menu as I watched the lights of Chicago slip past the window. "Good-by, Chicago, city without a heart," I thought, "hello, New York!" Immediately I felt better. Then I smiled shyly at the lone gentleman seated across the table, who had already informed me that he was in Drawing Room A.

THE SEARCHING YEARS

1919 – 1925

MY *DÉBUT* IN THE CHICAGO THEATRE had been a question of too much too soon. At a tender age I had burst like a meteor onto the stage of the Cameo. Without the arduous years of singing and dancing in the "line," without the heartbreaking "trek" from manager to agent, agent to manager, I had begun at almost the "top," thanks to my natural endowments, the force of my personality and the keen perception shown by Mr. Flinchy and the *maître de ballet*. Perhaps I was "spoiled," perhaps I had expected unreasonably that my Chicago reputation would precede me to New York, perhaps I was simply accustomed to being the "big frog" in a "small puddle." I don't know exactly what the reason was, but Gotham was a tougher "nut" to "crack" than I had anticipated in my distress and *naïveté*.

I arrived in Manhattan at the beginning of 1919 when New York was just emerging from the dread war years. And what a season that was! The "theatre district" stretched from Sheridan Square in the "Village" all the way up to Ninety-sixth Street. There were more stars on Broadway than I could count. John and Lionel Barrymore were appearing together in *The Jest*, while their sister Ethel starred in Zoe Aiken's *Déclassée*. Elsie Janis and her "gang" were back from the front, as was Irving Berlin, who was singing his own songs

A travelling costume à la Irene Castle

twice a day at the Palace. Hazel Dawn and Enid Markey were appearing in that hilarious farce *Up in Mabel's Room*. A revival of *Floradora* was being prepared. Ruth Chatterton appeared in *Moonlight and Honeysuckle*, Peggy Wood in *Buddies*, Irene Bordoni in *As You Were* and Fay Bainter was a "sell out" in *East Is West*. *Lightnin'* was well on its way to establishing a record run. E. H. Sothern and Julia Marlowe were co-starred in *The Taming of the Shrew* (by William Shakespeare), for lovers of the antique, and such new names as the Theatre Guild and Alfred Lunt and Helen Hayes (playing together in Booth Tarkington's *Clarence*) were being heard for the first time. George White had created his *Scandals*, starring pretty Ann Pennington, and John Murray Anderson the *Greenwich Village Follies*, with Bessie McCoy, the "Yama-Yama Girl," to compete with the Ziegfeld *Follies* and Shubert's *Gaieties*. Even Theda Bara came East that year to try her luck on the "Gay White Way."

Surely with so *much* activity in the theatre, I thought, there would be room for little me.

As all thespians will, I found living quarters with two other girls in show "biz." They had a small flat, in an old brownstone house, on West Eighty-ninth Street, and they were more than glad to have a third member in the *ménage* to share expenses. Although I was grateful for any show of friendship in a city as cruel as New York, I felt instinctively, from the very outset, that these girls (they shall remain nameless) were not in my class. One functioned as a "bit" player at a film studio in Astoria. The other was a chorine at a very ordinary burlesque theatre. As I have said before, I have nothing but the greatest respect for burlesque—*as it was then*—but I felt that I should strive to go onward and upward in the arts rather than remaining in a "rut." The girls laughed at me when I told them of my dreams of being a "Glorified American Girl" costumed by Ben Ali Haggin in Florenz Ziegfeld's *Follies*, or even of assaying a dramatic rôle. They were both coarse in the extreme and, as I have mentioned heretofore, without ambition or desire for the finer things of life. They made all manner of fun of me and called me "Marilyn Miller" or "Maxine Elliott." Yet, in the fashion of the *hoi polloi*, they were good-hearted and saw to it that I had no lack of attentive gentlemen escorts.

It has been said that success is not a matter of *what* you know but of *whom* you know. This is not strictly true. Yet it has long been my observation that the route to the "top" can be made shorter, smoother and swifter through valuable social contacts. Most of the "dates" procured for me by my two new *confrères* were distressingly vulgar and uncouth, with a large store of "smutty" stories and very little notion of how to behave in the presence of a lady. I endured their company out of politeness and because I still harbored the wan hope that one of them might be able to further my career in the realm of either pure drama or light operetta. One evening, however, my roommates introduced me to a gentleman who was "associated with David Belasco." He did not impress me as a "force" in the living theatre. Instead, he seemed callow, ill bred and overly familiar. But he spoke with considerable authority about Mr. Belasco, his theatre, his stars and his plays (lovely Ina Claire was then "packing them in" in *The Gold Diggers*), and added, "Dave is putting together a new play, *The Theatre Through Its Stage Door*. Why don't you drop around to the Belasco tomorrow afternoon and I'll give you some pointers?"

Thrilled, I put on my loveliest creation and appeared at the Belasco Theatre at the appointed time. It was dark and empty and I saw no evidence of actors or of a play in rehearsal. But my "sponsor" met me, explained that Mr. Belasco had been "unavoidably delayed" and had left instructions for him to "coach" me in the part of a young *ingénue* to improve my "reading" for Mr. Belasco.

The young man took me to Mr. Belasco's office, showed me all of the interesting curios and memorabilia on display and asked me to recline on the sofa to rehearse a love scene. He would, he explained, substitute for the leading man. The "lines" were all but nonexistent. (I knew that Belasco plays had a paucity of dialogue.) But it seemed to me that this importunate young gentleman was carrying the famed Belasco "realism" to an extreme never before seen in the theatre—at least not before a mixed audience. After several hours he complimented me on my "performance," said that I had been "swell" (an example of the sort of language he employed) and told me to return the following afternoon. The next day when I appeared, this young man explained that Mr. Belasco had wanted to see me but that he had been called upon to deal with Mrs. Minnie Maddern Fiske and had left instructions for me to rehearse the "rôle" once again. This I did with some trepidation. I was then instructed to return the next day when, I was told, Mr. Belasco would surely see me. He did. When I arrived at the theatre, my "patron" informed me that Mr. Belasco had been once again "detained" but that I was to rehearse the love scene on the sofa once more. I am an actress who loves to "throw" myself into a part and I have no idea how much or how little time elapsed when suddenly the office door burst open. There stood Mr. Belasco, his pale complexion white with rage. Instead of admiring my performance, he flew into a rage and demanded to know how a lowly usher dared to bring his "doxie" into the producer's private office and use it as a "place of assignation." My tears and explanations were to no avail, I was thrown bodily out of Mr. Belasco's office and my gentleman "friend," who had claimed to be "associated with David Belasco," was summarily discharged from his job as usher. Oh! The bitter humiliation! I never saw Mr. Belasco again.

I made several attempts to secure an appointment with Mr. Dillingham but he had always "just gone for the day." Then, one freezing morning, I arrived, clutching my scrapbook, just as that great producer was marching out of the theatre. "Mr. Dillingham," I announced, "I have just arrived in New York from Chicago." Getting into his limousine he said, "And I am just departing for Europe." Two ships that pass in the night! Had it not been for our unfortunate timing, who knows to what artistic heights the two of us might not have soared?

Dressed in my best one day, I went to the New Amsterdam Theatre to discuss with Mr. Ziegfeld the possibility of my appearing in his famous *Follies*, starring Bert Williams and Eddie Cantor. The stage doorman was most rude and uncooperative. I was just about to depart when I saw Mr. Ziegfeld approaching. He was besieged by girls, all of whom were trying, as was I, to catch his attention. On the spur of the moment I chose to faint at Ziegfeld's feet. "She's fakin'," the doorman said in harsh tones. To prove that I was not, I kept my eyes tightly closed until I felt myself being carried and laid out at full length on some soft surface. Then I heard a car door close. "Ah," I told myself, "Mr. Ziegfeld has placed me in his smart *equipage* and is undoubtedly taking me to his lovely home, where he and Miss Billie Burke can discuss my career in privacy." My eyelids fluttered. "She's comin' to," a most uncultivated voice announced. When I opened my eyes I saw that I was not in Mr. Ziegfeld's limousine at all, but in a police ambulance! It was a matter of weeks before I managed to extricate myself from the psychiatric ward.

The winter of 1919 was one of the coldest in memory of man, but I found even more numbing the blank stares of stage doormen, the curt dismissals of casting directors, the unfeeling "Mr. Harris is out" or "Nothing today" from managers' receptionists.

By summer I was nearly insane with worry and frustration. My poor savings were going rapidly and I had not been able to establish myself in the liv-

COHAN & HARRIS *Present*
MRS. FISKE
COMEDY OF MOONSHINE
NEW LAND MAKE BELIEVE

Nelly of N'Orleans
By Laurence Eyre

Under the Direction of
HARRISON GREY FISKE

STAGE
DOOR

ing theatre of Manhattan. And then it happened! Nervous and depressed, I decided to "treat" myself to dinner at a "posh" restaurant and hang the cost! I chose Reisenweber's and, dressed in my finest, presented myself to the *maître d'hôtel*, demanding a table for one. He looked me up and down, as though I were the lowest filth on earth, and said, with a sneer, that "unescorted ladies" were "not admitted" when suddenly I heard a familiar voice cry "Belle!" It was none other than D. Winifred ("Winnie") Erskine.

"Come on and join the party, kiddo!" she called. Drawing myself to my full height, I said to the rude servitor, "Excuse me, I must join my roommate from boarding school." But you can imagine my feelings when I saw who "Winnie's" gentleman friend was. It was George Jerome Musgrove!

Quivering with shock and indignation, I was about to withdraw when Mr. Musgrove said that "a lot of water had gone under the dam" and to let bygones be bygones. Seeing the dinner he had ordered, I acquiesced and, lulled by wine, even agreed to spend the weekend with him at Atlantic City talking over old times. It was while strolling the Boardwalk together that he informed me of a new theatrical connection. He had become involved with a producer who was putting on a musical extravaganza called *Swamp Lillies,* and, knowing of my many gifts as a mannequin, he secured for me the position of a "show girl." We rehearsed all through the heat of that torrid 1919 July. And, tired as I was at the end of each day, I was forced to accompany Mr. Musgrove to his rooming house every night for further work on my part. We were scheduled to open on August 7, 1919. At last I would be receiving not only recognition as an *artiste*, but a salary as well (in those days one practiced without pay). I was atingle with excitement when I arrived at the theatre that night only to find it dark and deserted. There was to be no opening. The actors in New York had "walked out" in a mass "strike." Twenty-three Broadway theatres were closed—including ours. Nor would we have opened anyhow. Mr. Musgrove, it was discovered, had "blown town" with the box office receipts and "Winnie." I was broken-hearted.

Burst like bubbles were my dreams of being a star, of taking a little apartment of my own, away from the immorality and vulgarity of those with whom I was forced to share living quarters. With tears streaming down my cheeks, I walked all the way back to West Eighty-ninth Street (I had no car-fare) and the distasteful place known as "home."

But when things looked the darkest, a faint glimmer of hope appeared. The roommate who worked at a motion picture studio in Astoria then told me of a "super spectacle" which was in the process of being filmed and said that attractive girls were needed. My only previous encounter with the cinema, at the unscrupulous hands of Mr. Musgrove, having been so tragically disillusioning, I was dubious of appearing again on celluloid, but I needed money in the worst way and I could honestly say that I had had motion picture experience. Thus I commenced—in a very minuscule fashion—my real career: that of a film star. Each morning I would awake at dawning and take the subway to picturesque Astoria, Long Island, where we of the cast would get into costumes and makeup and prepare for a strenuous day of "shooting."

The work was hard, the hours long, the discomfiture intense. Swathed in furs and velvets I would swelter through "take" after "take" under the hot lights of a studio in "Injun Summer" when, for example, we were filming *Minx in Mink*. Or, blue with cold, I would frolic on the icy beaches on "location" at Montauk Point in March, pretending that it was the *plage* of Biarritz in August. The pace was killing and the pay low, but I was learning things about my camera "angles" and technique that couldn't have been bought for a million dollars. And what a thrill to see myself as others saw me, projected onto the silver screen to millions of people in thousands of theatres all over the world!

My detractors have often accused me of being "unselective" in my friends. If this is at all true, it is because I am genuinely democratic and feel that I and the lowliest stagehand or "grip" are all God's children created free and equal under His Master Plan. Other "extras" may have criticized me severely behind my back for "playing up to" the electricians and cameramen on the "lot," but this was because I was so intensely interested in learning the myriad mysteries of movie making. I wanted to know how best I could be lighted, how better to bring out my good features in "close-ups" if ever I should be called upon to appear in one. And, sensing my spirit of true cooperation, it was not long before Floyd, the cameraman, was using me almost exclusively whenever he wanted an extra for a human interest "shot." Naturally this caused envy and consternation in the ranks of the "extras" and "bit" players. Never once considering that talent and willingness to learn had anything to do with my good fortune, they berated me harshly for what they called "messing around" with Floyd, our genius of the camera. Let them think what they will—has-beens and nobodies that they are today—at least I did not "toady" to the stars and directors as they did.

During the long months I worked at Astoria I appeared in more than two dozen pictures as an "extra." Some of them are unforgettable masterpieces,

Early Silents

Astoria

"Thou Shalt Not . . ."

"Weird Wives"

"Sodom"

"The Decline and Fall of the
Roman Empire"

"Arabia"

"Gomorrah"

"Gay Husbands"

"Saudi-Arabia"

"Plutarch's Wives"

"Forgive Us Our Trespasses"

even today, and I rank films such as *Sodom, Thou Shalt Not . . .*, *Weird Wives* and *The Decline and Fall of the Roman Empire* as celluloid classics in which I am proud to have taken part—even as an unknown, poorly paid and without acclaim. But the handwriting was on the subway wall, so to speak. I could see, with half an eye, that the film products being ground out in Astoria were sadly lacking in the scope and splendor of the rival Hollywood productions.

During the severe shortages of the war, Fort Lee, New Jersey, had changed from the metropolis of the motion picture art to a veritable "ghost town." The Biograph Studios on Fourteenth Street in Manhattan, the Edison Studios in the Bronx, Vitagraph in Brooklyn—all of them had deserted for the "Sunshine State." The Los Angeles Chamber of Commerce was shouting "Every epoch-making picture has been produced in Southern California," and who could gainsay it? Hollywood was the coming place and I did not want to be left behind.

California had everything in its favor—space, climate, all sort of natural settings for "location" work, the biggest stars, directors, writers, producers and budgets. I was at a low ebb in March 1921. I had caught a severe chill while chained to a rock in Long Island Sound for the filming of *Thou Shalt Not . . .* I was beginning to find the cramped living conditions, the unladylike conduct of my roommates, the grossness of their men friends and the bad weather of New York unbearable. I was almost ready to give it all up and return to my stellar *niche* in burlesque when Floyd, the cameraman who had taught me so much, announced that he had just signed a contract with the mighty Metronome studios in Hollywood. He had purchased a new Moon *coupé* and he invited me to drive across the country with him. It would be a chance, he said, to see the country, "crash" Hollywood and have some fun along the way. I leapt at the opportunity. Pleading a sick headache, I remained in the little apartment one evening after my roommates had gone off on some low round of revelry with their vulgar "sheiks." Then, borrowing all the suitcases in the flat, I packed up everything I thought I might need on the "coast" and took a taxi to Floyd's little bachelor "digs" in the Bronx, so that we could get an early start the next morning. "California, here I come!" I said, as I settled back in the Yellow Cab, and, prophetically, the ticking of the meter and the clicking of the skid chains on the slushy New York pavement seemed to repeat after me in unison, "California, here I come!"

Never having been west of the Mississippi River, I was thrilled at the sights of golden California. The palm trees, the orange groves, the mountains, the beach at Malibu, the quaint Spanish-type mansions of the stars—all of them seemed to say "Belle, this is for you." I was agog with wonder as I glimpsed the palatial homes of such luminaries as Gloria Swanson, Pola Negri, Mabel Normand, Mary Miles Minter, the Gish Girls, the Talmadge Sisters, Corinne Griffith, "Doug" and Mary. "Someday," I kept repeating to myself, "someday, Belle, all of this will be yours."

But I was soon to discover that the glitter and glamour of gilded Hollywood is only for the few. Although I was to know it well in later years, when the world was at my feet, Hollywood in 1921 meant little more than hardship, struggle, deprivation and heartache to lonely little Belle Poitrine.

Through Floyd's connections at Metronome, I was called on occasionally to do extra work, but the film colony of California was not the "big, happy family" that it had been in Astoria. Girls, girls, girls poured into the Los Angeles station with every train—each of them with but one desire, to "get into pictures." And among them came young women of the lowest sort, devoid of talent and morals, but possessed of pretty faces and easy virtue. Not fired by a burning ambition, as was I, to make histrionic history, many of these unfortunate girls came to the "coast" only because they "smelled" big money and visualized Hollywood as an ideal place to ply their iniquitous trade (the "oldest profession"). Can you imagine my feelings as a sensitive dramatic actress to be classified with such loathsome types?

However, Floyd did what he could to protect me from the stigma usually attached to "extra girls." So that I would not have to associate with the low-type young actresses who thronged the theatrical "boarding houses" (many of which were little better than *bordellos*), Floyd took a little "bungalow" off Sunset Boulevard and installed me in it, explaining to the understanding landlord that I was his "housekeeper." The arrangement worked nicely for a time.

Through Floyd's modest influence on the Metronome "lot," I secured employment as an "extra" at that great studio and appeared in several films with such stellar performers as Pauline Frederick, Barbara La Marr, Tom Mix, Wallace Reid and even the late, great Rudolph ("Rudy") Valentino. But, although I hoped and prayed for recognition, I was only "one of the mob" and never a star, or even a "bit" player. Alas, Floyd—although a superb photographer—did not carry the weight in Hollywood that he had in dear, friendly little Astoria. In fact, owing to studio "politics," he was soon reduced from doing "B" pictures to filming low "slapstick" comedies and two-reel "shorts."

Suddenly our little home—parlor, bedroom, kitchen and bath—changed from nest to cage. There we were, two great creative *artistes* thwarted by the cruel indifference of "filmdom" to our talents. Tortured by our own frustrations, what had started out as a beautiful friendship, firmly founded on affection and understanding, became enmity. Floyd turned surly and sullen by turns. Although prohibition had been in force for more than a year, Floyd sought solace in the "bottle." And what bottles! These were not the delicate vintage wines that I had learned to sip, in moderation, whenever I dined or supped, as any true *gourmet*. Floyd bought the cheapest, vilest, strongest "redeye" or "rotgut" he could find. The effect on him was that of the terrible draught that transformed kindly Dr. Jekyll to cruel Mr. Hyde. He would become maudlin and then abusive, often striking out at me for no reason at all. I could not bear to see so fine a person sink so low, and Floyd's unspeakable conduct was also having a deleterious effect on my own career. Happily, I have more inner resources than the average person. If Floyd could no longer help me up the ladder to success, I would find someone who could. For the first (and last) time in my life, I sought the professional assistance of an agent (or "ten per center").

Although I have long been known as an astute judge of human character, I would be the first to admit that I am not infallible. I have made mistakes, and one of them was in my selection of an agent, whom I shall call "Bernie." He was small, lithe and dark with button-black eyes that seemed to penetrate right through me. I recall now that his gaze often made me uncomfortable. However, I was desperate to advance in motion pictures and I was also gullibly impressed by the "setup" of "Bernie's" attractive little office: Chinese with thick Oriental rugs, low divans and soundproof walls and ceilings, by his precisely clipped "Jack" Gilbert mustache and the big diamond ring which he wore. (I beg the reader to bear in mind that I was little more than a child during the latter months of 1921.) "Bernie" took a great personal interest in me, which was flattering. Through his efforts, I appeared as an "extra" in Marvin McQueen's *Gay Husbands,* playing a depraved society girl, and in Cecil B. DeMille's great spectacle *Plutarch's Wives* in which I appeared as a concubine. But I was still a long way from stardom and whenever I complained of this, "Bernie" would take me out to dinner and then for a long drive in the mountains to "cool off."

Either unable or unwilling to recognize that my evening engagements with "Bernie" were purely business, Floyd became almost insane with jealousy

every time my agent's name was so much as mentioned. Returning quite late one night, after "Bernie's" Marmon roadster had developed motor trouble, I discovered that the locks had been changed. I felt then that it was high time to move on.

Just why I chose to return to cold, cruel New York which had rejected little me and which I, in turn, had rejected only a few months before is something I can never explain. Perhaps it was because Dame Chance has regarded me as one of her favored "children" and, in ways that may seem inexplicable in moments of despair, has always delivered me to the right place at the right time no matter how dark my prospects may have seemed. I suppose there is just something of the Eastern fatalist about me.

At any rate I arrived in New York with only a few dollars. I had no friends, no place to go and, to make matters worse, it was raining. With two of my precious pennies, I purchased a newspaper to put over my head and there, right on the front page, was a photograph of my dear old "chum" from boarding school, "Winnie" Erskine. "Party Girl Released From Hoosegow" the headline screamed, and there, big as life, was a photograph of dear old "Winnie," modishly garbed by the House of Tappé, stepping into a smart electric brougham as she waved to cheering crowds. In my absence "Winnie" had become a legendary New York hostess whose fame was to be rivalled only by Texas Guinan and Belle Livingston! The accompanying article stated that darling "Winnie" was now proprietess of a fashionable *boîte de nuit* called the Club Audubon (or "Bird House" as it was affectionately known). I knew then and there that my troubles were over. Instead of setting off on foot to find cheap, cramped lodgings, I went to the station ladies' room, removed—as best I could—the grimy traces of my four-day trip in a dirty railway coach, freshened my georgette dress with the peach-colored maribou trim and took a taxi directly to the Club Audubon.

"Winnie," after the initial surprise had worn off, was of course delighted to see me again although, in her typical brusque fashion, she did her best to disguise her pleasure. Over delicious and colorful Pink Ladies I told "Winnie" as much of my recent history as seemed pertinent and, "laying my cards on the table," begged her for a position at the Club Audubon. In typical "Winnie" fashion (she has always fought a losing battle to repress her generous instincts) she was dubious at first, but when I reminded her of the "madcap" pranks I could recall, such as her setting fire to our boarding school, the accusation of shoplifting, the "French leave" she had taken with Mr. Musgrove, she relented and offered me a place amongst the "show girls" of the Audubon. In addition, she also took me into her luxurious apartment on Riverside Drive which she and her *fiancé*, Alfredo ("The Violinist") Pizzicato, shared in a purely platonic "design for living." Al was actually the owner of the Club Audubon but, because of his shyness and the true patrician's dislike of publicity, he preferred to "take a back seat" and pretend that it was actually "Winnie's" property.

And so, once again back on dear old Manhattan Island, I resumed my career as supper club *diseuse*. Club Audubon was always thronged with its loyal members (let me state here and now that it was *not* a common public restaurant, but an exclusive social organization where the members were scrutinized through a little window in the front door and where membership cards, evening dress and total decorum were *de rigueur*) and, because of Mr. Pizzicato's many eligible gentleman friends, I was never to want for a cluster of attentive *beaux*. However, the one who appealed to me most was a Mr. Barouch. He was dark, vital, ever so good-looking and one of history's unsung mathematical geniuses. If I have one weakness, it is "mind over matter." I have always bypassed handsome men for intellectual men because I find their conversation so very stimulating. Mr. Barouch was doubly blessed and our association was to prove both profitable and pleasurable. Hardly a day went by when, through some mysterious mathematical formula sprung full-blown from his intricate mind, Mr. Barouch would not telephone to advise me to bet a large sum of money on such and such a horse in some particular race. The steeds of his selection never failed to win. He also advised me on certain business transactions, not publicly known, but privy to a chosen few—Canadian rye "futures" was one of his favorite investments, and I turned many a bright profit through his sage counsel. Even when it came to the prize ring—although I know and care nothing about fisticuffs—through some arithmetical alchemy known only to himself, Mr. Barouch would often advise me to wager money on a particular fighter, at the most favorable "odds," and could even tell me in which round the pugilist of my choice would be proclaimed the victor.

Owing to Mr. Barouch's many connections, I was able to lease a very pretty apartment on Central Park South, decorated in the Renaissance manner, where Mr. Barouch was a constant visitor. I knew very little about his personal life but he was extremely filial and spoke often about his dear mother out in Yonkers—"my old lady" was his affectionate soubriquet. You can imagine then my stupefied horror when, after more than two years of the most cordial relations, Mr. Barouch's body was dredged from the Harlem River. The circumstances surrounding his untimely death have ever been veiled in mystery. But I feel sure that it was a suicide. Some men are simply too brilliant to live.

With Mr. Barouch no longer a part of my life, I continued to perform at "Winnie's" Club Audubon. (One must do something to forget one's sorrows.) As the name of the establishment suggests, ornithology was the *leitmotiv* of the Audubon and each of our elaborate "floor shows" dealt one way or another with our winged friends. They would be given titles such as *Peacocks on Parade* or *Fine Feathers*. The big winter gala of 1925 was called *Birds of Paradise* and featured, as its star, a gifted female impersonator with the appropriate name of Ned Crow! In the *grande finale* I appeared as "The Raven" in an exquisite costume of jet black plumage inspired by the designs of the Viennese genius, Ernst de Weerth, for the fairies in Max Reinhardt's production of *A Midsummer Night's Dream* and executed by a talented taxidermist in Hack-

ensack. While "Winnie," perched atop the piano, recited Edgar Allan Poe's grand old poem, I did a neodramatic exotic dance number with a fierce fluttering of chiffon wings that quite "brought down the house." As a production "number" it was unforgettable.

One evening when I was in my dressing room, relaxing after the exhausting demands of my solo, I was surprised to see the door burst open. There stood a tall slim gentleman unbuttoning his faultless evening clothes. He had a long, thin, sensitive face reminiscent of the paintings of El Greco. He wore a beard and had an extremely high, intellectual forehead.

"Oh!" he said.

"Yes?" was my frosty reply. I was accustomed to countless admirers flocking to my dressing room after each performance, but they had always been considerate enough to knock before entering.

"I'm most frightfully sorry," the stranger stammered. "I was looking for the men's room. Nothing here seems to be what I expected."

"And what did you expect?" I asked haughtily.

He then explained that he was an English gentleman totally absorbed in the study of nature lore. He had mistaken "Winnie's" gay club for the Audubon *Society*. In his confusion and total ignorance of American usage, he had not understood the witty chicken yard labels on the doors of the two restrooms and had wandered, hopelessly lost, through the basement of the building until coming to my dressing room door, upon which some "wag" had scrawled "water closet" because of a leak in the sewer main that sometimes caused my accommodations to be flooded during inclement weather. I explained his mistake, directed him to the proper portal and thought no more of the incident.

But later that night, as I was going home, I saw the bearded Briton standing out in front of the Club Audubon. He was having an altercation with the doorman and a cab driver. He kept saying, "But I want to go to the Tolliver-Fanshaw, my good man. Tolliver-Fanshaw. It's a large club on a very big square. I can't remember the address." When he saw me, he doffed his hat and then said, "I can't seem to make you Americans understand anything." I will admit that with his English accent and slight speech impediment, it was not always easy to get the "gist" of his every remark. However, I was more cultured than the underlings at the club and, in my usual friendly fashion, attempted to assist this stranger on our shores. Patiently, the British gentleman spelled out the address to which he wished to be taken. "Tolliver-Fanshaw," he repeated. "T-a-l-l-i-a-f-e-r-r-o, Tolliver. F-e-a-t-h-e-r-s-t-o-n-e-h-a-u-g-h, Fanshaw. Tolliver-Fanshaw." I recognized it as the forbidding men's club (razed in 1929 to make way for a large apartment building) right next door to my own little place on Central Park South. I explained matters to the driver and soon we were chatting merrily in the back seat of the cab.

This aesthetic English gentleman was named Cedric Roulstoune-Farjeon. Because I was the only person in New York who could understand him and because we were "next-door neighbors," he became my constant companion for the next two weeks. Poor "Cedie," he seemed so alone and lost and friendless in a huge metropolis like New York, not "speaking the same language," living alone in a gloomy men's club like the Talliaferro-Featherstonehaugh. He was not interested in life on the Gay White Way, in the nightclubs and "speakeasies" and fashionable restaurants. "Cedie" loved beauty and beauty alone—birds, nature, poetry and music. Perhaps his worship of beauty is what brought us together. We would take little strolls through Central Park or along the Palisades. Together we would visit the zoo, the Museum of Natural History, the Aquarium, poetry readings or the lovely dance recitals of Paul Swann. It was very restful.

When "Winnie" inquired as to my whereabouts, I told her that I was seeing a good bit of Cedric Roulstoune-Farjeon. "Jesus," she said. "And he's an Honorable!"

Knowing little of the British aristocracy in those faraway days of 1925, I said haughtily, "He certainly is. He's never once laid a finger on me." "Winnie" just laughed in that coarse way of hers and made a very crude remark. But I felt extremely touched and flattered that an English intellectual gentleman, such as Cedric Roulstoune-Farjeon, would be interested in me for my mind alone. Yet "Cedie" seemed to draw great spiritual strength from my mere presence, and there were times when we sat for hours on end in my little Renaissance parlor without uttering a single word. I had also acquired the gift of being a "good listener" and this was very important with "Cedie" as he was extremely shy and inarticulate which, coupled with his almost incomprehensible accent and defective speech, made listening a full-time job. But during the "lavender hour" one afternoon in 1925 "Cedie" timidly asked me—or at least I *thought* he was asking me—to become his wife.

I cannot, even today, quite express my feelings for dear "Cedie." I loved him, yes, but was I *in* love with him? He was so sweet, so gentle, so refined, so different from any of the men I had known. He could awaken the maternal feeling in my breast, but could he ever kindle the flame that guttered there? I frankly did not know. He went on to say something about being cooped up in the country a good deal of the time, about living on an allowance, about having very simple wants in life—poetry, music and nature. Of course I loved the country and cared little for pomp, circumstance and fashion's folly. But did I really want to give up my promising career to start afresh in an alien land with a husband whom I barely knew? I repeat, I honestly did not know. As I bade *adieu* to "Cedie" at the door of my apartment I said, "Give me twenty-four hours to think it over." He said—or at least I *believe* he said—that he would.

Club Audubon was hectically gay that night with celebrities crowding every inch of space. "Jimmy" Walker was there as were "Al" Capone, "Legs" Diamond, Marilyn Miller, John Barrymore, Zelda and Scott Fitzgerald, "Freddy" McAvoy, "Al" Jolson, Jeanne Eagles, Mrs. Patrick Campbell, Mistinguett and the fabulous Ruth Brown Murray. Also in the throng of festive celebrities were two insidious men who would never have been granted membership in such an exclusive circle. They were "Izzy" Einstein and "Moe" Smith, the notorious prohibition agents, who had disguised themselves as Roumanian diplomats in the *entourage* of Queen Marie and had thus—*quite illegally!*—gained admission to the club.

I was in the midst of my Raven "number" when there was a piercing blast of a whistle and someone shouted "This is a raid!" I darted off the floor, raced to my subterranean dressing room and, using all of my strength, managed to escape, like the martyred Jean Valjean, through the sewer. When I reached home—clad only in my costume and a light evening wrap from Martial et Armand—I found a note from "Cedie." But I was too exhausted to read it. Like a weary animal, I tumbled into bed and slept until the following noon.

Upon awakening I sent the elevator man out for some newspapers as I was curious to learn the exact fate of "Winnie" and her club. But upon opening the New York *Graphic* I was shocked to see a large photograph of none other but "Cedie." The accompanying article stated that "Cedie's" father, "the

ninth Earl of Baughdie, and third richest man in the British Empire," had passed quietly away, "leaving his enormous holdings to Cedric Roulstoune-Farjeon, his only son." I realized then and there that I *must* marry dear "Cedie," if only to be of some solace to him as companion and helpmate when he, poor, shy boy, took on the staggering burdens that went with the earldom. I telephoned his place of residence but learned that he had sailed for England that morning.

With trembling hands I opened his note. It read: "Must return to England. Pater dead. Knowing you has been an experience. Farewell. Cedric." Poor darling! He must have been beside himself with grief over what he imagined was my indifference when he wrote those few lines of farewell. Of course I could see it clearly. The only possible answer was Yes.

Through an influential acquaintance at City Hall, who was able to cut through miles of "red tape," I had a passport issued immediately (although the photograph did not do me justice and my age was put down incorrectly). I threw some things into a valise, telephoned the news of my engagement to the newspapers and raced down to the Cunard Lines. Just eleven hours after "Cedie" had set sail for our gracious ancestral seat, I was following. True love had come my way at last. I would sacrifice my career for the man I loved and for the ancient lineage of the proud Earls of Baughdie.

CHAPTER SEVEN

THE TOAST OF LONDON

1925-1927

Taking "Cedie" by surprise · "Gretna Green" · Little me as a Lady
"Cedie's" mother (Britannia, Lady Baughdie) · My new "empire" · The Baughdie Diamonds
The London social whirl · My famous parties for famous people · Momma's
surprise visit · A mishap at the Sanctuary · My nervous breakdown

BY A STRANGE QUIRK OF FATE, "Cedie" had taken the *first* ship sailing to England from New York, I had taken the *fastest*. Thus, landing at Southampton, I had ample time to run up to London, purchase a smart outfit—beige with fox trimming dyed to match—at Mme. Lucille's, arrange for credit as the future Countess of Baughdie and notify the press of my forthcoming nuptials. Since the fabulously wealthy Earls of Baughdie had always created considerable interest throughout Great Britain, the reporters were more or less telling *me* of my plans. (The announcement of our engagement in the New York newspapers preceded me to London and had already caused quite a "stir.") Besieged by reporters, I travelled to Liverpool to surprise dear "Cedie."

Always a poor sailor, he looked paler and sicker than usual as he tottered down the gangplank. The sight of me, waving up at him, was just too much for poor Cedric. He collapsed completely. While reviving him, I carried on the interview for both of us, and as soon as "Cedie" was able to get to his feet, we were whisked off to a quick civil marriage service at the nearest registry office. Once able to "shake" the reporters, we repaired to Claridge's for our honeymoon.

As a young girl—a child bride, if the truth were known—our "Gretna Green" elopement was not the sort of romantic wedding I had so long desired.

In the Music Room—Park Lane

For a member of the distinguished Baughdie clan, a magnificent marriage ceremony in Westminster Abbey, attended by the royal family and the "cream" of London Society, would have been my due. But, with poor "Cedie's" late father barely cold in the family mausoleum, such ostentation seemed in the most questionable taste to me. My bridegroom was all but incoherent with sorrow, shock and *mal de mer*. And so it seemed wisest to wed as simply and rapidly as possible without taxing unduly his already overburdened mental capacities.

That night, in our simple but attractive suite at Claridge's, I put on my loveliest new *négligée* (a diaphanous creation also purchased from Lucille's), sprayed myself liberally with *Nuit de Noël*, and prepared to give myself wholly to my virile new husband. It would be my duty to the Empire, I realized, to produce a male heir, and as quickly as possible. Such is the stuff of which we British noblewomen are made! "Cedie" still looked quite shaken when he saw me. I took his thin, delicate hand, placed it on my breast beneath which my heart was beating with excitement and expectation, and said to him, simply and eloquently, "Dearest husband, I am all yours. Do with me what you will."

Then Cedric paid me a beautiful, beautiful tribute merely mumbling: "We'll muddle through somehow, old girl." When I tiptoed timidly to our nuptial bed, he was fast asleep.

We lingered on at Claridge's for many weeks. My new husband was a great clubman and spent a good deal of every day and each evening in the vicinity of St. James's in those exclusively male strongholds, the West End Clubs. When we were together he seemed scarcely able to grasp the fact that we were man and wife and that I was all his to do with as he chose. In his absence I was able to entertain myself by "snooping" about the many interesting shops which London has to offer—Asprey, Worth, Molyneux, Cartier, Boucheron—I was like a child in a toy store! As the new Lady Baughdie, it seemed my duty to have at least one full-length portrait painted so that if *Country Life* or the *Tatler* or British *Vogue* should telephone to request something for publication, they would not find me shorthanded. In order not to seem to "play favorites," I commissioned likenesses of myself from Augustus John, Marie Laurencin, Boldini, Sir William Orpen and Eugene Speicher. John Singer Sargent, alas, had just passed away.

When the paintings were finished there was simply not room enough in our tiny suite to hang them all. I was growing restive at Claridge's, cooped up in six minuscule rooms, and wanted to settle down in a little place of our own—as what new bride does not? We had been wed for nearly two months

and I had not yet been introduced to "Cedie's" widowed mother or any of his family or friends. Whenever I mentioned this to "Cedie" he became uncommunicative, and distant, and usually departed for one of his many clubs. Nor had I been the recipient of any of the uxorial tenderness a "honeymooner" naturally expects. However, I waited patiently, knowing that "Cedie" would soon "snap out of" his nervousness and timidity.

However, the occasion of my first interview with my new mother-in-law was not far off. Perusing the Court Circular in the London *Times* one morning, I observed that the Dowager Countess of Baughdie had moved into the family townhouse in Park Lane. I resolved then to pay a surprise call. Knowing how conservative would be the Dowager Lady Baughdie's feelings about proper mourning, I chose for my "weeds" a somber and stunning creation all in black—a jet and fringe dress, black pearls, sheer black hose with jet clocks and a full-length monkey fur cape with muff and hat to match designed by Louiseboulanger. That I looked outstanding was abundantly evident. As I made my way on foot along Brook Street to comfort my bereaved mother-in-law, every head turned.

I had not previously known of the existence of a town property among "Cedie's" many holdings and I must admit to being awestruck by the *façade* of the Park Lane house. It was far more splendid than I could have imagined in my wildest dreams of *richesse*. Two footmen opened the door to me and Fidgets, the butler, took the visiting card which I produced from my Dorothy bag. He stared at the card, stared at me, lifted his eyebrows and seemed almost to stagger toward the reception room to which he led me. "How stunning this big old house would be," I recall thinking, "if only it could be redecorated by someone like Ruhlmann or Joseph Urban." I sat decorously on a fragile Hepplewhite settee and gazed across the room at a portrait of a woman who looked remarkably like my "Cedie." She was wearing court dress of the Victorian period and a breathtaking set of diamonds—necklace, tiara, earrings and bracelets. "This," I said to myself, "must be my dear husband's mother. How I'm going to love her! And those must be the fabulous old Baughdie Diamonds!" I had time to think no more. A tall, stately *grande dame*, the image of "Cedie," swept into the room. Like little me, she, too, was in the deepest mourning. Upon seeing me, she swayed in the doorway and grasped at a tapestry to regain her balance, so overcome by emotion was she.

"You?" she said in shaken tones. "My son married *you*?"

"Yes," I said, rising with a sweet smile. "I am the little bride your Cedric chose in far-off New York. But you must call me Belle and I'll call you Mum." ("Mum" is very British and I was already speaking like an English aristocrat.) At that, my mother-in-law fainted dead away. Her physician was summoned and I was ordered from the house as I could be of little help in this emergency.

When I told "Cedie" of our meeting and how well it had gone, he was most distressed and hurried right around to Park Lane. ("Cedie" and his Mum

above: "Cedie," Mum and the Baughdie Diamonds
below: Little Me and same —1926

were very close, even though he was forty years old and she was nearly eighty. I always like to see a son so devoted to his mother, although in this case the mother may have wielded too strong an influence.) When he returned he said that we would have to get out of England immediately and began packing.

Even though I was sick with worry about his Mum, I dutifully obeyed my husband. Besides, I had never been to Europe before. Accompanied only by the chauffeur, Cedric's secretary, his valet and my maid, we set off to visit our shooting box in Scotland (which I did *not* like). From there we travelled to our little *pied-à-terre* in the Place Vendôme in Paris, France, which I adored as it was so convenient to the smarter shops and dressmakers. When the cool weather came, we moved onward to our dear little villa at Cap Ferrat, then to the apartment in Rome for Easter—a sacred experience—and finally to the Baughdie *palazzo* in Venice. But even though all of these lovely pieces of foreign real estate belonged to "Cedie" (and thus to little me), I did not feel that

With "Cedie," Park Lane

any of them was really "my home." As the wife of a peer exercising his own peerage, my *duty* lay in London at the house in Park Lane and at Baughdie House, our famous "seat" in Hertfordshire, where I could "put down roots," serve as a hostess to the man of my choice and bear his children. Not for little me the fruitless, rootless existence of the expatriate.

Without telling "Cedie," I wrote to his Mum inquiring after her health and stating that I thought that "Cedie" and I would return to London for the "Season" where she could arrange to have me "presented" at court and where I planned to take my rightful place in Society. By return mail I received a most unsettling reply. Britannia, Lady Baughdie, seemed to have taken leave of her senses. She called me vile names—words I did not even understand—and stated that I was not to return to England under any circumstances. I knew then that my mother-in-law's recent bereavement had affected her sanity and, rather than tax poor "Cedie" with this problem, I took it to an attractive lawyer I had met while dining at Quadri's.

He informed me that with "Cedie's" father laid to rest, "Cedie" was now the Earl of Baughdie and "head of the family"; I was *The* Lady Baughdie, mistress of all the Baughdie properties, their furnishings and heirlooms; my mother-in-law, it appeared, was just the Dowager Countess of Baughdie and entitled to little more than a lifetime of retirement in the dower house at our country seat. Realizing that life in London had become too much for the poor old lady, I told "Cedie" very definitely that I was returning to England, by the next ship, to see that his Mum received proper treatment at the hands of a loving daughter-in-law and to make sure that the proud name of Baughdie would be better known than ever before throughout the realm. "Cedie" decided to accompany me.

While Syrie Maugham was "doing over" the Park Lane house, I established poor Mum (by then raving) in the dower house at Hertfordshire, promised her that I would have the roof repaired as soon as the manor house had been redecorated and, wearing the famous Baughdie Diamonds, "made my curtsy" to King George and Queen Mary who, like all of London Society, were speechless at the sight of me.

Thus my long career as one of England's reigning hostesses began. Because of the terrible shyness and reserve of my husband, because of his afflicted speech and his interest only in matters concerning ornithology, ichthyology, botany and music and poetry of his own composition, "Cedie" was not easy to "bring out" socially. As with almost every other important quest in my life, I discovered that my ascendency in the British "social whirl" would be largely a matter of "going it" alone. But I was ready, willing and able to face the challenge.

I had given up my promising dramatic career to devote full time to my dear husband and the sons I hoped someday to bear him. This I regretted in no way. But when I considered the few people who made up Cedric's "social set"—drab bachelors interested only in birds, fish, flowers, music and poetry and those Peers of the Realm who were over the age of eighty—I decided to make some drastic renovations. (Mind you, I adore the Arts because I am an artistic and creative individual. But I felt that the tuneless tunes and rhymeless rhymes of "Cedie" and his *coterie* lacked the appeal of such lovely old favorites as Joyce Kilmer's *Trees* and Victor Herbert's "Ah, Sweet Mystery of

Life," to name only two vivid examples.) It seemed to me that with the "Bright Young Things" all over London, with the Embassy Club, the Kit Kat Club, the Savoy Grill—true gathering places of the intellectual *élite*—but minutes away from my Park Lane doorstep, our social "circle" could easily be enlarged. And even though I had retired from the theatre, I saw no reason to bar thespians of note from my salon. A True Society, as Momma always said, is nourished by its intellectuals and artists. If I would electrify London's "Old Guard" by welcoming to my drawing room such gifted *artistes* as Noël Coward, "Gertie" Lawrence, Ivor Novello, the Lunts and Vesta Tilly in the august company of darling David (Prince of Wales), then the "Debrett Set" would simply have to be shocked. After all, lovely Lady Diana Manners, daughter of a Duke, managed to blend Court Circles with the "Green Room." If one English aristocrat could "pull it off," why couldn't another—particularly one with far more experience on the "boards"—do it even better?

Thus I set out to enliven and enhance England's *haut monde,* and who, pray tell, was better equipped to do so? I had boldness and youth, unlimited funds and a wardrobe and collection of the fabled Baughdie jewels that were—when I wore them, at least—truly stunning.

Syrie Maugham had redecorated the townhouse in London very prettily, indeed, with masses of her famous white (no wonder she was called "The White Queen") and glowing pastels. The Chippendale pieces had been smartly "pickled" and the Dutch marquetry work sprayed white—a great improvement, I thought, although Mum suffered a severe setback when she saw it. (This was purely out of spite and brought on by her envy of me as her successor.) I had nothing but the greatest admiration for Mrs. Maugham's stately and serene rooms, but what two women of taste can ever agree about anything as deeply personal as the proper setting for one of them? Dear Syrie's creations were exquisite, but I felt that they lacked sufficient expression of my own unique personality. They looked cold, professional, "interior decorated." And so, paying off Mrs. Maugham, I set about adding a few individual touches of my own. The Gainsborough in the Adam Room I replaced with a large Tony Icart study of me in white *crêpe de chine* posing with two white Russian wolfhounds, a white "Peke" and a white swan. Finding the drawing room a little too sterile, I had all of the Boule furniture sprayed a delicate pink and scattered gay beaded sateen cushions, in shades of cyclamen, on all of the sofas. The big polar bear rug was especially noteworthy when dyed rose. The ugly Chinese wallpaper in the halls was steamed off and replaced by etched plate

glass mirror tinted blue. Even though dear Syrie had had all of the telephones done in white, I still found them unsightly and covered each with a large French doll in a hoop skirt. When I had completed the "personalization" of the house, I had it all photographed and sent to the press. It created quite a furor, and Mrs. Maugham, always modest, retiring and willing to share the glory, wrote to me and asked that her name not be mentioned in connection with the house as "the final excrescence shouts Belle Poitrine and does not even whisper Syrie Maugham." Say what one will about gentlewomen "in trade," it is always a rewarding experience to work with a true lady.

I have often felt that, if my dramatic career had not demanded every moment of my time, I might have enjoyed an unparalleled reputation as an interior decorator and arbiter of taste. In fact, many professional "taste makers" preferred not to compete with me and graciously declined the commissions I offered. As Elsie de Wolfe (the late Lady Mendl) once said, when I consulted her about refurbishing Baughdie House in the country, "No, thank you, my dear. God Himself couldn't do anything to improve *your* taste."

A lot of people said that they couldn't wait to see what I'd done to the Park Lane place so I decided to launch the *new* townhouse and the *new* Lady Baughdie at one gala party. It was an enormous crush and people who didn't usually go everywhere appeared, open-mouthed, at my reception and said they wouldn't have missed it for a million pounds. The *Tatler* wrote that "the architecturally perfect old Baughdie house in Park Lane and its new mistress simply have to be seen to be believed." British *House & Garden* wrote nothing, saying that words failed them and that the four pages of photographs spoke for themselves. By the end of my first Season in London I was quite the talk of the town and had filled up two scrapbooks with press cuttings about the "unbelievable new Countess of Baughdie." My true goal as a brilliant social leader was now within my very reach.

However, nothing runs entirely smoothly. Cedric, my husband, was no help. At each of my brilliant functions he seemed more withdrawn and embarrassed than at the last. When I tried to reason with him and would say, "But what are you, one of the mightiest lords of England, ashamed of?" he would flush and skulk off without answering. When I showed him the youth-

Like those other noblemen, Lord Berners, Prince Louis Ferdinand and Duke Ellington, "Cedie" was a gifted composer

ful, flattering dresses that had been run up by such great *couturières* as Patou, Maggy Rouff or Lucille, to my own specifications, he would color and say, "Don't you think it's a bit much?" Unlike many pace-setters in the world of high fashion, I have always dressed to please *men*, not other women. For whom, after all, did Our Maker put ladies on earth but men? But unfortunately it was becoming painfully evident to me that the gentle, cultivated, shy husband I had sacrificed so much for was not, in the truest sense of the word, a man at all. My readers will find it difficult to believe, but not once since the perfunctory kiss—his first—which he had given me on the occasion of our marriage had "Cedie" ever made a single demonstration toward me! As a warm-blooded, affectionate young woman, I was both hurt and puzzled. I sensed Mum's evil power at work to destroy our marriage, and this was one thing I would not endure.

Mum's malign influence was felt all the way from the dower house in Hertfordshire, even though I had given orders for her telephone to be disconnected, so that its incessant jangling would not upset the long period of peaceful isolation I had planned for her. However, there were many important social functions for which our invitations never arrived. I was mystified at first to learn that the Duchess of This was giving a dinner to which we had not been summoned, or that the Marchioness of That had neglected to include us among the guests at a ball. Then it occurred to me that Mum, from the country, was paying one of the servants to rifle our mail. Once I had accepted this shocking fact, I simply took "Cedie" to every important party in London just as though the invitations had reached their proper destination. The stunned silences, the blank looks of admiration for my elaborate *toilettes* at each brilliant *soirée* were enough to assure me that we had been meant to be included among the merrymakers.

With a house in town for formal entertaining and with Baughdie House not too far distant for relaxing weekends, I set about to plan a series of brilliant luncheons, dinners, house parties and balls, bringing together the most famous, most talented, most beautiful and most distinguished members of British society. My parties were soon the talk of the town.

There was, for example, an afternoon of poetry (this was mainly to amuse dear "Cedie" who seemed restive at the time) to which I had invited Edith, Osbert and Sacheverell Sitwell to entertain. Owing to an unfortunate mix-up with the postal system (Mum's fine Italian hand, I could swear), the Sitwells never received their summons to appear at my salon and I was left with only "Cedie" to fill in with his own verse. He was surprisingly effective and the guests who were there said that he was "every bit as abstruse as Miss Sitwell would have been." It was a brilliant afternoon—my dear husband's "day in the sun."

My great friend Gertrude ("Gertie") Lawrence simply doted on me. In her honor I planned a Limehouse Evening (will anyone ever forget her rendition of "Limehouse Blues" in *Charlot's Revue*?) with all the guests to be dressed in Oriental costume. But just as the evening had reached its height, darling "Gertie" telephoned to say that her car had broken down. When I offered to send one of mine, we were disconnected and the call could not be traced. I was frightfully disappointed, but of course I understood.

Another "pal" of mine was Lady Peel, that superb *comedienne*, Beatrice ("Bea") Lillie. Both being noblewomen and seasoned "troupers," we had much in common. I had planned a dinner party in her honor, but just before the guests were due to arrive dear "Bea" sent a note around to explain that she had developed an allergy to tarts and her doctor would not permit her to attend. Good old "Bea," always thinking of her hostess, even though I had ordered *Bombe Belle* for dessert that night.

Noël Coward, always my favorite, was invited time and time again for weekends in the country, but his heavy schedule of travel always made it impossible to accept.

Nor was there any dearth of royalty flocking to my remarkable rooms. I had planned a gala dinner honoring King Carol of Roumania and his dear friend the lovely Magda Lupescu, and, wanting the Roumanian monarch to have others of his own "ilk" present, I graciously asked the English royal family to take "pot luck" with us, *en famille*. Unfortunately, Carol was called back to the Continent the day before the party and an equerry from the palace telephoned to say that pressing political matters would prevent darling George and "Maisie" from attending. How often affairs of state can intrude upon life's simple pleasures.

And so it went! One gay gathering of celebrated people after another! The time fairly flew!

One lovely autumn afternoon when we were staying at Baughdie House in the country, I had learned that the Prince of Wales would be motoring past our very gates on his way to a function at Cambridge. Impetuously, I sat down and wrote a little note telling him to drop in for a hearty country tea with just the family—"Cedie," Mum and little me. In reply a secretary sent a letter to

Baughdie House stating that H.R.H. very much appreciated the invitation but seriously doubted that time would permit him to accept and not to count on his presence. Knowing how diffident the prince was, I took great pains to "underdress"—just an old tweed suit from Molyneux and the Baughdie Diamonds. "Cedie" was in homespuns and gaiters and even Mum had been "spruced up" in a black serge Mother Hubbard and a cameo I had lent her from the Baughdie collection. I was waiting impatiently in the hall when I saw a large Daimler rumble up the drive. Instructing the footmen to throw open the doors, I sank into a deep court curtsy with my forehead nearly touching the marble floor. From this position I heard the car door open and a strangely familiar voice say, "Pretty swell layout, I'll tell the cockeyed world." I looked up with a start and there stood Momma!

No words of mine can express the feelings that surged through me when I saw darling Momma once again. We had not seen one another, or written to one another, since I had left Venezuela, Illinois, as a tiny little girl more than ten years ago. (Like me, Momma is an abominable writer—when it comes to letters.) For all either of us knew, the other could be dead.

"Momma," I said, after the initial shock had worn off, "how did you know where to find me?"

"You been in all the papers, kiddo," she said, producing the *American Weekly* section from the old Chicago *Herald-Examiner*. There indeed was an article describing my fortuitous marriage into *Burke's Peerage*, as well as a description of the Baughdie holdings.

"How nice of you to drop in this way," I said graciously, always the dutiful daughter. "Will you be able to dine with us?"

"I'll say," Momma replied. "Tell the hired man to unload my trunks." Momma had come to England for a long stay.

Of course I adored my mother and naturally I was delighted to see her again. But I could not help noticing how very far apart we had grown over her lengthy absence. It also occurred to me that East is East and Middlewest is Middlewest and never the twain shall meet. Momma simply wasn't "right" for Court Circles and vice versa. In her jocular, good-natured way she made all manner of sport of poor "Cedie," calling him "Nancy" or "Mushmouth" or sometimes just "Seedy." Her presence in the manor house made my dear husband extremely nervous and even more withdrawn than ever. Thinking per-

haps that Momma and Mum might hit it off, being of the same generation, I had Momma's things moved over to the dower house. It was a disaster! Momma's warm, Gallic ways—the age-old customs of the New Orleans aristocracy—were totally alien to "Cedie's" mother. The dower house was not large and, after twenty-four hours under the same roof with the Dowager Countess of Baughdie, Momma was back at the manor house bag and baggage.

I suggested that Momma might enjoy taking an extended tour on the Continent, but she said that she'd spent so long trying to find me that she wasn't going to let me out of her sight again. It was as I had suspected. However, Momma was quite anxious to move into the London house, never having cared for the rural life. I felt that this would not be wise at that time.

What with Momma, "Cedie" and Mum all at swords' points, I found myself becoming nervous and "edgy" in the extreme. After having been "cooped up" in Baughdie House with the three of them for nearly a month, I finally suggested a brisk stroll around the estate and, as "Cedie" had complained of a hawk or some other bird of prey molesting his "feathered friends" in their sanctuary, I carried a shotgun hoping to exterminate the intruder. Momma was being excessively jovial that day. She had taken to referring to "Cedie" as "Marjorie the Bird Girl," although he could not understand her hearty Southern accent. This was indeed fortunate, as Momma had a frightful "tiff" with Mum and she was saying "To hear the two of you talk, I wouldn't know which one was the mother and which one the son. Except Marjorie's got a beard. But you're catching up fast, eh, Britannia?" It was ghastly!

We were approaching the bird sanctuary when I stopped to powder my nose. A mist was rising and I urged "Cedie" to lead Momma and Mum onwards to show them his new ornithological specimen, a Scarlet Crested Curmudgeon, I believe. He brightened at this and hastened on. They were approximately fifty feet beyond me when a terrible accident occurred. In picking up my shotgun, it accidentally went off! I heard a cry and then everything went black.

I don't know how many hours later I was revived to consciousness in my bedroom. "What happened?" I breathed. "Where am I?" The local physician was standing over me. He took my trembling hand gently in his and said soothingly, "Lady Baughdie, there has been a terrible, terrible accident."

"Yes?" I said. "You can tell me."

"Whilst walking near the sanctuary today," the doctor explained, "your gun went off, killing . . ."

"Yes?" I said, wide-eyed with fear.

"Killing your poor husband's Scarlet Crested Curmudgeon. A sorry, sorry loss."

"And . . . and the others?" I whispered.

"Don't worry your head about us chickens, honey," Momma's voice rang from the far end of my bedroom. "Britannia and Marjorie and me is all safe as church."

Lifting my head weakly, I could see the three of them standing there in the fading light. It was then that I suffered my complete nervous collapse.

CHAPTER EIGHT

UNKIND HEARTS

1928

My lingering illness · Trouble with Mum · "Only a bird in a gilded cage" · I try democracy
A living death · Our unfortunate *bal masqué* · A strange encounter at Worth's · The reappearance
of Mr. Musgrove · A secret *rendezvous* · "Cedie" and Mum pay a surprise visit · Divorce!
Dishonored · The Baughdie Diamonds · Homeward bound

I LANGUISHED FOR SEVERAL WEEKS in a private nursing home on the lovely Devon coast, lingering between life and death. The unfriendly, interfering attitude of my mother-in-law, the icy indifference shown me by "Cedie" and Momma's contentious ways had all but broken my poor sanity.

The only thing that got me back on my feet was a letter from Momma, postmarked "London." In it she said that she was coming to spend the Christmas holidays with me and that "Cedie" had welcomed Mum into the Park Lane house where she was acting as hostess in *my place!*

I had neither the time nor the patience to wait for the next train to London. Instead I hired a car and arrived in Park Lane in the middle of the night. Just as I had feared, Mum had "taken over" completely. She was even sleeping in *my* bedroom and had had the effrontery to remove the etched mirrors from the ceiling and to have disposed of my unique golden swan bed, my glass furniture and the magnificent portrait of me painted by that great Irish master, James Reynolds. She had replaced my exquisite things with her ugly old Queen Anne furniture which I had long ago consigned to the servants' quarters. As she was senile, demented and quite lame in the bargain, I could for-

Back from the nursing home

give her childish spite, her pathological jealousy of me. But I could never con-
done her wanton destruction of so much beauty.

However, the changes Mum had wrought in the house were as nothing
compared to the "job" she had done on my husband. Never overly warm,
"Cedie" was now cold to the point of ignoring me entirely and, when I told
him that either Mum or I must go, he said merely, "Shall I have your maid
commence packing?" I was too furious even to dignify his rude remark with
any sort of rejoinder.

And so all of us dwelt in acute disharmony in both houses. Even if I do
say so myself, Momma is a lady and a living example that "breeding will tell."
Once "Cedie" put her on a comfortable allowance, so that she could come and
go with some measure of ease, she made very little trouble and was away from
England more often than she was in it. Through one of the footmen, she had
met a very attractive Swedish gymnast and spent a good deal of time sight-
seeing on the Scandinavian peninsula.

I, however, remained, truly "a bird in a gilded cage." Shunned by "Cedie"
and his Mum, I did not fare too badly in London for I had a multitude of stimulating and socially prominent friends, but life in the country was almost unendurable. Left to my own devices, I did my best to make friends throughout
the countryside—not with the stuffy rural "gentry" whom "Cedie" and Mum
cultivated, but with the *real* people. As mistress of a large *retinue* of servants,
I tried to democratize my staff, starting with the young footmen. But I could
not get over the haunting feeling that I was being "watched." No sooner would
I get into a jolly conversation with one of them than Fidgets, the butler, would
appear and order the unfortunate youth to perform some irksome task in a
remote part of the manor house. Or, even worse, we would hear Mum stomp-
ing through the echoing corridors on her cane (later crutches, although I still
believe that her limping was simply a "grandstand play" for "Cedie's" sympathy) and the terrified young man would flee, leaving me to endure a long, unpleasant interview with my mother-in-law.

At other times, dressed in my prettiest, I would drive to "The Tooth and
Nail," the "pub" in our village of Baughdie Close, and strike up conversations
with some of the local men. They were a brawny, good-natured lot, never at
want for a salty joke or a friendly wink. But sooner or later Mum's big, black

A typical evening with "Cedie"—the library at Baughdie House

Rolls-Royce would appear in the village High Street and, with some transparent excuse about matching thread at the draper's opposite, she would again be spying on me.

So much for my days. The nights were totally unbearable. Shortly after dinner in the great cavernous dining room—simply *made* for gay banquets, but gloomy and oppressive when dining *à trois*—Mum would hobble off to her bedroom (she had entirely abandoned the dower house since the roof caved in) and leave "Cedie" and me sitting morosely in the vast library, where he would read his own privately printed volumes of poetry and I would attempt vainly to amuse myself. The lovely Jacobean combination cocktail cabinet and gramophone, which I had ordered from Heal's, was perennially "out of" needles and my new wireless always seemed to be "on the blink." (Sabotaged, of course.) At ten o'clock "Cedie" would mutter "Good night" and go to his bedroom next to Mum's, at the farthest end of the house from mine. Such was "life" at Baughdie House. I didn't blame Momma for staying away.

The climax of many, many months of tension came at Mum's eightieth birthday. In honor of the "great" event, a ball was to be given for "the whole countryside." Lady Bronwyn Haggis, an "arty" cousin on Mum's side of the family, suggested that it might be more fun if it were a masquerade ball with all the guests dressed as distinguished members of the Baughdie family. This, Cousin Bronwyn said, would please Mum especially as she was such a "demon" on genealogy and had such pride in the family history. It didn't sound like a very festive evening to me, but at least there would be someone else in the house that night besides "Cedie" with his poetry and Mum with her crutch.

About that time I noticed that the dampness and the smoke from all the fireplaces in Baughdie House were beginning to make my jewelry look extremely dull and I decided to have the famous Baughdie Diamonds cleaned. But instead of sending them to a jeweler in London, I took them myself to a little shop in nearby Hemel Hempstead—*anything* to get away from Baughdie House, even if just for a "breather." The man in the small jeweler's shop admired these historic gems inordinately and, while they were being "freshened up," told me an interesting story about their origin. It seems that Charles II, a dead king with an unmanageable page boy bob, had been enamoured of a young actress known as Barbara Bulbous, the "Bawd of Backshot Street." She had given him an illegitimate son and, in return, King Charles had given her the famous diamonds and had granted the boy, Barstead, the title of Earl of Baughdie. "What could be more historical," I asked myself, "than for the present Countess of Baughdie, and owner of the famous Baughdie Diamonds, to go to the party attired as the founder of the family fortunes?"

After doing a great deal of research, I happened upon a picture of Barbara Bulbous as she had appeared in a sylvan *masque* written especially for Charles's fiftieth birthday. There she was, a statuesque blonde like little me, wearing the very diamonds that were mine and dressed as Aphrodite, a Greek goddess of Love.

On the evening of the party I made a careful *toilette* and waited until all of the guests had assembled before making my "grand entrance." Their costumes did not seem very original or exciting to me. "Cedie" was dressed as Lord Pughtred Baughdie, the sixth Earl, and Mum appeared as the death mask of his wife, Lady Fistula Baughdie. Watching from the top of the stair-

*I pay my respects to
another great actress*

*With the Dowager Countess of
Baughdie—pour le sport*

case, I felt certain that my costume would cause a sensation, but I had no idea that it would create a scandal.

Just as I descended the stairs, there was a roll of drums and a man's voice called out, "We will now unmask." At that moment I appeared and announced in the loud clear tones which I had mastered in my early elocution lessons that I was "Barbara Bulbous, the Bawd of Backshot Street" and founder of the family.

Mum toppled over with a crash—and once again it was only to get attention. But this time she was well repaid for her trouble as "Cedie" fell right on top of her and the impact broke the old lady's good leg. There was no question about it. I was awarded first prize. The next morning I received a very sarcastic note from "Cedie" suggesting that "it might be better" if I were to "move to the house in London" while he "nursed" his "poor, long-suffering Mother" back to health "free from distracting influences." As Momma and her friend, Bengt, had just returned from the calisthenics festival in Stockholm, I was delighted.

About that time Momma "got it into her head" that she, too, would like to be presented at court. As the Countess of Baughdie, it was up to me to "launch" her, and I thought—and rightly—that this might "take some doing." However, I was honestly able to say that Momma had never been divorced and, as quite a lot of other American ladies were also being presented around that time (1928), I was able to slip Momma in without too much trouble.

Momma was thrilled and, even in my depression, I was able to derive

Momma at the Court of St. James's—1928

some vicarious pleasure from her childlike joy. She had chosen presentation dresses in every color except white, which she disliked, and was happily telephoning Malcolm Arbuthnot and Bertram Park for "sittings" so that this great occasion could be photographed. But I had become heartsick and despondent at the "turn" my marriage was taking. The hollow grandeur of life in London Society—the false friends and empty decorum—had made me *blasé* and jaded. Despite Momma's nagging and goading, I held off until the last possible moment before ordering my dress for Momma's "big night."

But, being a loyal daughter, I put on a "brave face," got into my white Rolls-Royce town brougham and asked to be driven to Worth's. (I might explain here that each member of the family had Rolls-Royces in his or her own individual color to "keep them straight." Mum's particular Rolls-Royces were always black, "Cedie" chose dark blue, fun-loving Momma's "Rolly-Polly," as she called it—stingy "Cedie" had allowed her only one!—was "fire engine" red and *my* cars were all snow white, so that I could find them in the fog.) As I was about to enter the House of Worth, an attractive older stranger tipped his hat and said, "Belle! I'd know you anywhere."

"I beg your pardon," I said with dignity. "Many people know *me*, for I am the Countess of Baughdie. But I am afraid that I do not recognize you, sir."

"Perhaps, then," he said, "this will refresh your memory." He handed me a small white pasteboard object which I took to be a visiting card. I whipped out my lorgnette to scrutinize his face when my eye fell upon the "visiting card." I stepped back with a start. "Mr. Musgrove!" I gasped.

It was not a visiting card at all, but a "still" picture developed from the horrid cinema in which I had innocently appeared with the notorious Houlighan brothers so many years ago.

"I am no longer connected with photography," Mr. Musgrove said in an odious, "oily" way. "I am now an art dealer and I have in my hotel room, Lady Baughdie, many pictures which I feel certain you would be interested in buying. I am stopping at a small private hotel not far from Soho Square, your ladyship."—Oh! The sardonic way in which he said that!—"Shall we take your car or walk?" Before I could answer I was once again in the rear of my "Rolls" with Mr. Musgrove's heavy hand on my thigh.

The *true* story of what happened in his squalid hotel room on that afternoon, which will live in infamy, has never been told. The journalists, always on the "lookout" for a sensational "scoop" involving the aristocracy, have distorted the facts and dragged my good name through the mud to such an extent that even *I* am not now quite sure of what *did* happen. However, I will tell, for the first time, the *real* story of what occurred with Mr. Musgrove and how certain unscrupulous people were able to twist it into a sordid and scandalous event.

I went to Mr. Musgrove's room and sat on the only chair there while he showed me hundreds of "stills" in all sizes—some of them hand tinted, and not very artistically, at that—and then told me that if I did not give him an outrageous sum of money, he would flood the market with them and my career as undisputed social leader of England would be forever ended. At the very thought of the horrendous scandal this would create, I swooned dead away. (Bear in mind, please, that I had been under tremendous emotional strain for the past year and more.) I "came to" only at the loud sound of pounding on the door. When I did so, I discovered that I was disrobed and in bed. Mr. Musgrove bounded for the cupboard, but it was too late. There was a blinding flash of light and there stood "Cedie" and Mum. Pointing his finger at me, "Cedie" said "Jack Hughes!"

"His name isn't Jack Hughes," I replied. "It's George Musgrove." Then I fainted again.

Naturally the court would not believe my simple story. I was branded as *déclassé* and by March 1929—just four months later—I had been divorced by Cedric, the Tenth Earl of Baughdie. Imagine! He was not even gentleman enough to let *me* divorce *him*! The press had a "Roman holiday" besmirching my good name and digging up trivial facts from my past which, when printed out of context, were damning out of all proportion. After all I had done for England, the judge was merciless with me. I was left with only my clothes, although I had had the foresight to send Momma across the Channel with my jewels. If my readers can believe it, "Cedie" was even caddish enough to demand back the Baughdie Diamonds, saying that they were "heirlooms" and not my property at all!

Penniless, I was even forced to sell a few things to get together my fare back to America. On the first of April 1929 I set sail—heavily disguised—for "the land of the free and the home of the brave." I had with me just ten dollars, twenty-six pieces of luggage, some other sentimental mementoes and the strong resolve in my heart never again to set foot on English soil.

Standing at the rail, watching the shores of Great Britain recede, I felt as

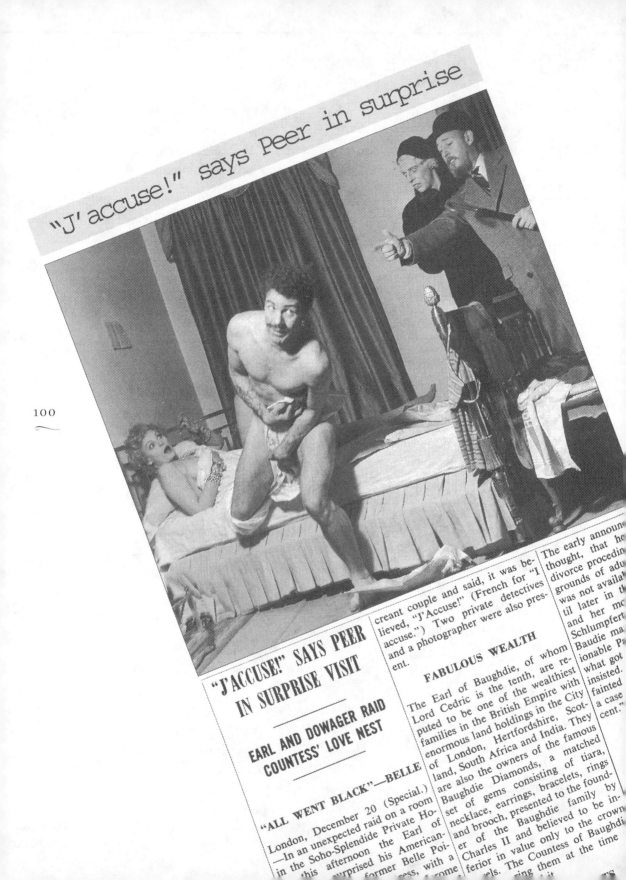

100

"J'ACCUSE!" SAYS PEER IN SURPRISE VISIT

EARL AND DOWAGER RAID COUNTESS' LOVE NEST

"ALL WENT BLACK"—BELLE

London, December 20 (Special.) —In an unexpected raid on a room in the Soho-Splendide Private Ho- this afternoon the Earl of ...urprised his American- ...former Belle Poi- ...ess, with a ...rome

creant couple and said, it was be- lieved, "J'Accuse!" (French for "I accuse.") Two private detectives and a photographer were also pres- ent.

FABULOUS WEALTH

The Earl of Baughdie, of whom Lord Cedric is the tenth, are re- puted to be one of the wealthiest families in the British Empire with enormous land holdings in the City of London, Hertfordshire, Scot- land, South Africa and India. They are also the owners of the famous Baughdie Diamonds, a matched set of gems consisting of tiara, necklace, earrings, bracelets, rings and brooch, presented to the found- er of the Baughdie family by Charles II and believed to be in- ferior in value only to the crown ...els. The Countess of Baughdi ...ing them at the time

The early announc... thought, that he divorce procedin... grounds of adu... was not availa... til later in th... and her m... Schlumpfer... Baudie ma... ionable P... what got... insisted. ...fainted ...a case ...cent."

"blue" as indigo. A tear slid down my cheek just as another woman, also heavily veiled, thrust a crudely wrapped package into my hand. "Here's the ice, honey," she said.

"Momma!" I cried.

"Not so loud," Momma said. "You're not officially out of England yet."

"Oh, Momma," I sighed, "I feel so terrible. I've disgraced you. Here I stand, a fallen woman. The first *divorcée* in the family."

But good old Momma had a ready answer at hand. "That's only natural, honey," she said. "You're the first one of us ever to have been married."

With that she was off, and I watched this game American gentlewoman gaily clambering down the ladder to go back to shore with the pilot.

Feeling a little better, I put on the Baughdie necklace, the tiara, the bracelets and one or two other baubles and walked bravely into the first-class bar for a bracing "Sidecar."

CALIFORNIA, HERE I COME!

1929

ALL OF MY LIFE—ever since infancy when the lonely whistle of the old Rock Island Line served as my "lullabye"—the very word "travel" has spelled "magic" for little me. I am never so happy as when boarding a train, a plane, an ocean liner, a yacht or just a simple limousine. My pulse quickens with the hustle and bustle, the whistles, the throb of motors, the hiss of steam, the very thought of new faces, new places, new worlds to conquer. I find travel a challenge and, with little me, the answer to the challenge is always "Yes!"

Disgraced, dishonored and dismissed I may have been by the "stuffy" standards of Cedric, his vicious old mother and their cruel *coterie*, but I still had my youth, my good name, my wardrobe, the Baughdie Diamonds and a new life to live in the good old U.S.A. Finishing my third "Sidecar," I began to feel much better. How thrilled I was to be going places, doing things in the company of gay, urbane people. I smiled at the lone, older gentleman who was sipping a Moxie at the next table. As I had not yet inspected my accommodations, I looked, in vain, for the waiter to present my bill. He was nowhere to be seen. "I shall simply settle with him later," I said to myself. Leaving the bar, I sought the route that would take me to my stateroom in a section known as "steerage" and deserted the quiet and comfort of first class.

I become Mrs. Morris Buchsbaum in a simple ceremony at sea

First class! Never, no matter how rich or how poor I may have been, had I ever travelled any other way! Even as a little girl, on the many short trips I took with Mr. Caruthers, from Venezuela to Ottawa, we always went by Parlor Car (and occasionally in a Compartment). As a result of my desperation to quit England, and of the sheltered life which I had always led, I had naïvely ordered the cheapest possible accommodation aboard the *Euremic,* little wotting that there could be such worlds of difference between "A" Deck and that pestilential hole below the water line called "steerage." What a shock! I could scarcely believe my eyes—*or my nose!* Instead of a trim cabin for one or even two—for I am a democratic person and should never have objected to sharing quarters with another lady of refinement from my own walk of life—I found a sprawling, brawling mass of humanity spilling out from tiers and tiers of crude "bunks." Steerage was not, as I had expected, a group of less expensive staterooms for the indigent voyager, but instead, one vast dormitory shared by men, women, children—even *animals*—alike!

Hardly anyone there spoke English and when I innocently asked which berth had been reserved for me, the whole ship shook with harsh, ribald laughter. In steerage it was a question of "first come, first served" and because, like any civilized lady of fashion, I had lingered over an *apéritif* in the bar, I had been allotted a squalid upper "bunk" in the most central, most public section of the "room." The trunks, suitcases, hatboxes and shoe trunks into which I had crammed my few poor possessions had already become "public property." I gasped as I saw unwashed peasant women pawing over the lovely creations I had ordered from such august establishments as Worth, Chapel, Poiret and the Boué Soeurs and my heart fair stopped beating when I saw two disgusting babies crawling over the exquisite chinchilla coat which I had ordered from Revillon Frères as Cedric's farewell gift to me.

Nor could I make my protestations understood. My fellow steerage passengers were foreigners of all sorts—Italians, Russians, Turks, Poles, Hungarians, Roumanians, Germans, Arabs—with little or no command of English. The only thing that lured them away from my beautiful Vuitton luggage—each piece marked with the Baughdie arms—was the announcement of luncheon.

Luncheon! How can I dignify it by that term? Instead of the spotless china, crystal, silver and napery I had come to expect as the due of any ocean traveller, proffered by smiling, servile waiters, this dreadful "meal" consisted of an undecipherable *ragoût* dished out of common enamel buckets! I had not the heart to eat.

Intolerable conditions in steerage!

Ever since Cedric's caddish intrusion on my privacy in that grim hotel room, I had felt "queer" and out of sorts. Never strong (in fact poor Momma despaired of ever being delivered of me), I had suffered dizzy spells, nausea and general lack of appetite, although my weight had increased alarmingly. Howsomever, I had reasoned with myself, could anyone undergo the severe emotional strain of my sensational divorce without showing marked physical symptoms? I had more than once arranged appointments with Sir Julian Catheter-Cowper, the great Harley Street diagnostician, only to cancel them because of the desperate pressure I was under in trying to assemble the few precious mementos of my loveless marriage to that brute, Lord Baughdie. (Try as I will to forgive and forget the terrible injustices done me, I must state that Cedric—under the pernicious influence of his mother—acted as no gentleman would over the most picayune personal effects such as jewelry, secondhand furniture, automobiles and real estate! I mean, some men are just plain *small*!) But today, surrounded by the noise, the odors, the congestion, I was in no mood to partake of the midday repast.

While the odious rabble swarmed around the serving table like swine at a swill trough, I quickly consolidated my poor possessions and locked my luggage. It was at this moment that I elected to move my trunks and valises to a corner of this revolting room where I could "keep an eye" on them. By exerting all of my frail strength I managed the smaller pieces but, alas, how was a weak female, unused to hard physical labor, to move heavy trunks? In desperation I tugged and pulled at the smallest of them to no avail. It was then that I first became aware of the Sofa Brothers, a Turkish knife-throwing team on their way to fulfill a carnival engagement in the United States.

The Sofa Brothers—Nadir and Faik—were splendid physical specimens in their middle forties (or so I should judge). Like me, they spoke English—of a sort—and they leapt to my aid with what I took to be a splendid show of chivalry. They were exceptionally tall and muscular with bristling mustaches and a notable array of artistic tattoos. Talkative in the extreme, they explained to me that they had travelled the wide world over in such variegated capacities as sailors, wrestlers, boxers, stevedores and acrobats. They "walloped" my trunks to the safe corner I had selected. I thanked them kindly for their willing assistance and made to dismiss them, but the Sofa Brothers did not understand. When I went to the ladies' restroom (a place sordid beyond my meager powers of description) to freshen my make-up, I found them waiting for me outside the door. When I stepped out onto the mean little bit of deck space reserved for steerage passengers for a welcome breath of fresh air, the Sofa Brothers were at my side. And when I tried to improve my troubled mind by perusing the pages of a new Michael Arlen novel, I discovered both Nadir and Faik leering over my shoulders and whispering indecent suggestions in their guttural, broken English.

With each unrepeatable word my heart contracted in terror! They had done a trivial favor for me and now, it seemed, they expected, as their repayment, a woman's most priceless gift! Against two brutes such as the Sofa Brothers, where could I, a lone, frail female, turn for protection?

I glanced nervously around me and realized, at once, how wise I had been in forgoing luncheon. In the angry seas of the North Atlantic the *Euremic* had begun to pitch and toss like a tiny cork. My shipmates in steerage, many of whom were sailing for the first time, now had ample reason to regret the noxious meal of which they had partaken—not to mention the assorted fruits, wines, breads, cheeses, cakes, sausages and other indigestibles which they had brought along. Such moaning and retching and praying and babble of heathen tongues I have never heard, and, as the sanitary facilities were primitive at best, I was close to illness myself in the very proximity of these piteous cases of *mal de mer*. Hopefully I looked for some sign of nausea in the lascivious countenances of the Sofa Brothers. But there was none! *Au contraire*, Nadir was munching on a vile concoction of vine leaves and sesame seeds, while Faik was attempting to ply me with his evil-smelling bottle of Arak. And these predatory lechers were the only two able-bodied men in the whole of steerage! I realized then that something must be done, and, making a flimsy excuse to my two pursuers, I took a long, circuitous route to the purser's office.

Accustomed as I had become to the courtesy and subservience of the British working classes, I expected a short, civil interchange with the purser, after which I, and my belongings, would be transferred to more suitable quarters. What a shock! This young officer was a curly-haired cockney of about my age, rather good-looking, in a common way, and with a definite "gleam" in his eye. Feeling that I could deal with him, I said, "Good afternoon, sir. I am Lady Baughdie."

"The *ex*–Lady Baughdie, I believe," he said with a horrid leer. "The photos don't 'alf do you justice, they don't."

"Photos?" I asked, not comprehending what he was getting at.

"That's right, Belle old girl," he sneered, extracting a tattered newspaper cutting. "Like this one of you in bed with that Yank."

The insolence! Cutting him short I said, "Thank you. But I am not here to discuss photography, merely a change of quarters."

"Oh, I'm afraid that will be impossible," he said, eyeing my *décolletage*.

"And why, my good man?" I inquired icily.

"Good is right, dearie," he said. "One of the best you'll ever know. Why not give me a try?"

"I have no time for your badinage, sir. I am prepared to purchase a berth in first class."

"'Fraid not. First is sold out. So's second. But 'ow about bunkin' in with me?"

Realizing that the *hauteur* of a lady to the manner born was wasted on this churlish oaf, I relied upon my delicate femininity. "But, sir, can you know what a throng of cutthroats, thieves, ruffians, procurers and common prostitutes frequent my quarters? It is your duty to protect me from the passengers in steerage."

"It's also my duty to protect the first-class passengers from *you*," he sneered. "But if you'd care to spend your nights in my cabin—cozy like . . ."

In utter defeat, I gathered my wrap around me and marched out of his office, stumbling over the Sofa Brothers as I retreated. My cheeks burned with fury. To think that I, so recently the toast of London, could now be so insulted by common sailors! Feeling like Marie Antoinette (a heroine with whom I have often been compared) as she mounted the reeking garbage cart to be carried to her tragic death in the Place de la Revolution, I descended into the gloomy pit that was steerage with Nadir and Faik Sofa jostling me obscenely.

Somehow I managed to endure the rest of the afternoon, fending off, as best I could, the bestial advances of Nadir and Faik. But, at an hour when I knew that on the promenade deck the elaborate tea service would be cleared away to make room for a gala cocktail hour, an even more obnoxious repast was flung out at the "cattle" crowded into steerage. By this time the misery was such that only the Sofa Brothers were able to eat. With such sickness all about me it is miraculous that I, too, did not succumb. But with the aid of my *étui* of smelling salts and a *mouchoir* liberally soaked in *eau de cologne*, I was just able to keep on an "even keel."

By ten o'clock that evening, however, I felt that I could stand my appalling surroundings no longer. Those who could sleep (a pitiful minority) snored and those who could not moaned and gagged with every roll of the ship. Babies cried. Arguments broke out. There was a constant traffic past my "bunk" to the convenience. And, what is worse, I was always conscious of the burning eyes of the Sofa Brothers boring through my very frock! I felt most unwell and I knew that the only thing to settle my delicate digestion would be a bottle of champagne. I also recalled the purser with a bit more kindliness. Although outspoken and "fresh as paint," he was a well-set-up lad and there could be little doubt that his quarters—no matter how humble—would be far preferable to these. However, I resolved, I would consider that problem after the "inner woman" had been lulled with a glass or two of "bubbly."

Locking myself into the ladies' room, I changed into a filmy dance dress, put on my chinchilla coat and all of my more important jewels. Thus dressed, I felt that a lady of my aristocratic bearing would have no trouble being served in the first-class bar. Carefully avoiding the Sofa Brothers, I darted up the companionway and marched bravely toward the bar.

As the sea was very rough and many of the passengers "under the weather," this convivial gathering place was empty of all save the distinguished older man I had seen drinking Moxie earlier in the day. He nodded and I rewarded him with a winning smile, ill though I felt. Selecting a table quite near him, I had the odd feeling that I had seen him someplace before— New York, California, London, Paris, Venice, the Côte d'Azur?—and the premonition that I would see a great deal more of him in the future. But who, *who* could he be? In my confusion I dropped my bag.

"I beg your pardon," he said, retrieving my purse.

"Granted soon as asked," I replied with a "toney" Mayfair lilt. (How many refined British expressions had become second nature to me during my years in England!) I could not help noticing how his gaze rested on the Baughdie crest, done in delicate beadwork on my bag. I hoped that I had not fallen prey to a common fortune hunter.

"Travelling alone?" the stranger asked.

"Yais, quaite alaone," I said in the elegant accent that was so naturally mine.

"I didn't see you by the dining room tonight, girlie."

"I dined in my quarters," I said quite truthfully. "Between you and I, one has to be most cautious of the types you meet on shipboard, don't they?"

"You're telling me?" was his cryptic reply.

Perusing the wine list through my lorgnette, I cast him a helpless little smile. "I'm so unaccustomed to ordering champagne, sir, perhaps you could assist me." In a moment he was seated at my table.

"Where," I kept asking myself, "have I seen this man before and who is he?" I asked one or two leading questions (Momma always told me that men enjoying talking about themselves) but the ruse got me nowhere. However, he abandoned his Moxie for champagne and I felt that he was not exactly miserable in my company.

How right I was. About midnight my companion said, "In the bar here is so gloomy. Maybe we could go to your cabin and order there another bottle."

My cabin indeed! Could this distinguished stranger but *see* it! Thinking fast I said, "I would love to ask you there but the place is a perfect sight!" (How true!) "My maid is quite overcome with *mal de mer* and unable to finish unpacking. However . . ."

He leapt at my suggestion. "You wouldn't mind maybe we should go to my place?"

I demurred and then, smiling, I said, "Is it a suite or just a stateroom?"

"It's the Verandah Suite," he said, "and should I tell you how much these *schmucks* are charging by the day you wouldn't . . ."

"In that case, sir, it will be perfectly proper."

I watched casually as he signed the bar chit and there was the name— Morris Buchsbaum! At last everything came into focus! Here was Morris Buchsbaum, the owner of the mighty Metronome Studios, where once I had worked as a humble "extra." I could remember seeing him as he observed the mammoth slave market "set" for *Gomorrah* and his eloquent criticism, "It stinks." Morris Buchsbaum, the star-maker! I could recall now reading that Mr. Buchsbaum had returned from Madrid with that torrid Spanish actress, Magdalena Montezuma; from Stockholm with glacial Svenska Flicka; from Warsaw with fiery Pola Bara. Suppose that he should come back to Hollywood with . . . No! The very thought of it was too much to bear.

Mr. Buchsbaum's suite stunned me with its opulence—its modernistic *boiseries*, the stunning murals by José Sert. "Oh, this *is* nice," I said, carelessly flinging off my chinchilla coat.

"Careful, I don't want you should catch cold."

"Oh, but it's so warm and toasty in here," I said, seating myself on the sofa with him.

"In that case," Mr. Buchsbaum said, "I'll leave the door open." He crossed the sitting room and opened the door wide onto the corridor. Even though he was a man whose entire professional life had been spent in the company of the most beautiful women on earth, I could not quite understand his seeming indifference to my nearness. Was this to be the story of Cedric all over again?

"A fella in my position," he said, "they can't be too careful."

"And just what is your position, Mr. B . . ." I stopped quickly. He had never told me his name.

"Uh, camera supplies," he said hastily.

"How interesting," I said. "You mean things like the cinematograph?"

"X-rays," he said. "Of course with an English lady like you, it's different. But some of the *nafkas* you meet—on a boat, on a train."

"It must be frightful," I said. "Poor, unfortunate women."

"Unfortunate women! Think of the men!"

I did so, and thought at some length of my host, Morris Buchsbaum of Metronome Studios—the "Bachelor of Beverly Hills," the famous "lone wolf," the recluse who refused even to be photographed for fear that self-seeking young women would "get at him." Rapidly I reviewed the men who had been in my life: Mr. Caruthers, sweet and kindly, but merely a "hick town" *entrepreneur*; George Jerome Musgrove, talented, perhaps, but a man who had allowed greed and avarice to overcome his dedication to Art; Fred Poitrine—my own darling husband—"nipped in the bud" so soon that one would never know what artistic triumphs might or might not have been his (Fred whistled exquisitely and, when released from his stifling inhibitions, did the most realistic barnyard imitations); Floyd had been a gifted cameraman but too quixotic, too lacking in self-discipline to grow in stature "in tandem," as it were, with little me; the "agent," whom I can only refer to as "Bernie," was simply a rat; the late Mr. Barouch, while a genius at numbers, had no time for art or for any science less perfect than mathematics; and Cedric, the Earl of Baughdie—while artistic himself—had been too repressed, too anxious to force me into the mould of his mother to accept the fact that the heart of a great *artiste* beat beneath the "social butterfly" who had captured London. I had given too much of myself to these men and they, in return, had taken, taken, taken, giving me nothing! But now, for the first time in my life, I was *vis-à-vis* with a man who had not only genius and vision—the soul of an artist—and the power to appreciate another *artiste,* but who also had a colossal studio all set up and running efficiently. I scrutinized Mr. Buchsbaum through my lashes. Where others saw a squat, balding, middle-aged man, plagued by myopia and sebaceous cysts, I saw (I was born with a caul and have always had the happy— and ofttimes tragic—gift of second sight) the pure, clear light of greatness shining from behind this unprepossessing *façade*. It was love at first sight!

Rising, I made to pour more champagne into Mr. Buchsbaum's glass, but a sudden motion of the ship caused me to overturn the whole magnum onto his coat and trousers.

"*Ay!*" Mr. Buchsbaum shouted, leaping to his feet. "This suit cost . . ."

"Oh, sir, how can I ever apologize?" I cried. "Remove your suit immediately and I shall ring for the steward to have it cleaned and pressed."

"Can wait," he said philosophically.

"Not a second," I said, propelling him toward the bedroom. "Take it off at once while I ring for the steward. I insist!"

Protesting, Mr. Buchsbaum went into the bedroom and closed the door. Having not a moment to spare, I ran my hands frantically through my perfect *coiffure* and, gritting my teeth, tore at the delicate lace bodice of my Paquin dress. I then overturned several chairs, our glasses and a vase of Fuji "mums." When the room seemed in perfect disorder, I then pressed all the bells summoning the steward, the stewardess—anyone who would come. "Help," I screamed dramatically, "help!"

The timing was extraordinary. Mr. Buchsbaum appeared at the bedroom door clad only in the suit of one-piece "B.V.D.'s" just as the staff appeared at the entrance to the Verandah Suite.

"So!" Mr. Buchsbaum shouted, "you think a *poobliker* like you can pull such a trick on Morris Buchsbaum? Throw this tramp out," he directed the steward. *Imagine!*

"If you please, sir," I said, "I am an English lady."

"Already I got all kinds ladies—English, French, a Gallician *Polska*, a *Spanierin*. Back home by Beverly Hills they all try this—blondes, brunettes, redheads, young boys, old men. Anything for a seven-year contract. But a *koorveh* like you . . ." His speech was halted by the singing of metal. A glistening knife flew through the air, removing the tip of Mr. Buchsbaum's ear and imbedding itself into the tulipwood panelling. "*Oi weh!*" he gasped. "*Turkishers! Goyim!*" There, standing in the open doorway, were Nadir and Faik Sofa. I became Mrs. Morris Buchsbaum in a simple ceremony at sea, performed by the captain a few minutes later with the Sofa Brothers, quite mystified and protesting loudly in Turkish, as our witnesses. After that Morris always called me his little Turkish Delight.

Once joined in matrimony, Mr. Buchsbaum was placed in the ship's hospital to have his wounded ear treated. He was faint from loss of blood. In the interests of safety, I had the Sofa Brothers confined to the "brig" and I saw to it that the purser who had been so unspeakably forward was dismissed.

With the Verandah Suite all to myself, I found the balance of my journey pleasant in the extreme. As we passed the Ambrose Light, my new husband was just able to get out of his hospital bed and become acquainted with his little bride, and no words of mine can suitably describe his reaction when I imparted to him my exact ambitions as a motion picture actress. However, Mr. Buchsbaum—dear Morris—sighed deeply and said, "If only we should get off this boat you could be Rin-Tin-Tin and I'd die a happy man already." (One has only to recall what an enormous "draw" at the box office the late Rin-Tin-Tin was to appreciate the profoundness and flattery of Morris' tribute to his blushing bride.)

There was a great reception by the press awaiting us at the pier. (I had had the foresight to radio the Public Relations Department of Metronome Studios to prepare an ovation as Morris Buchsbaum had not only discovered a fabulous new star, but had *married* her.) After the photographs and interviews were over, Morris and I were driven to the Plaza, where he attempted to carry me over the threshold in the grand old tradition. But it was not Morris' lucky day. He wrenched his back terribly and had to be put into traction at Mt. Sinai Hospital.

However, I was able to while away the lonely hours of my honeymoon getting acquainted with such beloved old sights as Saks, Bergdorf Goodman, Jessie Franklin Turner, Tiffany's and the Central Park Casino. By the time my darling husband was able to be moved, I felt like a new woman. And indeed I *was* a new woman. I was Mrs. Morris Buchsbaum, wife of the most important, most influential producer in all of Hollywood!

CHAPTER TEN

MARRIAGE AND MOTHERHOOD

1929

My lovely home · Casa Torquemada · Nesting · I discover my
interesting condition · Momma rushes to my side · A bride in April, a mother
in September · Baby-dear's premature birth · A modern madonna

OUR ARRIVAL AT LOS ANGELES was met by an even greater ovation than
the one which greeted us in New York. As dear Morris was still strapped to a
stretcher, it was agreed that we would steal off the train in darkest anonymity
at the Pasadena station. Therefore I arranged with Manny, the "P.R." man for
Metronome Studios, to have the press and all available "extras" meet us there.
It was a glorious sight! The Metronome Philharmonic and Massed Chorale
were on hand to sing the triumphal cantata especially written to greet me as
"first lady" of the Metronome "lot." It started out almost as a hymn: "Welcome, Belle, come to be our lady fair ..." and then turned into a rousing an-
them of praise and devotion to Morris and little me. I was presented with the
keys to Pasadena, Altadena, Hollywood, Beverly Hills and downtown Los Angeles. Morris was then put into an ambulance from the Pines of Rome Hospital, while I was helped into an exquisite *phaéton* by none other than Dudley
du Pont, one of the leading male stars of the Metronome Studios, and driven
in *cortège* to our lovely home in Beverly Hills, while being pelted with roses
and oranges. In the end *both* of us were carried over the threshold—Morris on
his stretcher and I by two assistant producers.

A quiet evening with Morris

With Morris safely bedded down under the constant surveillance of male nurses, there was naught for me to do but explore the wonders of my new home, Casa Torquemada. It had served as dear Morris' bachelor quarters for many years and was rivalled in splendor only by "Doug" and Mary's "Pick-fair" and "Falcon's Lair," home of the late Rudolph ("Rudy") Valentino. After my years as a "bird in a gilded cage" at Baughdie House, the Casa Torquemada seemed ridiculously small and cozy to me with its fifty pretty rooms, but this pleased me greatly. I had had my day as the lofty English *châtelaine* and what pleasure had it given me? None! I was, after all, American through and through, fun-loving and democratic and always ready for a "lark" in the traditional "Yankee" way, whether it be a dinner for fifty in our quaint Sala Alhambra, a plunge in our pool (copied from the famous Spanish Baths of Caracalla) or a quiet game of mahjong in our casual *Hacienda Méjicana* playhouse. I called Casa Torquemada my "castle in Spain" (although I thought of it privately as my "cottage" in Spain). To me it represented the place where darling Morris had spent so many lonely years before I happened into his life, and I was determined to bring the California sunshine, as well as the spirit that is *me*, into its gloomy rooms.

Having exerted an enormous amount of creative effort into improving the *décor* of my English husband's properties, and having received nothing for my pains but scorn, criticism, abuse and the wine of "sour grapes," I resolved to leave my new home just as Don Jaime Jesús y María Gonzáles y Fitzsimmons (famed Panamanian "set" designer for Metronome Studios) had planned it. A cheery smile, a buoyant spirit, the crystal shimmer of laughter were to be *my* only improvements on the interior decoration. But not long after we were married I learned to my great surprise that at least one room would have to be remodeled—a nursery!

The occasion of my great discovery that I was going to have a baby (I call it "B-Day") was the celebration of dear Morris' return to the "lot." Finally able to be on his feet after six weeks of excruciating pain, my beloved husband and I were fêted at a banquet luncheon held in the producers' dining room at Metronome. All of the studio's top-ranking stars and executives were in attendance. Morris was seated at the head of the long table (decorated in ferns, orchids, baby grapefruit and festoons of film) between that so-called "Spanish beauty" Magdalena Montezuma and lovely Helen Highwater, while I was flanked by dashing Dudley du Pont and "Tex" Lonestar, the cowboy hero. All of the studio "top brass" made toasts and charming speeches of welcome which went on for several hours. The day was extremely warm and I had, perhaps, been wrong in choosing to wear my pink-dyed fox coat with the blue broadtail lining. But the colors were certainly appropriate! I had asked the Public Relations Department to prepare a little extemporaneous speech of thanks for me to deliver to the studio "family," and had committed it to memory perfectly. But I never got to make my speech. When I heard my name called I tried to rise and found that the banquet hall was spinning around my head. I took a final sip of my Orange Blossom to steady myself but it did no good. I felt myself falling, falling, falling, and I landed right in the lap of Dudley du Pont! When I "came to" the studio physician said very simply, "Congratulations, Mrs. Buchsbaum. You are about to provide Metronome with the answer to Jackie Coogan." I was so overcome with the news that I was not able to speak but only to offer up a little prayer of fervent thanks. "Jesus," I said. Then everything went black again.

With the knowledge that a new little life was stirring beneath my heart, everything about me changed. I had always lived—if it could be called "living"—with a constant, gnawing fear of motherhood. That is to say, fear that I could *never* become a mother. Because the life of my beloved first husband was snuffed out by the senseless horrors of war after so brief a time together, I had been denied even that one living, breathing, smiling souvenir of dear Fred Poitrine—his child. And, as eager as I had been to provide a tiny heir to the Baughdie title and estates, the coldness and indifference of Cedric had made the thrill and pride of maternity impossible for me. But now, in this lush land of klieg light and Vitaphone, my fondest wish was soon to be gratified—sooner even than I had expected—and I was about to become a mother. I dreamed now of being a kind of Roman matron bearing sons, sons to carry on the family name and to take over the burdens of the studio like the Warner brothers. I was absolutely numb with joy, and as for Morris' emotions, they were indescribable. All he could say was "I can't figure it out. How could I be such a *schlemiel*?" (In moments of overpowering feeling dear Morris often reverted to the picturesque language of his Central European birthplace and delivered his many little endearments in the romantic Magyar tongue of old Hungary.) Needless to say, I was given the very finest medical advice, as the little unborn Baby Buchsbaum was widely considered one of the most astonishing and noteworthy phenomena of the film colony. A brilliant Viennese physician, whose name was later to be made nationally famous by the Fleischmann's Yeast Company, took complete charge of me. Because I was so delicate and very, very young to become a mother, he advised the greatest caution and said, "At your age this won't be easy." But I was prepared.

It was during the long summer of my pregnancy that I received a precious visitation. While serving tea to Helen Highwater, Dudley du Pont and Carstairs Bagley in the garden, I heard the muffled roar of a motor and there, coming up the driveway, was a familiar sight—Momma's old red "Rolly-Polly"! My hand went to my heart. "Oh, my God, no!" I breathed, and shut my eyes tight. But when I opened them again, there was Momma. She had found me once more!

The bond between a mother and her daughter is a wonderful, mystifying thing. I am always amazed at how darling Momma never fails to find her "baby" and rush to my side. Although we can be the width of the world apart, although years may pass without even the exchange of a post card, a Mother Always *Knows,* and whenever one of my marriages is mentioned in the newspapers—no matter how casually—sooner or later Momma always appears. Because I am a trained actress, I was *just* able to control my emotions, to introduce Momma to my new friends and to suggest that she might enjoy staying at the Ambassador or the Garden of Allah. But naturally Momma would

With Momma—expecting

hear none of it. Her place was by my side as My Time drew near, she said, and she vowed that she would sooner sleep on a billiard table at Casa Torquemada than let her "little baby daughter" out of her sight once again. Morris' face was a study when he returned from the studio that evening and was introduced to his brand new mother-in-law.

As she always does, Momma simply took over. Like the mothers of such stars as Mary Pickford, Mary Astor, Jackie Coogan and Mary Miles Minter, she soon became a Hollywood legend. What a godsend she was in helping me plan for the arrival of our "little producer," as we called my unborn baby. Because I was very ill during my pregnancy, and because I was utterly inexperienced in motherhood, darling Momma was able to do everything—even to preparing the baby's nursery. Momma's sense of style is rivalled only by her sense of economy, and it was she who got the baby's quarters redecorated in the most unusual taste, without costing anything except for her commissions. Metronome had just released its first all-talking costume drama, a life of Beau Brummel called *Gorgeous George,* starring Basil Thyme as Brummel, Vivienne Vixen and lovable Carstairs Bagley as the Prince Regent. Because there was a dear little nursery setting used in the film, Momma had it all crated up and moved from the studio to the Auto-da-Fé wing of Casa Torquemada, which was rechristened the Regency Room. Although I had anticipated something more along the lines of pink, and maybe commissioning Walt Disney to paint some cute murals on the walls, I agreed with Momma that no other baby in America would have anything like *my* baby's nursery (incidentally, the "set" designer won an Academy Award that year, but for a different picture and at the Pathé Studios). Helen Highwater and Carstairs Bagley personally supervised the refurbishing of the suite in Pines of Rome Hospital where my precious baby would be born. There was nothing to do but wait.

But the waiting period was not to be long. Although my baby could not reasonably be expected until Christmas time (the perfect gift for Morris—a man who had everything), I felt my first twinge during the gala *première* of Magdalena Montezuma's first talking picture, *The Loves of Ethelbert Nevin.* I had felt uncomfortable all evening long but I bravely tried to keep my jangled nerves in check. However, just as Magdalena appeared on the screen to sing Nevin's beautiful "My Rosary" (her voice was so untrue and her "Spanish" accent so thick that naturally the whole song had to be "dubbed" by a cousin of the late Grace Moore) but just as Montezuma appeared, something inside me snapped. I stood bolt upright and screamed. All the lights went on and the *première* was at an end. I was rushed to the Pines of Rome in the very nick of time.

The agony and indignation I suffered giving birth to my precious child are indescribable. But what mother would not go through it again and again and again if only for the ecstasy of holding for the first time her own dear little cuddly "bundle from heaven"?

After nearly half an hour of the most excruciating torture in the delivery room, my screams became so unendurable to the kindly obstetrician that he said, "For God's sake, shut her up." A mask was put over my face and the next thing I recall was being eased gently into my bed as the pearly dawn began to peer through the palm fronds outside my window. It was a perfect September morn.

"My baby," I whispered to the nurse. "Where is my baby? It's not..."

"Oh, no, honey," the nurse said cheerily. "She's just fine. One of the biggest, healthiest kids we've ever delivered."

But of course this kindly "Lady with the Lamp" was only trying to allay my fears. Morris and I had been married in April. Here it was only September. How could my treasured child be anything but a poor, wizened premature baby with hardly the strength to exist? I found out later—for I am one who insists on the truth no matter how great the cost—that my poor tiny tot weighed but eleven pounds at birth, hardly big enough to survive the cruel shock of being born! The child was placed immediately in an incubator and kept there, hovering between life and death, for nearly three-quarters of an hour.

Then at last, as I could hear the breakfast trays clashing discreetly in the corridor outside my suite, my nurse came into my room, her plain, wholesome face radiant with joy. "It's a beautiful little baby girl, Mrs. Buchsbaum," she cried, "and she's going to live!" I fell back onto my pillows in a torrent of relief and slept all the rest of the day.

BABY-DEAR AND I (actually our daughter was named Isabelle, but to me she will always be Baby-dear) went home to Casa Torquemada and the Regency Room a month later, when Baby-dear was strong enough to be moved. She then weighed nearly thirteen pounds and was pronounced "out of danger" by the retinue of pediatricians whom I had insisted on retaining. They felt that she had a good chance of survival. Mademoiselle, her governess, was installed and we were safe and sound at last. "Just Morris and me and Baby makes three," I kept humming.

I decided that Baby-dear would be raised in the simple high Anglican

A modern madonna—Little Me, Baby-dear and Mademoiselle

faith that had been such a comfort to me during my turbulent years as Lady Baughdie—at least I had got *that* from the ruins of my English marriage. For her spiritual mentors, I chose dear Carstairs Bagley as godfather and my adorable Helen Highwater as godmother for a beautiful, beautiful christening, just as soon as Baby-dear and I would be strong enough to face the ordeal. (Unhappily poor Helen had just returned from the Keeley Cure Rest Home at the time of the ceremony and was forced to have her stand-in hold Baby-dear during the ceremony while her attendant held her.)

Now I had everything—or almost everything—any woman wants: a beautiful home, a devoted husband, a darling baby daughter. I could rest on my laurels now and devote my entire energies to the one thing all women desire but few achieve—a career in motion pictures.

Baby-dear's christening—we thought Epicipull was nicest.
far left: "Helen's stand-in"; middle: "Helen"

CHAPTER ELEVEN

MY NAME IN LIGHTS!

1930-1931

My triumphal re-entrance at Metronome as Mrs. Morris Buchsbaum · Early "talkies"
Elocution lessons · Poitrine speaks! · All work and no play · Famous stars I have known · Stardom
at last! · I am Hester Prynne in *The Scarlet Letter* · Script difficulties · My gala *première*

CERTAIN OTHER ACTRESSES, who shall remain nameless, have found a certain amount of comfort in stating that I, Belle Poitrine, "married" my career. What they mean to imply, I can only assume, is that, as the wife of the most fabulous producer in motion pictures, I had but to express the whim that I would like to be a star in order to become one overnight. How laughable! Let me state, here and now, that no amount of "pull," no amount of money, no amount of publicity and advertising will make anyone a star unless he or she has that "certain something" to create public adoration. Don't ask me why, I simply had it. Some do, others do not. However, if it eases the pangs of jealousy for my "knockers" to believe that I used undue influence to attain my position as one of the "all-time greats," far be it from me to deprive them of their bitter pleasure.

For the "record," however, I would like to say three things in my own defense:

1. First of all, I was a seasoned actress with many years of experience on both the legitimate stage and in films, when I reappeared at Metronome Studios intent on rising to stardom.

My triumphal return to Metronome

2. Unlike Anne Sten, Simone Simon, Jane Russell, Faith Domergue and others, I did not *begin* my American talking picture career in star status. Instead, mine was a slow, steady climb from featured player to supporting player and then to star—after the position had been earned by dint of hard, diligent work. I worked in eleven films over a period of nearly two years before my big "break" finally came. Can one call that "undue influence"?

3. Although I may appear to be "telling tales out of school," I would like to make it clearly known to my detractors that my husband, Morris Buchsbaum, did *not* want me to go into films! In fact, he literally got onto his knees and *begged* me not to pursue my career at Metronome!! At first I was shocked, but I quickly understood how my husband felt: Morris wanted me for his very own. I was his wife, his hostess, his *confidante*, his guiding hand in every important business deal, his advisor and constant companion. Moreover, was I not the mother of his child and heir? Sobbing into his pillow he said brokenly, "I will be a ruined man if you make so much as one picture at my studio!" I tried to comfort him. "Nonsense," I said soothingly, "it is wrong for you to be so selfish, Morris darling. Because I am your private joy, you are unwilling to have me become a public delight. But there is enough of little me for all to share. As a creative *artiste,* Morris, you know how cruel it is to deprive the public of an idol, especially when I am perfectly capable of being a goddess to you and an inspiration to the millions of Little People whose lives will become richer because of my talent and because of your magnanimity in sharing me with them." He continued sobbing the night through, and he was still a broken man when I insisted on accompanying him to the studio the following morning.

So much for my receiving any favors not granted to lesser actresses!

My return to Metronome, as an employee, was a triumph in every sense of the word. Manny and the publicity department had done a wonderful job. All of the studio's top-ranking stars were waiting at the gate to greet me— many in full costume and make-up, looking unreal and "other worldly" against the hurly-burly of Buchsbaum Boulevard. Even Magdalena Montezuma, the biggest box office attraction of Metronome, was on hand, appropriately dressed in one of the garish costumes she wore as a French strumpet in *Grue of the Rue de Trop.* For some reason of which I am totally ignorant, Magdalena has never liked me. However, on this occasion she was civil enough, although I couldn't help remarking how very tired she looked (from overwork she would have you believe) and how unbecoming her costumes were (although this was intended as a criticism of the gown designer).

Relaxing on the "set" of "Papaya Paradise" —
Lyons Maine, Letch Feeley, Little Me and Carstairs Bagley

Metronome Momentous Moments was there to record the event for newsreel audiences all over the world. I made a brief, gracious speech of thanks and then got back into the limousine to be driven to the script department, where I was to be shown the available properties about to go into production and choose the one I most preferred. But while rolling past the great sound stages, the bustling outdoor "sets," I was once more struck by the odd quirks of fate. To think that less than ten years ago I was an unknown little "extra," pounding helplessly, hopelessly, at the employees' entrance for a "bit" part and today I was riding along the main thoroughfare of this great studio in the owner's private car, about to be given my "pick" of all the available female rôles. How often I've said it, but I'll say it again—Life *is* odd!

As I was a bit "rusty," from not having acted in several years, and as I did not wish to appear "grabby" by selecting a very large part for myself, I finally settled on the rôle of Tampa-tampa, a native girl in a South Seas epic called *Papaya Paradise*. Helen Highwater was once again well enough to work and was appearing in the feminine lead—an American missionary's daughter who redeems the son of an English duke, even though the young man (magnificently enacted by Dudley du Pont) has "gone native" and is little better than a beachcomber. Cast as the island storekeeper was my especial favorite, that great character actor, Carstairs Bagley, and I was especially drawn to the appearance of a newcomer to films, a most compelling boy named Letch Feeley, who had come from a filling station in Pamona by way of the Pasadena Playhouse. One look at this young man and I knew that he had "what it takes"—real star quality; I can spot it anywhere.

Although no screen test was required for my being cast in *Papaya Paradise,* I did not wish to appear as one having special privileges and I graciously consented to appear with Mr. Feeley in his test. And I must say that in his tapa-cloth sarong he was most impressive. The scene we did for the test was a very emotional one in which I, as Tampa-tampa, tell my native *fiancé* of an impending hurricane, tidal wave and volcanic eruption. Mr. Feeley was very nervous but, of course, I was not. In my best pidgin English I read my one and only speech:

"Great god Jujube angry at white sinners. Big fire and water come. Must sacrifice native virgin to appease angry god."

Poor Letch Feeley! He was so nervous that he "blew up" in his "lines" four times. Seeing that the director was growing very impatient, I asked for a "break" and took the young man to my dressing room for a relaxing drink. We were alone together for only half an hour but it worked wonders. He went through the next "take" with "flying colors." We sat together in the darkened screening room when they showed the "rushes." From all quarters I could hear such remarks as "look at those legs!" and "what a body!" and "a perfect Apollo Belvedere." I am accustomed to praise but I felt so sorry for poor Mr. Feeley. Nobody remarked about him at all! However, he got the part! I dropped him off at his rooming house and, as he stepped down from my car, he pressed my hand and said, "Mrs. Buchsbaum, I owe it all to you." Somehow I felt good all over, just realizing that I had helped this young "unknown" up one rung on the ladder to success.

The *Papaya Paradise* company was just "one big happy family." It was great fun working with such lovable old "pros" as Highwater, du Pont and Bagley. Helen, ever up to her fun-loving old tricks, had a portable bar rolled onto the "set" every morning at ten and, even on "location" at Malibu Beach, the whole project took on the air of a big picnic. Both Dudley du Pont ("Cuddly Dudley" as the wardrobe men called him) and Carstairs Bagley took to young Letch Feeley like "ducks to water," and they both outdid themselves inviting him to their homes in the evenings for extra rehearsal sessions so that he would be perfect. The film was a great success—both commercially and critically—and one reviewer even coined the word "soporific" to describe it. This, I suppose, was meant to combine "superb" and "terrific," but the term certainly caught on as I have heard it used many times—once or twice even applied to my own performances—since those carefree days in the sarongs and leis of *Papaya Paradise*.

But I was not satisfied to bask in the glory of my success as a simple native girl. I was determined to *grow* as an actress. Talking pictures were now all the "rage." If you were a star you had to *talk*, and I did not wish to be left behind like "Jack" Gilbert, "Connie" and Norma Talmadge, Vilma Banky and others who, for various reasons, did not take kindly to "talkies" or vice-versa. I had had only one line in *Papaya Paradise*, and the storm sound effects had been so loud that not very much of my speech could be heard. Still, I was not entirely satisfied with the *timbre* of my voice. Feeling that a beautiful speaking voice is the hallmark of every great actress—*and* of every great lady—I engaged the services of Dame Florence Fleming, a retired star of the London

Poitrine speaks! I learn to talk refined

stage, to give me lessons in speech. My progress was even swifter than I had hoped in my wildest dreams for, after six sessions, Dame Florence said, "Miss Poitrine, it is foolish for me to continue taking your money as there is absolutely *nothing* that *anyone* can do to *your* voice."

With the talking-picture craze, so came the popularity of big movie musicals such as *The Hollywood Review, Happy Days, Broadway Melody, Gold Diggers of Broadway*, the *Fox Movietone Follies* and a host of others. Metronome was planning its own all-star revue, *The Broadway Barcarole of 1930*, in which such New York "headliners" as Marilyn Miller, "Al" Jolson, Helen Morgan, "Fanny" Brice and "Bobby" Clark were appearing for brief "turns." All of the most important stars on the Metronome "lot" were also asked to do specialty "numbers." To be in the *Barcarole* gave a performer a great *cachet* at Metronome. I was eager to join in the fun although none of my own specialty material seemed quite suitable for family entertainment—or so Morris said. But to show that I was neither a "snob" nor stand-offish, I said that I would be perfectly willing to lead the "show girls" out in the beauty parade. This spectacle was called "A Gay Bouquet of Old Broadway"—a lovely number written especially for the film by George Frederick Handel and "Herbie" Resnick. Each girl represented a different flower and I was cast as Broadway Rose. It was great fun and after our taxing routine was finally filmed and "in the can," the dance director, Ares Mars, paid me a beautiful compliment by saying "Belle, you're the only broad in Hollywood who can telescope one day's shooting into three." However, I did not allow flattery to turn my head and I was always wary of it, knowing that many sycophants hoped to get to dear Morris and to improve their positions by "soft soaping" little me.

Other rôles which I played during 1930 were Anne Boleyn in *Oh Henry!* with a truly stellar cast. Carstairs Bagley was a perfect "scream" as Henry VIII—off camera as well as on. Because she claimed to be Spanish, Magdalena Montezuma played his first wife, Catherine of Aragon; Vivienne Vixen was Jane Seymour; Nan Badian was moving as Catherine Howard; Laura Gray played Anne of Cleves and Alida Freeborn was Catherine Parr. Such a collection of talent and beauty that the critic for the New York *Times* was moved to headline his review "Westminster Was Never Like This." Another critic spoke of the film as "the Westminster Kennel Club," obviously a misprint. Next I assayed the rôle of Cynthia Plantagenet in *Bottle Babies*, which attempted to show what happens to débutantes when they get in with the wrong set. After that I had the great pleasure of playing with young Letch Feeley once again.

He had become—very briefly, as I had other plans for him—the sixteenth Tarzan. Together we tried to bring some standards of art and dignity to a silly animal picture called *Tarzan's Other Wife*. In it I played Daphne, the title rôle. However, I was indignant at the waste of talent for such rubbish as this. As I said to Morris, "Letch Feeley has a lot more than shows in that Tarzan costume and *I* want to make use of it." "B" pictures indeed! I wound up the year with an extremely moving performance as a girl who had gone wrong in a shocking *exposé* picture entitled *Penal Institute*. It certainly woke up the public to the conditions in reformatories and if you think I am simply "blowing my own horn," I quote Mae Tinee, film critic for the Chicago *Tribune*: "A truly shocking picture in this day and age . . . Belle Poitrine's performance will certainly put drowsy customers right where they ought to be." So much for my first year as a real actress.

When 1931 finally came around I was ready for it! I had a year's solid experience—six pictures—"under my belt," and my confidence was fully restored. I was at sort of a lull in my career, owing largely to the lack of challenging new material. Nothing on hand at Metronome seemed quite right for me when a grand opportunity presented itself. Magdalena Montezuma was scheduled to make a picture called *¡Viva Tequila!* The story concerned two sisters in Mexico, during a revolution, who become involved with a young American aviator (Dudley du Pont). Both sisters fall in love with the pilot. The revolutionary forces are marching on their village. He can save only one. He saves the star (Montezuma, naturally!) and the younger sister valiantly stays behind to be raped and slaughtered by the enemy. My dear friend, pert little Lupe Velez, had been engaged to play the younger sister, Dolores, but at the last moment a prior commitment made it impossible for her to accept. As I lived in a Spanish house, why would I not be perfect as Dolores? Morris was maddeningly uncooperative, largely, I believe, because most of the picture was to be "shot" at a distant "location" in Mexico, and he was so insanely jealous of me that he could not bear to let me out of his sight. Finally, I won, had a long session with the director and the part was mine.

If I had known then what I know now, perhaps I would have done Morris' bidding. Never before or since have I met such a vicious, egotistical and despotic star as Magdalena Montezuma! To begin with, she was madly envious of my youth, my beauty, my talent, my rapid rise and my position as Mrs. Morris Buchsbaum. But that was only the beginning! What really enraged Magdalena was my portable dressing room. Marion Davies may have had the

"Early Talkies"

above: As Anne Boleyn in "Oh Henry!" with Vivienne Vixen and Carstairs Bagley. left: As Broadway Rose in "The Broadway Barcarole of 1930" with Helen Highwater as Virginia Creeper. below: With Helen Highwater in "Bottle Babies"

above: With Letch Feeley in "Tarzan's Other Wife." I played Daphne.
below: Pixie Portnoy, Letch Feeley and "Yours Truly" in "Sawdust Circe"

above: Magdalena Montezuma, Little Me and Dudley du Pont in "¡Viva Tequila!"

first portable dressing room in Hollywood, but Belle Poitrine had the *largest!* As a going-away gift to myself I had ordered it—*them* to be accurate—from the Mack Truck works. My dressing room was two orchid-colored Mack Trucks which, when backed together, made a lovely little suite. Compared to my new quarters, Montezuma's old White trailer looked sick!

Like many persons of Latin extraction (although there is some very legitimate doubt about this), Magdalena had a strong streak of jealousy in her make-up and she certainly took it out on little me! Poor Dudley (our male lead) kept saying that he felt as though he were in No Man's Land, between two enemy forces.

I, for my part, tried to behave like a professional *and* a lady. I was always polite with a cheery, personal pleasantry of some sort or another on my lips. I was punctual, helpful and courteous to everyone connected with the film. When Montezuma claims that I tried to undermine her confidence by making remarks about her costumes and make-up (and I know that she does so to this day), it is simply the work of a sick, warped mind trying to twist a kindly, constructive criticism into a deadly insult. The *truth* behind these stories is simply that, as the producer's wife, I wanted everything to be perfect and if a certain dress made Magdalena look thick in the middle (she has a tendency toward plumpness, if not downright obesity), if her make-up looked matronly during the daylight sequences (when she was *supposed* to be a girl of twenty), I said so to be helpful and in the interests of having a first-class production. Her famous story about my having "stripped her naked" right on the "set" is also a gross exaggeration. What actually happened is that Montezuma arrived late on the "set" (quite "hung over," if the truth were told, although it is not generally known that she drinks to excess) with a long thread hanging from her costume. After saying "Good afternoon, Magdalena" (I was being jocular and good-natured, as it was nearly eleven in the morning and we had been called for eight o'clock!), I remarked that she looked tired and that her extra sleep hadn't helped enormously. All of this, of course, she greeted with her typical sneer. Then I noticed this loose thread and said, "Wait a minute, darling, I don't want you to ruin still another scene." I pulled at the thread and the next thing I knew, her whole costume simply disintegrated and she was standing only in her shoes!! But I can hardly be blamed if "Señorita" Montezuma was so unfastidious as not even to wear undergarments when she was on camera. In fact, I even said that her costumes would fit far better if she wore a really firm foundation. Montezuma was livid. She stormed off to her rickety old dressing room in hysterics and work had to be suspended for the day.

After that she was insupportable. She talked and rattled her castanets during all of my scenes. I know it was she who put the itching powder in my cold cream and who sent me on a wild goose chase, all the way to Taxco, after a certain telegram signed "Ronald Colman" appeared under my dressing room door. She also tried to work against me through the director, and this I know for a fact as I was in his hotel room myself when she telephoned to arrange an assignation with him! But the lowest trick of all was trying to curry favor with the critics at my expense (as well as creating a terrible loss for the film itself!) and this Magdalena did all too thoroughly, as almost every review compared my performance most unfavorably with hers. Needless to say, we were not on cordial terms when the picture was completed! I am too big a person to endure such pettiness and such childish display of ego and "spleen." I resolved, then and there, that the next time I appeared with Magdalena Montezuma, *I* would be the star and *she* the supporting player.

But after that bad start the rest of my 1931 films were pleasure itself. The first, *Sawdust Circe,* was a circus story starring lovely Pixie Portnoy and that great clown, Stuart Harris. But, in the rôle of a trapeze *artiste,* I got not only featured billing but also the pleasure of playing opposite Letch Feeley once more. I had never met a young man quite so accomplished—and he seemed to grow with each performance. It was a happy company and the work went smoothly with only one unpleasant incident to mar our enjoyment—the young stunt woman who did my dangerous trapeze work for me fell to her death! I was dreadfully upset but Letch came to my dressing room to comfort me and stayed quite a long time. As he pointed out, she was insured. It made me feel a great deal better in my mind.

My next film was also a joy although, spiritually speaking, it took a great deal out of me. It was a great Biblical pageant entitled *Jesus Wept.* Dear old Carstairs Bagley was cast as Pontius Pilate and I played the unsympathetic rôle of his mistress. Darling Carstairs! What a lot I learned from him! He was the grandest of all the grand old character actors in Hollywood.

Many people have made cruel fun of Carstairs Bagley simply because he felt more comfortable in women's clothes during his off hours. I, for one, see nothing amusing or unusual about that. I—and millions of other women—relax in *slacks.* Why, then, was it so wrong for poor Carstairs to take his leisure in the lovely creations designed and made for him by the late Omar Kiam?

above: As Pilate's mistress in "Jesus Wept" with my darling Carstairs.
left: In "Jolly Roger" with Letch and Carstairs

With Letch and "Tex" Lonestar in "Caw Girl"

(Or "Omar the Tentmaker" as Dudley du Pont used to call him because of Carstairs' great *avoirdupois!*) Cheerful, witty, generous, outgoing and always eager to help younger actors, Carstairs Bagley's mysterious death, in that unwholesome hotel for men during World War II, left an empty void in "filmdom" and in my heart.

But I digress! *Jesus Wept,* although boycotted by both Catholic and Protestant faiths, was a reverent and moving film and its loss of nearly seven million dollars does nothing to persuade me that I was wrong in urging Morris to produce it.

Next came my only "horse opera," and although it was a Grade "B" Western, I was at last the leading lady. The film was called *Caw Girl.* In it I played the title rôle, that of an Indian princess, head of the Oklahoma Caw tribe. I fall in love with the leader of a wagon train (Letch Feeley) and because of my great and enduring love for the enemy white man, my people turn on me and torture us, until we are miraculously saved from a hideous death by "Tex" Lonestar (as General Custer) and the U.S. Cavalry. A trite story, you will say, but one which I found very touching.

In my next picture—the last before achieving stardom—I was a full-fledged feature player with my name given the same importance as Carstairs Bagley's and (I insisted on this because he was such a talented boy) Letch Feeley's. As I said to Letch one day in my dressing room, "Isn't life odd? I played opposite you in your screen test for *Papaya Paradise* when we were both unknown and now here we are, not two years later, still playing opposite one another with our names in lights!"

"Yeah," Letch said.

This film was called *Jolly Roger.* It was a buccaneering saga something like the ones "Doug" Fairbanks and "Jack" Barrymore used to make. Kindly old Carstairs, who wouldn't have laid a hand on Letch in anything except affection, was again the blackest sort of villain. I was the damsel in distress and Letch the bold, romantic pirate. A lot of the picture was filmed at sea, actually on an old sailing ship, and I remember the long, moonlit nights lying out on deck with Letch and listening to him talk of his love of the sea, and spinning dreams about the boat he hoped someday to own. We were six weeks over our shooting schedule but I didn't mind. *Jolly Roger,* while not a great critical success, was a *fun* picture to make and even turned a modest profit.

Because of the financial success of *Caw Girl* and *Jolly Roger* (both of them low-budget pictures), I felt that now I was ready to star in a vehicle tailored expressly to my needs and I said so to Morris. He put up a "howl" when I suggested hiring someone like Noël Coward, Somerset Maugham, Frederick Lonsdale, Philip Barry—a "name" author who was *au courant* with the pressures of contemporary life. Morris was most unreasonable and suggested that I employ the services of his nephew, Sheldon, in the Metronome script department, as no one else would. I was furious. I told him that if a common "greaser" like Magdalena Montezuma could have her pick of such famous writers as Ernest Hemingway, William Faulkner, Willa Cather and Elinor Glyn, why should I, his own wife, have to put up with a nobody like Sheldon? I said that I intended to have a "name" author, too. With that Morris tossed a copy of *The Scarlet Letter* at me and said that I could probably play it to perfection. I asked Momma, Helen Highwater, Vivienne Vixen and some of the other girls in my set if they had ever heard of this Hawthorne and they said they thought they had. Lynn Caine was almost sure of it. Dudley du Pont had read the book and explained the story to me and I thought it was cute and certainly had some good scenes in it for the leading lady. The only thing I objected to was that it was so old-fashioned. I had been in so many costume pictures recently that I felt a change of pace would be good for me. So I told Morris that I liked the story and to go ahead and buy it for me, but that I did want some changes made and to get hold of the author for some story conferences. Morris just laughed and said something to the effect that Hawthorne didn't live in Hollywood but was eccentric and hung around a Public Domain where they couldn't call him, and that I could do anything I liked with the script.

What a challenge! I admired the character and the nobility of Hester Prynne and I thought the title was very catchy. Otherwise I wanted a free hand to bring the story up-to-date and to make a lot of changes. So many men in the story department at Metronome said that *The Scarlet Letter* was a great classic and that it was a sacrilege to touch it that I decided to handle the script myself. (They'd certainly taken liberties with the Bible, but just try to change one comma in some old book about a girl having a baby in Massachusetts and they're all up in arms!! That's the sort of help one used to be forced to endure on the Metronome "lot"!)

What I did to *The Scarlet Letter* is now history. I have been both lauded and criticized for "taking liberties" with the work of "Nat" Hawthorne, who was the only person involved not to make any comments, either "pro" or "con," about my film. Suffice it to say that I transformed it from a dusty classic, about dead people in a dead age, to a vital, living story about a girl everyone could understand. In modernizing the story, I kept the essentials—Hester Prynne is a good, lively, spirited girl who makes a mistake, pays the price and ends up happily married—and mercilessly cut out the "deadwood." As this was my first real starring vehicle, I wrote in parts for the people on the Metronome "lot" whom I knew I could trust (too many others had made the mistake of "showing their hands" to me in the past). Helen Hightwater was scheduled to appear but suffered an unfortunate relapse and was once again placed in a sanitarium. I gave Carstairs Bagley a "fat" character rôle and offered a specially written part to witty Dudley du Pont. However, he said that he had been put out on loan to Alexander Korda (later Sir Alexander Korda) and had to go to England for a long time on the very next boat. I was sick with disappointment, but that, alas, is life in show "biz." I went to Morris and demanded—and got—Letch Feeley as my leading man. With a "team" like that, how could any picture help but be a huge success?

As you may remember, *my* version of *The Scarlet Letter* was a college musical set in a big coeducational university called Allstate. Hester, the daughter of a man who renounced a fortune of millions to become a minister, is working her way through college (this was the time of the depression and I felt that she would lose sympathy and "audience identification" if she was just a pampered coed in some radical school like Vassar or Foxcroft) selling subscriptions to *College Humor* and she is also captain of the cheer leaders' team. She meets Brick Barclay (the new name I gave the hero, as Letch didn't like the one "Nat" chose), who is captain of the football team. They fall in love at a beautiful formal ball held in his fraternity house and, having drunk too much "spiked" punch, Hester allows Brick to take liberties with her that she would never have otherwise permitted. The next day she is horrified when she finds out what she has done and realizes that she is pregnant, and that a hard society girl is wearing Brick's "frat" pin and that he is the son of a millionaire and would never consider finding happiness with a poor girl. Hester is sick with worry but she puts on a brave face, avoids Brick whenever he tries to "date" her or even "cut in" at a dance, and she goes out to cheer the Allstate team on to victory against Plymouth U. It is then that she faints and Brick, realizing how much he loves her and that her unborn child is his, picks her up in his arms and tells his millionaire father that if he can't marry Hester he won't finish the game for the old *alma mater*. The father recognizes Hester as the daughter of his old college roommate, the man who lent him enough money

to get started in business, and gives the young people his blessing. With Hester cheering him on, Brick goes in to make the winning touchdown in the last minute of the game. Then Hester, wearing proudly the big red "A" of Allstate, leads the team and student body in a big victory snake dance culminating in their wedding under the visitors' goal post. I felt that it brought home a real message for the youth of America.

It took us more than four months to film *The Scarlet Letter*, I insisted on a closed "set" with only Manny, head of the publicity department, permitted to visit. Morris ranted and raved about the budget, but I wanted my *chef-d'oeuvre* to be the one flawless film of my career. And it was. Why should I, a serious *artiste*, care for Morris' hysterical outbursts over deficits when I have in my scrapbook reviews such as "Devastating..." "An unbelievable four hours in the theatre..." "Belle Poitrine brings to Hester Prynne all the innocence and virtue of a John Held flapper..."

After a carefully planned campaign of advertising, publicity, personal appearances and interviews, *The Scarlet Letter* had its world *première* at the Buchsbaum Baghdad in New York's fabulous Times Square on New Year's Eve.

The *première* was a very exclusive invitational affair. All the top stars of the Metronome "stable" were invited (with one glowing exception) as were rival producers, stars, international celebrities, critics and leading "opinion-makers." I was terribly disappointed when Louella O. ("Lolly") Parsons telegraphed that she had suddenly been taken ill. Walter Winchell was also suddenly unable to attend and President and Mrs. Hoover regretted that they had a prior engagement. Otherwise it was a *succès fou*. The showing began promptly at eight (I am one star who won't put up with latecomers) and ended on the stroke of midnight. Although I had seen "rushes" and screenings of *The Scarlet Letter* many times before, I was dissolved in tears at the beauty of my performance and even my "hardboiled" husband, Morris, sobbed brokenly in the seat beside mine, muttering softly in his quaint native tongue. The rest of the audience was so touched that they were unable even to applaud at the end of the film.

When I stepped out of the theatre onto Times Square, pandemonium broke loose. From the wildly cheering populace of New York I knew that I had arrived. Never before was any actress given such an ovation. As the shouts, whistles, horns, sirens, serpentine and confetti swirled around me, I knew that this was something more than the work of Manny and the "boys" in the P.R. department. This demonstration was far beyond something staged in the name of publicity.

"Morris," I breathed. "The shouting! The cheers!"

"It's 1932, *nafkeh*," he said affectionately.

1932—those magic numbers—the year of Belle Poitrine's elevation! With my head held high, I waved to the multitude who had turned out to pay homage to little me. It was a new year and *I* was a star of the first magnitude!

CHAPTER TWELVE

A DIFFICULT YEAR

1932

Stardom · My heavy "shooting" schedule · Busy days · The hectic
social whirl · I become a leading Hollywood hostess · Famous feuds of Filmdom
Baby-dear · A part-time mother or a full-time star? · Re-enter Mr. Musgrove!
A dreadful accident in the gun room · Trial by jury

NO POOR WORDS OF MINE can ever describe the international furor caused
by *The Scarlet Letter*. Editorials, petitions, sermons, radio lectures—there was
even talk about having a bill passed in Congress concerning the adaptation of
classics—appeared everywhere. Overnight Belle Poitrine became a household
word. I was delighted and paid no attention to dear Morris' morose muttering
that all publicity is not necessarily good. I think he was still jealous of "sharing" me with the public.

Naturally I wanted to make another picture while I was still "hot," as the
saying goes. But I didn't want to make just *any* picture. Instead I required a
superb vehicle which would bring out my best qualities and show me off to
the greatest advantage. (I have always had trouble finding material that is
suitable for my talents.) I was totally "stymied" until I received a letter from
my dear old "chum," Dudley du Pont, written from the Savoy Hotel in London.

Darling, darling Belle—

Caught you and that cute Letch in The Scarlet Letter *at the Odeon.*
Too divinely unbelievable! You are the absolute dish of London—
where, ça va sans dire, *you are still most vividly remembered.*

With Letch in "Paradise Lost"

Ducky, don't spread this around to those old bitches in H'wood, but I think I've found the film divine for you and Prettykins to do next. This old side-kick of mine, Milton, has written the most heavenly thing called Paradise Lost and it's a natch for pix!

Unlike Scott Fitzgerald and other writers I could—but won't—name, Milton is absolutely buried in St. Giles's and wouldn't make a bit of trouble about your changing bits about. He's a perfect pet, although there is unpleasant talk about his being blind now and again. However, if you rush $10,000 to me I can promise you that Milton will be as still as the grave and not lift a pinkie to interfere with anything you want to do to Paradise Lost.

Ivor and I rather see you and Lover Boy in simply celestial things by Lanvin and then a flashback to the Garden of Eden with the two of you in absolutely minuscule *rhinestone fig leaves and things too divine . . .*

Isn't that like darling Dudley, always taking time to think of his friends? Without even consulting Morris (who would have thrown cold water on the whole idea) I sent Dudley a check for his friend Milton and got right to work on plotting *Paradise Lost.* As Dudley suggested (if he had not chosen to be an actor, he might have been a famous author—what an imagination!) I did part of the story in the present where Eve is a rich Junior Leaguer who wants to lead Adam, a young, idealistic architect, astray (with flashbacks to the Garden of Eden) until the modern Eve happens to stumble into the Four-Square Gospel and get saved. In the end she and Adam marry and settle down happily on a big ranch, with a lovely apple orchard. The film created a furor and I was once and for all established, not as a "one-shot" star, but as a performer who could be counted on to do truly unique films.

I was driving myself too fast, working too hard, but I loved it for I am one of those truly dedicated *artistes* who will sacrifice anything for his career. In addition to my actual "shooting" schedule there was a constant round of activity—posing for "stills," interviews, publicity "gimmicks," radio engagements, personal appearances, goodwill tours, addressing the Belle Poitrine Fan Clubs, which Manny started all over the world. It was a busy life.

In addition to my hectic career, I still had to make the "social rounds" of Hollywood. Sympathetic, friendly and gregarious, I was naturally popular with everyone in the movie colony and always at the center of some gay "high jinks."

I had so many, many good friends that it is now almost impossible to name them all. Jean Harlow simply doted on me, for example, even though she was under contract to M-G-M and we were considered "deadly rivals" by all those who did not know what dear friends we were in real life. Darling Jean! How can the millions of "fans" who saw and adored this fabulous "blonde bombshell" on the silver screen ever hope to understand what a shy, timid, retiring creature she was in real life? Although she worshipped the very ground I walked on, she was so shy that she never once accepted an invitation to one of my fabulous parties at Casa Torquemada—nor did she ever invite me into her own modest home for, despite what the "fan" magazines said (many times they simply made up the "facts" they published), Jean never entertained. She was even too timid to telephone me or to return my many calls. However, she did adore me and to prove her great friendship she gave me the formula for making her hair platinum blonde! If that isn't a sign of one woman's devotion for another, I ask you, what is? But a tragic thing happened. The day after my beautician had "platinumed" my hair it began falling out in fistfuls! By the end of the week I was totally bald. I was beside myself with grief and anger at the stupidity of my hairdresser (who claimed in court to have followed Miss Harlow's secret formula to the letter). For the next six months I wore a platinum wig and had to go to Max Factor's twice a day for treatment.

But I must not take my readers on a sentimental *détour* down Memory Lane. On with my story!

In Hollywood's halcyon days there was the perfect basis for a truly *chic* Society—beautiful women, handsome men, gifted writers, artists, directors and creative people of all sorts. There was plenty of money and almost no crippling income tax to rob those talented ladies and gentlemen who had sacrificed so much to earn it. There were big mansions, glossy cars, servants galore, the most breathtaking gowns, furs and jewels—all overly abundant in Southern California's faultless climate. With these perfect ingredients for a Society, then, why was there none as I had always known it in England? The reason, my friends, is because Filmdom lacked a Social Leader, a true "arbiter," an experienced woman of the world to mould all these outstanding members of the "liveliest Art" into one cohesive social structure.

True, Hollywood had a couple of Marquises de la Falaise de Coudray and quite a few Princesses Mdivani from time to time, but what was really needed was a real aristocrat to take over the reins of social leadership. And who, pray (with the possible exception of Aileen Pringle), had had more experience in

A Day with

UP WITH THE BIRDS!
No lolling abed for glamorous Belle Poitrine, lovely Metronome star. Belle is awake at dawning rarin' to go.

ALL THE COMFORTS OF HOME!
Belle examines her reflection in the specially built lavender portable dressing room on the set.

READIN' 'N' 'RITIN'
Hard at work revising a script. Belle is one of the most literary stars in Movietown.

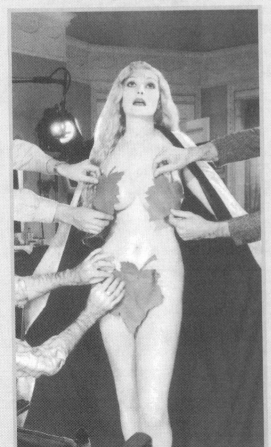

PRACTICE MAKES PERFECT
Rehearsing with young Metronome leading man, Letch Feeley. Belle says that no one can play love scenes like Letch.

FITTINGS! FITTINGS! FITTINGS!
One of the lovely and intricate costumes for Paradise Lost. *No unsightly wrinkles for our Belle.*

BELLE POITRINE

Intimate Lives of the Stars by Sell U. Lloyd

CATCH AS CATCH CAN
No time for a fancy banquet. Belle roughs it at lunch on the set of Paradise Lost.

NEVER TOO BUSY
FOR AN INTERVIEW
Gracious Belle grants a newspaper interview right in the midst of her heavy shooting schedule.

BEST DRESSED?

HOMEWORK
A devoted mother, Belle Poitrine writes to her daughter every day—even if it's only a postcard.

GOODNIGHT SWEETHEART!
A tender kiss for hubby, Morris Buchsbaum, before our popular star steps out.

SEEIN' STARS!
A star must be seen as well as see in Filmdom. Belle chins and gins with the Al K. Halls (he produced Dr. Damon's Doings).

court circles than little me? Therefore, I felt it my duty to take the throne of Hollywood's Social Queen.

As darling Dudley du Pont said, "There are plenty of queens in Hollywood, pet, but with *you* as empress—hotcha!"

Keeping peace among my devoted subjects was not a simple task. There were rivalries and jealousies, constant toadying and jockeying for my favor. The existing friction between such stars as Mary Pickford and Joan Crawford (for a time step-mother and step-daughter-in-law), Marion Davies and Norma Shearer, Gloria Swanson and Pola Negri, Dolores Del Rio and Lupe Velez, the Bennett sisters, Lilyan Tashman and Ina Claire is already public property. The frequency of marriage, divorce and remarriage made the seating of my famous dinner parties more than a little difficult. Transvestism, unnatural practices, nymphomania, excessive drinking and even narcotics addiction were not conducive to a truly smart social *milieu*. Yet I always tried to remind myself that these gilded boys and girls of the silver screen had not all had my Advantages—my aristocratic lineage, my gentle birth, my careful rearing, my grounding in the arts, my proximity to the Court of St. James's: all the generations of breeding that go into the makings of a true leader of society.

But if my parties lacked the decorum that I felt was my due, they certainly lacked nothing in high spirits and gaiety! Casa Torquemada was "GHQ" for the "revels" of Hollywood's Smart Set. When not working on a picture, I loved nothing better than to entertain casually at cocktails every day beginning at noon. There would be merry "pranks" at the pool, luncheon for anyone who wanted to eat, plenty of extra bedrooms for the siesta period (although no one was ever sleepy at *my* house!) and, if we didn't all choose to go on to the Cocoanut Grove or the "Troc" or some other gay *boîte de nuit*, a buffet supper with more intimate entertainment later on. And, working or not, my Sundays at home were famous. Letch Feeley was always on hand to act as auxiliary host (there is no use trying to disguise the fact, Morris Buchsbaum was *not* a social asset). Carstairs Bagley would be the first to arrive and the last to leave. Whenever he was in this country Dudley du Pont was always at my Sundays, bringing with him a small army of the extra men who always make a party "go." Momma, although lacking many of my attributes as a social arbiter, had a certain following of her own and could always be counted on to amuse simple men like "Tex" Lonestar and other cowboy favorites. Stars such as fun-loving Marjorie Josa, Vivi Weaver, Elaine Adam, exotic Bita Dobo, Nan Badian, pert Lucile Sullivan, darling Bessie Otis, Lila Lewis, Pixie Portnoy, Jane

Lambert and Baby Betsy Kerr were usually shedding their radiance. Of dashing leading men I could almost always count on Leslie Copeland, Duncan McGregor, "Al" Apatia, Sir Gauntley Pratt, Stuart Harris, Lyons Maine and dozens of others. It was a veritable paradise for an "autograph hound." The fun started right after church and didn't stop until time to get to the studio on Monday morning.

However, one unsettling incident did occur during one of my famous Sundays at Home that gave me pause. Late one afternoon Letch and I were coming out of the *Hacienda Méjicana* playhouse, after a prolonged game of backgammon, when I noticed a tiny baby girl toddling across the lawn toward the pool. Nobody was paying any attention to her until there was a terrible splash and the poor child fell in fully dressed. There was great laughter (someone was *always* falling into the pool, and the more elaborately garbed the funnier it was) and Lyons Maine, who happened to be naked anyhow, dived in and pulled the child out.

"Heavens," I said, "whose is that little girl? Some child under contract?"

"It's yours," Carstairs said, and, wrapping Baby-dear up in his tea gown,

he carried her into the nursery and to Mademoiselle. (He was such a kindly man.)

The shock was too great for me. I was put to bed under sedatives and allowed to see no visitors except for Letch (we were rehearsing a new film and the schedule could not be broken). But lying there shattered from the terrible experience I had endured, I asked myself this frank question: "Which should you be, a full-time mother or a full-time star?" I pondered the answer for a long time and then I knew what I must do no matter how much heartache my sacrifice would mean. I would have to send Baby-dear off to boarding school. Would it be sporting, I asked myself, to deprive the millions of Belle Poitrine fans the pleasure of seeing their idol just for the sake of one small child? While there were thousands of capable women who could take the place of Baby-dear's Mommy, who could replace Belle Poitrine on the screen?

The knowledge of this terrible step nearly crushed the spirit out of me, but I knew what had to be done. Baby-dear was nearly two years old and I wanted her to get an early start—to enjoy the advantages of a classical education which had been denied me in my own girlhood.

Through the studio I was able to find a splendid Episcopal boarding school in Pennsylvania that would take Baby-dear. Willing to make any sacrifice for the sake of my little girl, I delayed "shooting" the new film for three days while I shopped frantically at Bullock's for the darling little uniforms and pinafores she would wear at Radclyffe Hall. I put in a night of anguish on the eve of her departure but I managed to "pull myself together" and put on my loveliest *peignoir,* and all of my jewels, so that Baby-dear's last memory of her Mommy would be one of a beautiful madonna.

"Baby-dear," I said, fighting back the tears, as Mademoiselle lifted her up so that I could kiss that precious little flower of a face, "you're going to school because Mommy wants you to get an early start. It's going to be much more fun than just being here with Mommy and Daddy and Gran. And it won't be forever. You'll be home for your Christmas holidays and we'll all have so much fun." I could endure it no longer. "Hurry now, you don't want to miss the big choo-choo train."

I stood silhouetted in the doorway as Baby-dear toddled after Mademoiselle toward the car. "Wave bye-bye," Mademoiselle said.

"Who's the big blonde?" Baby-dear asked. Then they were gone.

The wrench nearly killed me but, as we say in the theatre, "The show must go on!" I hurried to dress for the studio and for a tea the George Arlisses

were giving for Sir Thomas Lipton that afternoon. Only a mother can know what I felt.

My hectic life of business and pleasure continued at its usual breakneck pace. As I have said, Casa Torquemada was considered (by simple American standards) a showplace and as the Homes of the Stars have always attracted great throngs of tourists, I felt that I could make Casa Torquemada and its gardens into a force for Good by opening it to the public once a year and turning over the proceeds to my favorite charity. Thus I announced, in discreet newspaper advertisements, that my lovely home would be open to anyone willing to pay fifty cents on a certain day in September.

How well I remember that gruesome autumn day when the gardeners were preparing Casa Torquemada for the first "onslaught." Although the morning seemed fine, I recall distinctly that there was "something" in the air—a sense of foreboding—as I chose my prettiest gown in order not to disappoint the many pilgrims who would come to admire me and my lovely belongings that afternoon.

As the time drew near for the great iron gates to be opened, the atmosphere grew heavy, moist, almost suffocating. I don't know quite how to explain the sense of doom which I felt.

"Not a very nice day for the public, madam," the butler said to me. "I don't expect that we'll have many visitors."

How right he was! A clammy rain began falling. I stood in the doorway all ready to smile and wave cordially as the first visitors appeared, but I needn't have bothered. I was quite alone. The weather had kept them away. I was just about to retire to my bedroom to read *Film Fun* when I heard a strangely familiar voice. "Hello, Belle. You're looking good."

I wheeled about and there, at the other end of the terrace, was none other than George Jerome Musgrove!

"*You!*" I gasped. "What are you doing here?"

"The ad here says that anyone with four bits can take the grand tour of this mausoleum. For your favorite charity. What's that? You?"

Ignoring his uncalled-for remark, I said, "I'm sorry, but due to the inclement weather my house has been..."

"Ah, that won't do, Miss Schlumpfert. It says here in the paper 'rain or shine.' I came all the way over from Long Beach just to see how the other half live. Here's my fifty cents. Let's see the place."

"Very well," I said coldly, snapping the coin from his hand. "Follow me."

With great *hauteur* I led him through the house. He admired everything and was never at a loss for a "wise crack." But, much as I had suffered at this scoundrel's hands, I could not quite bring myself to detest him. Say what one would about George Musgrove, he still had a certain urbane wit and charm that had impressed me from the very first. He was no longer young. His hair had turned quite gray—though not unbecomingly so—and his pallor seemed ghastly. But otherwise he was his jovial old self.

"And this," I said, finishing off the tour, "is the gun room where my beloved husband Morris and I spend our rare moments alone together."

"Where do you and Letch Feeley spend them?" Mr. Musgrove asked rudely.

"If you have any questions about this room," I said, "I shall be glad to answer them. This completes the tour."

"One question, Belle. Do you mind if I sit down and have a drink? I see some genuine just-off-the-boat scotch over there. It's been a long time since I've had any. Plenty of bootleggers get to Sing Sing, but they don't deliver."

"Sing Sing?" I gasped, my eyes going wide.

"Yes, Belle," Mr. Musgrove said sadly, "I've just come from there—just been sprung." Appalled as I was to think that a "jailbird" had forced his way into my home, I felt a certain sympathy for poor Mr. Musgrove. Blackguard that he might be, he had always been able to rekindle a certain spark of affection which I still felt for him. I poured drinks for both of us and he explained that he had been railroaded into prison under a trumped-up charge of possessing obscene photographs. He then told me that he was "broke" and wanted to borrow five hundred dollars. When I replied that I felt it would be wrong to allow money matters to come between two such old friends, Mr. Musgrove turned ugly.

"Maybe the cops confiscated *some* of my old pictures—but not all," he said. "And I've got plenty left of you—movies, stills, black and whites and also a few hand-tinted enlargements."

"You're lying," I said steadily.

"Oh, yeah? They're right out in my room at Long Beach. How do you think Morris Buchsbaum or Will Hays or the Belle Poitrine Fan Clubs would like to see the movies *I've* taken of you?"

"You wouldn't," I said. "You couldn't. No man could be so heartless and cruel. I was tricked into posing for those pictures, but everything is different now. I'm a famous star, the devoted wife of a respectable producer, the mother of his darling little baby daughter." With a limp hand I gestured toward the beautiful portrait Bradshaw Crandall had painted of Baby-dear on her first birthday.

"So," he sneered, "Buchsbaum really believes it's his kid? Well, I could set him straight on that. And maybe I'll have to."

"What do you mean?" I asked, backing away from him in terror.

"Figure it out for yourself, Belle old girl. Just simple mathematics and then maybe you'll know who the father of the kid really is—if you can count to nine. Or is that asking too much?"

I heard a terrible roaring in my ears. The room began to revolve around me. I was revolted to think that this human vulture could suggest anything so low and despicable. And yet it had always occurred to me that Baby-dear's cunning little face—what I remembered of it—had a certain cast of feature that . . . Stumbling, I clutched out for something to prevent my falling. My hand touched an object hard, cold, metallic.

"As a matter of fact, baby, it might be a swell idea if you and me was to go upstairs to that fancy bedroom of yours and try it all over again. Maybe this time Morris could be the father of . . ."

I heard a deafening report, saw a flash of light, a cloud of smoke. The old Spanish duelling pistol in my trembling hand dropped to the cold tile floor—right next to the body of George Musgrove.

"What the hell's going on, honey?" It was Momma—darling, reliable old Momma—right at her baby's side when she was needed the most.

"Oh, Momma," I sobbed. "I've shot Mr. Musgrove."

"For Christ's sake!" Momma said.

Servants began appearing at the doorway. Mustering up all of my dignity, I said to the butler, "There has been a frightful accident. Please telephone a doctor—and the police."

Then dear, true blue Momma poured a stiff drink for me and a larger one for herself in the glasses Mr. Musgrove and I had used, thus destroying a bit of evidence, which would have only complicated matters. "Also," she said, "call Clarence Darrow and Louella Parsons."

My trial pushed Libby Holman right off the front pages and was widely considered to be the biggest Hollywood murder story since the mysterious passing of William Desmond Taylor. In as short a time as it takes to pull a trigger I had moved from the amusement section to the headlines! On the following day I was a current event.

I was questioned mercilessly by the police but I stuck to my story: Mr. Musgrove had entered my home uninvited and unannounced. (Perfectly

true.) He had made a menacing sexual advance and, in attempting to escape, I had accidentally shot him while protecting my virtue. (Also perfectly true.) It seemed to me that any mention of photographs would only obscure and complicate the real issue.

In my favor were the facts that my home had been open to the public that day, which explained how Mr. Musgrove could have been there; that Mr. Musgrove had a known record of offenses and had served two prison terms; and that I was a model wife and mother.

Damaging evidence was that I had been in the presence of Mr. Musgrove at the time of my London divorce. My fate hung in a delicate balance.

Schiaparelli did all of my clothes for the trial, and I must say that I looked lovely. My maid brought the entire collection to my cell along with a make-up man, Manny, the Metronome press corps, Metronome Momentous Moments, and three "still" photographers. My meals were catered by the Brown Derby. My lawyer was Jerry Gosling, the absolute "top" trial lawyer in all of "Screenland," and the studio loyally provided the services of ace director Gregory Ratoff to supervise the delivery of my testimony.

Thank heavens the weather turned fine in time for the trial! Never before in the history of Los Angeles County Court House have there been such queues of people waiting for seats. The crowds were so dense that the cameramen could hardly get through. After considerable haggling and arguing between Mr. Gosling and the District Attorney, an all-male jury was chosen and the trial began.

Momma made a splendid and imposing witness in a dear lavender outfit which Adrian had originally designed for Marie Dressler, a lorgnette and *my* sables. Through the dumb misery which I felt, I recall being quite surprised by the dignity and feeling Momma gave to her testimony. She was every bit as refined as Margaret Dumont and I wondered who had been directing Momma. Her only mistake, I felt, was in trying to swoon. In doing so she toppled off the witness stand, wrenched her knee quite badly and said a very undignified word. However, I could see that the judge, jury and spectators were all very favorably impressed. Darling Momma! What an actress she would have made had she been born at a time when it was considered respectable for a *bien élevée* young lady to pursue the drama as a career.

The trial went on for days, so it was fortunate that I had bought up the whole Schiaparelli collection. All the fashion magazines sent correspondents and Lilyan Tashman was furious about the coverage I got. During the trial I

Free!

fainted five times, collapsed twice, burst into tears on seventeen different occasions and wore a total of thirty different ensembles. Even if I do say so myself, I was sensational on the witness stand and several film critics said that it
was my greatest performance. The jury deliberated for less than half an hour.
When they came back there was no question as to the verdict. Twelve angry
men proclaimed me innocent. I stood up, turned to face the cameras, smiled
wanly, swayed and then collapsed for a final time into the arms of my trained
nurse. The newspaper reportage was unparalleled and was not even matched
in later years by Charlie Chaplin, Errol Flynn or Lana Turner. I saw to it that
Manny's salary was doubled.

As one last gracious gesture toward the man I had inadvertently shot, I
insisted on having Mr. Musgrove's body collected from the morgue and
turned over to me for decent, Christian funeral services. A private ceremony
was held at Forest Lawn with a few simple floral arrangements from the gardens of Casa Torquemada. (I felt that it was in extremely poor taste for Magdalena Montezuma to send Mr. Musgrove a ten-foot-square blanket of white
orchids! But what can you expect from a Spic like her?) After a eulogy, beautifully delivered by Aimee Semple McPherson, I followed the remains to the
crematorium and placed all of Mr. Musgrove's photographic work in the cas-
ket just before it was lowered into the flames. I felt it only right that it should
go with him. Under the circumstances, it seemed the very least I could do.

1932 had indeed been a difficult year but then everything turned out
for the best.

Magdalena Montezuma—the meanest Spic in pictures!

CHAPTER THIRTEEN

THE END OF AN IDYLL

1933

My blissful life with Mr. Buchsbaum · Toward a more varied career · Morris suggests that
I lend my talents to rival studios · Trying out for famous rôles · My desire to play Cleopatra
I reject Shakespeare · G.B.S.–another famous correspondence · *Nights on the Nile*
One terrible night · Mr. Buchsbaum's farewell tribute · Widowhood

MY "MURDER TRIAL"—the term by which the radical press tried to denigrate a powerless woman's last-ditch attempt to preserve her chastity—had taken a more terrible toll of both my husband and me than I realized at the time. When I was proclaimed "not guilty," dear Morris burst into tears and wept uncontrollably all the way home in the car. And I—once the terrible ordeal was over—fell prey to a complete *crise de nerfs*. So shattered was I that I felt totally unable to have my darling baby daughter come home for her Christmas holidays. The absence of her merry voice, her *staccato* little footsteps left me desolate but, under the trying circumstances, it seemed better for Baby-dear to have Morris spend Christmas with her at Radclyffe Hall while I passed a long, sad Yuletide with only Letch Feeley. who understandingly hurried to my side as soon as Morris was on the train.

In glancing over these last few pages. I feel that I have spoken mostly of my fabulous public career and very little of the rich, happy life of "togetherness" which I shared with my dear husband. Morris Buchsbaum.

The life of a great Hollywood film star is so hectic who can wonder that

above: Mr. Musgrove at Ossining
below: Ditto at Forest Lawn

the divorce rate is high? Yet I can truly say that my marriage to Morris Buchsbaum was one "made in heaven."

Because of the great difference in our ages, because Morris and I were each completely absorbed in careers that kept us apart for weeks on end, because Morris had waited fifty years before being "hooked" (as one unfeeling columnist so crassly put it), those who did not know us well scoffed at our marriage, giving it but a short time to endure. There are even those who have so little regard for the truth, so little feeling for two people "head over heels in love," that they had the gall to claim that I "tricked" my darling Morris into marriage! So much for those Philistines. I would simply like to state—and I believe that the facts prove me to be correct—that my marriage to Morris Buchsbaum was one of the few beautiful and enduring things in Hollywood. Who knows what we might not have achieved together had not The Greatest Director of All called my darling Morris to Location for Script Conference on His Truly Divine Picture?

Let me tell all sneerers, cynics and doubters right here and now that Morris Buchsbaum *worshipped* me! What other explanation could there be for a man's utter and complete selflessness?

To give just one example—and those who know the keen competition, the dreadful jealousies between producers in those days will appreciate this— Morris came to me at the beginning of 1933, right after my ordeal in the courtroom, and said: "Belle, we've been *shlepping* through hell together. You need a little change. Retirement maybe?"

I denied this fervently. Was I the sort to let Morris and the studio down?

"I was afraid you'd say that. Such a *hokachinik*!" Morris said sadly. "Everyone at the studio said you would." (They knew a "trouper tried and true" when they saw one.) "But maybe you should try a different type picture at a different studio. A *gonif* like Louis B. Mayer you should favor. You know, change your luck. Mine, too." How like that saintly man!

Having given me *carte blanche* to "test my wings" at a different studio for a picture or two, Morris even went so far as to make an adjustment in my contract to release me from Metronome and even offered to *invest* in any picture any other studio would be willing to make with me as its star. In fact, so big a man was Morris Buchsbaum that he even suggested that I go to Europe, taking Momma with me, to do long and intensive work on carving a career there! Of course I refused.

Thus "set free" of dear old Metronome with all of Hollywood to choose from, I was like a child in a candy store! I began "pounding the pavements" again—if riding from studio to studio in a Dusenberg town car can be called quite that. I felt that I needed a complete change of pace and, as so many exciting new projects were opening up around town, I was eager to try something entirely different.

At RKO, for example, they were filming that sweet story *Little Women* (a picture about four young sisters), which was being directed by my dear old friend and admirer George Cukor. "Katy" Hepburn was to star as "Jo" with a cast including Joan Bennett, Douglass Montgomery, Edna May Oliver, Spring Byington, Nydia Westman, Henry Stephenson and Paul Lukas. I suggested that, if the "script" could be somewhat rewritten to bolster the part, I would consider playing "Beth," the youngest sister who is literally too good to live. There was a great deal of talk about this all over the RKO "lot," but in the end the rôle of "Beth" went to Jean Parker. I guess that Hepburn was just afraid to appear with a real star.

Metro-Goldwyn-Mayer had a number of properties that interested me. *Peg O' My Heart,* for example, might well have been written with me in mind. However, through favoritism of the rankest sort, the rôle went to Marion Davies, a capable little actress but, as Morris said, not in my class at all. And just because she was Swedish, *Queen Christina* went to Garbo. In spite of the fact that Noël Coward was one of my oldest and dearest friends from the English "chapter" of my life, Paramount foolishly gave the lead in *Design for Living* to Miriam Hopkins. Although I was too good a sport to consult them, I know that the co-stars, Gary Cooper and "Freddie" March, the director, Ernst Lubitsch, and Noël all would have preferred me. By another fluke I lost out on appearing in *Reunion in Vienna* with John Barrymore. What should have been my rôle went to an unknown English actress named Diana Wynyard. However, "Jack" Barrymore paid me a compliment so eloquent that it almost made my loss worthwhile. "Belle," he said, "the only other actress I know who, today, could match your performance in that part is Sarah Siddons." Just imagine!

Another bitter disappointment—this time again at M-G-M—was *Dinner at Eight*—its all-star casting including precious Jean Harlow, "Jack" and Lionel Barrymore, "Wally" Beery, Billie Burke, Lee Tracy, "Eddie" Lowe and Marie Dressler. George Cukor again directed. One would have thought that with such a large cast something could have been written especially for me.

But no such luck. Darling Marie Dressler suggested that I might be carried in with an apple in my mouth, but I felt that if I could not have a truly meaty part I would rather stay out.

Because Baby-dear was in an Episcopal boarding school, I had a natural interest in religion. I offered my services as star of *The White Sister,* but for some reason that was never made quite clear to me, the rôle was given to Helen Hayes, a competent performer. At Paramount my desire to play a nun in *Cradle Song* was somehow ignored.

However, the same studio was planning an all-star production and everyone said that I would be absolutely fantastic as the star of *Alice in Wonderland* and staunch, reliable old Dudley du Pont and Carstairs Bagley even telephoned to encourage me to take a screen test as Alice. "Belle, darling, it would be *the* camp of the year," Dudley said. "*You* be Alice and *we'll* be the queens. Do it with us, for laughs." Those darling boys were so gay, how could I refuse? Just thinking of myself as the star of a huge cast that included Gary Cooper, Cary Grant, W. C. Fields, Edward Everett Horton, "Jack" Oakie, "Ned" Sparks, May Robson, Polly Moran, "Skeets" Gallagher, "Dick" Arlen, Roscoe Ates and Mae Marsh (who had thrilled me so in *Birth of a Nation*) sent chills up and down my spine. We rehearsed together for weeks and, while it didn't seem to me that Dudley and Carstairs were exactly right as the Red Queen and the White Queen, I appreciated their faith in me. Over drinks, Travis Banton designed the simple dress I was to wear in my test. (He said that it brought out all of my most girlish qualities.) On the day of our test the studio was mobbed with famous faces. I had been nervous about playing comedy, considering myself more of a dramatic actress, but any fears of mine were quickly quelled. The visiting stars and other "top" names shouted with laughter at my performance with Carstairs and Dudley. There was thunderous applause at the end of each "take." When it was all over, I was mobbed with admirers. Adorable Carole Lombard was laughing so hard that Clark Gable and Leslie Howard had to help her out. "*Alice?*" Carole gasped through tears of merriment. "Have you ever thought of co-starring with Shirley Temple?" No idle compliment when one recalls that sweet little Shirley was America's biggest box office attraction during the thirties.

Flushed with triumph, I returned immediately to Casa Torquemada to await the call from Paramount. Can you imagine my shock when the choice rôle of Alice went to an unknown *child* named Charlotte Henry! As for poor Carstairs and Dudley, the parts of Red Queen and White Queen were given to

Edna May Oliver and Louise Fazenda. The boys were very philosophical about it. "You can't fight sex," they said. Studio politics again!

However, I was rewarded by a call from RKO. They offered me the lead in *King Kong*. "But I thought that you'd already chosen Fay Wray," I said. "That's right. We want you for the ape." A practical joker! I slammed down the tele-

phone in a rage and told Morris that I was ready to return to Metronome. "Again the *hokachinik* begins. I could *plotz*," he said endearingly.

I decided that if I were to create a truly great film, once again I would have to find my own story. It was then that I stumbled across a fascinating historical character, Cleopatra. I learned at the time that Cecil B. DeMille was preparing just such a film with Claudette Colbert (a darling girl, but all wrong for the rôle); however, I was so angry at Paramount Studios for their shameful treatment of me that I decided to come out first with my own version of Cleopatra. Dudley du Pont, one of Hollywood's leading intellectuals, put me in touch with two versions of that great ruler's life. One was a play by William Shakespeare entitled *Antony and Cleopatra*. This I read and rejected immediately because I did not care for the lines and also because the story had an unhappy ending. The other one was written by an Irishman named George Bernard Shaw. This was called *Caesar and Cleopatra*. I preferred this version, but again I had very definite reservations. While I liked the idea of Cleopatra being a very young girl, I did not care for Caesar as an old man. Dear Dudley, trying as always to be helpful, suggested such leading men as George Arliss, Wallace Beery, Francis X. Bushman, George M. Cohan, Charles Laughton, King Baggot, Will Rogers, Cyril Maude and a roster of "name" character actors. However, I had someone more like Letch Feeley in mind as my leading man. Dudley said he understood exactly how I felt and reminded me that one of the last lines in *Caesar and Cleopatra* is when Caesar promises to send Cleopatra a sort of replacement who is "brisk and fresh, strong and young, hoping in the morning, fighting in the day, and revelling in the evening." That certainly described Letch! This character was Marc Antony. Dudley said that maybe Shaw had a sequel in mind. He suggested that I write to Mr. Shaw (Dudley knew him quite well and always called him "G.B.S.") at Ayot St. Lawrence. Dudley said that Shaw had had a number of famous correspondences with other great actresses and that any exchange between us ought to be worth its weight in gold. He and Carstairs Bagley dictated the letter, which they told me to begin "Dear George." Some weeks later I received a letter from the old gentleman which Dudley described as "too priceless." "While your mentality is ideally suited to Cleopatra," Mr. Shaw wrote, "your age would suggest the rôle of Ftatateetah—unless you were considering me to play Antony." It made no sense at all and, realizing that Mr. Shaw was almost in his dotage, I decided to take over the "script" myself, as I wanted to beat Paramount,

DeMille and Claudette with my own version of Cleopatra, called *Nights on the Nile,* which I thought romantic. Dudley said that he would help me on the "q.t." and that he didn't even want screen credit for his assistance. He said that it would be fun to play a character called "Paula Doris" but I told him that while that sort of thing might be "okay" on Sunset Strip, I didn't want it in a family-type picture.

We planned to write the whole scenario outside of Hollywood where there wouldn't be any "leak" as to our plans. Dudley chose Santa Catalina Island as "not too near and still not too far." I took several typewriters, Letch Feeley as "script consultant" and Momma as chaperone. Dudley brought his friend, Felice, a young Mexican bull fighter, and a Latin teacher from Hollywood High School to check on historical accuracy. Within two weeks we had the story "licked" although the Latin teacher kept saying that it was "glutted with anachronisms." Dudley pointed out that so were the stories by Shakespeare and Shaw and that he'd love to have a dollar for every inaccuracy in the DeMille "shooting script." I agreed. Knowing that Claudette would play Cleopatra as a brunette, I decided to play her as a blonde. I also chose to drop Julius Caesar from the picture (Carstairs Bagley, who would have been my choice, was appearing at the Chicago World's Fair that summer and was not available) and to focus entirely on the Cleopatra–Marc Antony love affair. I also rewrote the ending as it all took place so very long ago that nobody remembers exactly what did happen. Nor did I want Cecil B. DeMille to be able to accuse me of "plagiarizing" any of his picture. He never did.

Dudley suggested that it might be fun if we did everything on "location" in Egypt, but I settled for a stunning piece of real estate out on the desert not far from Palm Springs. This I named Belleville. On it I had built such permanent "sets" as the Sphinx, the Great Pyramids, the Library at Alexandria, the bazaars of Cairo, the royal palace, the Temple at Karnak, the Nile, the Suez Canal, Rome and the Vatican. I erected a "tent colony" for the six thousand "extras," stage hands and "grips," an apartment hotel for the supporting and featured players and little Egyptian-type villas for the executives and more important actors. I had a lovely house designed, in the Egyptian manner, for little me, and for Magdalena Montezuma a much smaller house out near the menagerie where we kept the elephants, camels, horses, mules, crocodiles, parrots and snakes. Magdalena had one more picture to do for Metronome before deserting poor Morris (who had made her a star) for a new studio.

Nights on the Nile

above: Marc Antony surprises Cleopatra bathing in the Suez Canal.
right: Cleopatra offers a basket of asps to Calpurnia, Marc Antony's faithless wife

right: All roads lead to Rome and to a happy ending for Mr. and Mrs. M. Antony! below: Cleopatra puts her pearl necklace in Marc Antony's champagne

Grudgingly, she consented to appear in *Nights on the Nile* to "wind up" her contract. To quote "Señorita" Montezuma's own ungracious words, "I'd play a dromedary to get out of my contract with this stinking pesthole filled with whores and faggots." Imagine! When I, myself, carefully supervised the activities of all the "extras" and "bit" players at Metronome! That was the sort of gratitude she showed to my darling Morris, to the studio and to *me*!

Momma suggested that Montezuma might be "perfect" as a camel. (She has such a sense of humor!) But for a so-called "star" with a big "name" and a weekly salary of $10,000, I had better uses. "Filmdom" was amazed to learn that I had been forgiving enough to cast Magdalena Montezuma in what was to be *the* picture of my career, after her abominable treatment of me in *¡Viva Tequila!*, but, as Dudley du Pont said in one of his many tributes to me, "Beneath Belle's whipped cream exterior beats a heart of solid granite."

I decided to do the "big thing" and give Magdalena the sort of rôle she really could "play to the hilt"—that of arch-villainess. She was to be Calpurnia, Marc Antony's faithless wife. I envisaged Calpurnia as a much older woman, of Nubian origin, to whom Marc Antony had been lovelessly joined as a boy by his wicked uncle, Brutus (Basil Thyme). As they are both of the Roman faith, divorce is out of the question, yet Calpurnia keeps right on dallying with slave boys of her own ethnic group until she finds out that Marc Antony has fallen in love with beautiful, young Cleopatra. Bent on revenge, she goes to Egypt to murder poor Cleopatra. Her low scheme is thwarted when Cleopatra innocently hands her a basket of asps (I used real ones for authenticity) and she is fatally stung. It was a "juicy" part and I even supervised Montezuma's costumes myself. How is that for magnanimity? If most of Montezuma's scenes had to be cut, it was only because of the great length of *Nights on the Nile*.

By sparing no expense and working seven days a week, around the clock, we finished the film that summer. I felt dreadful having to keep Baby-dear in boarding school during her holidays, but I knew that she would understand. We finished the picture on her third birthday and I went directly to Honolulu to rest from the crushing ordeal. *Nights on the Nile* had cost almost ten million dollars, but I knew that we had a "hit on our hands."

The *première* at the Buchsbaum Bessarabian in Los Angeles was a gala night indeed, *everyone* was there. A line of limousines and town cars a mile long waited to deposit celebrities at the entrance. Searchlights raked the skies. I had had the entire theatre redecorated in honor of *Nights on the Nile*, and rising above the marquee was a statue of me as Cleopatra just ten times life size. The film lasted exactly five hours and seventeen minutes. Every second of it was a milestone in movie history.

"What did you *really* think of it, darling?" I asked Morris as we left the theatre to face the spontaneous ovation Manny and I had prepared.

"Don't. Please," Morris whispered. "I'm speechless." And they have the nerve to say that man didn't worship me!

A huge party was planned for after the showing, but somehow I got separated from Morris in the throngs at the theatre and never went to the party at all. Instead, Letch and I drove to his little beach "shack" at Malibu just to have a friendly drink, talk over old times and the pictures we planned to make together.

I have no idea what hour it was when we were rudely roused from our *rêverie* by the jangling of the telephone. "Belle, honey," Momma cried, "you better come right home. It's Morris. He's dying!"

My heart was in my mouth as Letch's roadster screeched up the driveway at Casa Torquemada. I dashed to our bedroom. There was my adored and adoring husband lying, fully dressed, on the bed we had shared so blissfully. His evening shirt was open and a thin rivulet of blood trickled down its starched white bosom.

"Morris!" I cried. "Speak to me! What has happened?"

Half rising from the sa'tin coverlet and struggling for breath, he paid me his beautiful deathbed tribute. "*Nafkeh!*" he gasped. "Ten million dollars. Ten million simoleons! So it's nothing. Only *mazumen*, yet. Only Buchsbaum's *gelt* so a *schikseh nudnik* like the Poitrine should dress herself like some hootchy-makootchy Araber *koorveh* and make a real *mishmash* picture with some no-talent *goy putz* like Letch Feeley . . ."

"Morris, darling," I cried, "are you all right?"

"All right? Oi! You should ask. Ask me again I should tell you the answer. It's yes. All night long at the movie house . . . five *fablugene* hours at thirty-three thousand dollars a minute and a *gonif* like you asks Buchsbaum . . . Ay! Better I should *plotz* than see another picture with a *gurnisht* like you!" A convulsive shudder passed through his entire body. "*Ausgeschpielt*," he breathed. He sank back onto the pillows, lapsing almost completely into the vivid tongue of his faraway European childhood. But even at this moment my Morris could praise me!

Widowed again

"He's going fast, poor mockie," Momma said, standing breathlessly at the foot of the bed.

"The will," Morris whispered, raising his head weakly. "My will. The envelope I wrote to Faber, Farber, Ferber and . . ."

"You mean this, Morry?" Momma said, holding a stamped envelope over his head. "I'll take care of this for you. Don't you worry."

"Ah! The *dybbuk* . . . the *alte kockeh* . . . the . . ." Morris said no more. He was dead when the doctor arrived. A basket of asps—the ones I had used in *Nights on the Nile*—was found in Morris' bathroom. They said at the studio that my late husband had driven there immediately after the *première* of my picture and demanded the venomous reptiles "for personal use." My poor Morris, too moved by my performance to want to go on producing lesser films, had taken his own life! Sometimes a talent such as mine can be a curse!

Oddly enough, for such a keen businessman, Morris died leaving no last will and testament, no instructions as to the disposal of his enormous holdings. Although we ransacked the house in search of the vague document poor Morris had mentioned with his dying breath, nothing could be found. Perhaps his talk about a will had been just a figment of my imagination. Darling Momma, warming her old bones at the fireplace in her sitting room, had no recollection of his mentioning anything about it at all. Thus Morris' personal fortune, Casa Torquemada, the mighty Metronome Studios—everything he possessed became mine. It was when I heard this that I crumpled completely and had to be put to bed under full sedation in a state of total collapse.

True blue Dudley du Pont made all of the arrangements for what is still considered to be the most unusual funeral in the history of Hollywood. The entire "industry," I am told, turned out in one seething, sorrowing mass. But so shattered was I by shock, by grief and by fatigue that I remember nothing—nothing—of this farewell tribute to a great producer. I recall only that I was wearing a full-length gown of white mourning from Worth with five rows of ruffles at throat, cuffs and train; black lingerie and accessories from the Veuve Soignée Shop on Wilshire Boulevard; a modified Empress Eugénie hat created by Agnes; and Gunther's black fox capelet as loyal Letch Feeley helped me down the aisle at dear Morris' high requiem mass.

Very Sincerely Your
Leitch Seeley

CHAPTER FOURTEEN

ON MY OWN

1934

I become sole owner of Metronome · A new broom! · Keeping a brave face
in spite of my sorrow · Baby-dear · Seeking better material for my films · Difficult
authors who have known me · Loneliness · Letch · My wedding

SUCH WAS MY DESOLATION that I was unable to do anything for weeks. I finished out 1933 very quietly in a mountain hideaway, my solitude dispelled only by occasional visits from such old, tried and true friends as Letch. No chance again this year of having my precious Baby-dear home for Christmas. How unfair to the *psyche* of an innocent infant to invite her to pass the festive Yule season in a house of sadness! Instead, my secretary sent Baby-dear a letter of explanation, enclosing a generous check. Thus I brooded over my deep loss, in loneliness, while Morris' estate was inventoried and his many affairs put in order.

But I soon realized that I was being grossly selfish and negligent in my duty. Here I was, the sole owner of the world's greatest film studio, thinking only of my own troubles! Metronome, with its acres and acres of sound stages, was my domain. Its thousands of loyal employees my people. How could I "let them down"? Feeling just like the Dowager Queen Victoria, I drove sadly down Buchsbaum Boulevard to the Metronome Studios on the first business day of 1934. Except for the special black-tipped cigarettes I had ordered from Benson & Hedges, I showed no exterior signs of mourning. This, too (though criticized openly by my enemies), was meant as the ultimate sign of respect to

Letch at 23

my late husband. Morris had always hated me to wear black. "Like a crow you look!" he would scoff. Thus I affected bright, butterfly colors, painted a vivid smile on my trembling lips and turned a brave face to the world. How little they could know of my inner feelings!

Although Morris' personal fortune was solid and a source of great comfort and satisfaction to me (I had known so little financial security as a child that I especially wanted it for my own baby girl), I was dismayed to examine the books at the studio. For such an astute businessman, Morris had permitted many practices that stuck me as downright "slipshod." Even some of my own films, I noted with surprise, had been allowed to show distressing deficits. This I remedied by showing no quarter to the inefficient "bunglers" who had foolishly been entrusted with the fortunes of Metronome. I "sacked" them immediately and, after a long, disquieting talk with Momma, I saw the logic of placing her in sole charge of the studio's finances. Momma, I felt, with her native caution and thrift, could easily do the work for which Morris had paid a department of more than fifty shiftless and—*I* felt—dishonest accountants. Momma had her own unorthodox bookkeeping methods and often said that she didn't want any "nosey Parkers" prying into her records. This caused considerable difficulties some years later, but it worked splendidly for a time and represented a large saving in salaries, which I split between Momma and me, as all of the work would be on our shoulders.

As I deplore anything that "smacks" of favoritism or "nepotism," the next employee to go was Morris' nephew, Sheldon. Out of kindness, my late husband had placed this unpleasant and untalented youth in the story department at Metronome, where, instead of turning out unusual and original "scripts," Sheldon had done little but "carp" about the unsuitability of certain stories for me and vice versa. He had also been most unpleasant about Morris' passing, his funeral and his estate. Instead of rushing to comfort his "beloved" uncle's widow, Sheldon had done nought but create trouble and dissention. As most of the story department seemed to be more or less of Sheldon's "stripe," I discharged the vast majority of those "smart aleck" college boys at the same time. (Please do not misunderstand me. I have nothing but the highest respect and regard for education, but just because a boy has graduated with honors from Columbia, Harvard, Princeton or Yale, he has no right to sneer at the opinions of an internationally famed actress whose weekly salary is more than his yearly "take.") In their stead I placed Endive Kissner, my personal hairdresser for the past troubled year. Endive may not have had a fancy "Ivy

League" education, but she and I were interested in the same kinds of stories and we could see "eye to eye" on the sort of material that would be right for little me. As Momma always said, "A girl can learn a lot more useful information in beauty culture school than she can in some old convent!"

Magdalena Montezuma's contract had expired with 1933. However, when I arrived at the studio I found great heaps of her greasy cosmetics, her disgusting Spanish dresses, obscene foreign novels such as *La Catedral* and *Testamente Nuevo* all over her dressing room. These I deposited outside the studio gates, instructing *my* maid to telephone *her* maid as to their whereabouts. As far as I was concerned, Montezuma was a conceited, talentless troublemaker and her absence would mean a saving of more than half a million dollars annually! As my own duties had more than doubled since Morris' passing, I added her salary to my own.

"A new broom," they say, "sweeps clean," and that is just what I intended to do. Within a month I had bought off the contracts of those actors who had shown signs of jealousy, hostility or indifference to me. With such gifted thespians as Letch Feeley, Helen Highwater, Carstairs Bagley, "Tex" Lonestar, "Al" Apatia, Vivienne Vixen, Dudley du Pont—those who had shown me nothing but loyalty and friendship—things were different. They, and dozens of other true-blue fellow-performers were rewarded handsomely. (Alas, Baby Betsy Kerr's contract had to be bought off. At thirty, I considered her a little too old to assay further child rôles.) Carstairs and Letch were immediately elevated to full stardom. Letch's many outstanding gifts had been too often overlooked. Carstairs, I felt, would be the one logical actor in "filmland" to star in a series of movies directed at American youth. Dudley du Pont, one of the few actors I know with "horse sense" enough to save for a "rainy day," had planned to retire from pictures. He had, after all, started with D. W. Griffith and was rounding out his silver anniversary as a matinée idol. I would not hear of his going. I needed my friends! "But, cutie-pie," Dudley said in that frank, man-to-man way of his, "think of the ecstasy! A little decorating shop of my own. No more corset, no toupee, no more chin strap, no more good conduct clauses." By begging and doubling his salary, I was fortunate in getting him to stay on at Metronome as combination producer-director-advisor and talent scout.

By March the "deadwood" was cleared out and my "team" was in "fighting form." All that remained was to find a good vehicle for little me. The public reaction to *Nights on the Nile* had been so marked that Dudley, Endive, Momma and all of my most trusted advisors decided that I needed a definite

"change of pace." During an informal conference in the *Plaza del Cocktail* at Casa Torquemada, we were discussing all sorts of the most unlikely possibilities when witty Dudley said, "Darling, maybe if you changed sex."

"Ha!" Letch laughed. "She sure would be a pip as a man."

That started it! Still in his bantering manner, Dudley began reeling off a "never-never" plot about a beautiful young monarch of a mythical kingdom who, in order to avoid a loveless marriage, disguises herself as a boy and runs away on the eve of her wedding. She meets a virile young hunter (Letch Feeley) who is a runaway prince in disguise and they live together like brothers without his discovering her true gender until a lovely bathing scene in a sylvan glade. And so on until the happy ending where their two warring nations are united through their marriage. Dudley decided to call it *The Queen Steps Out*. There were a lot of objections. Letch didn't understand the plot. Momma kept saying that it was very familiar to her. But Endive and I loved it. Having great faith in first impressions and "snap" judgment, I told Dudley that he was to write and direct and that we would start work immediately. It was one of my finest films, of that I am convinced, but somehow it was "jinxed." There was terrible trouble with my camera "angles," with the bathing scene (during which Letch caught the most terrible cold and, in an unexplained fit of *pique*, blacked Dudley's eye) and with the Hays office.

The picture opened to wonderful reviews, for me, personally, at least. Percy Hammond wrote: "In masculine attire Miss Poitrine is every bit as convincing a male as her writer-director, Dudley du Pont." How's that for high praise? But the picture was beset by trouble. The publishers of George Barr McCutcheon's *Beverly of Graustark* brought suit for plagiarism and there was so much talk that Elinor Glyn, Paramount, M-G-M and several other studios were going to do the same thing that our lawyers felt it best to withdraw the film entirely.

I decided to seek greener fields for fresh material. Nothing Endive had read in *True Story* appealed to me. I tried to commission Frederick Lonsdale to write an original story for me, but he never replied to any of my letters. Through Dudley, I approached Ivor Novello to compose an operetta suited to my vocal range. "CAN PROSTITUTE ART ONLY SO FAR" was his cabled reply. Well! Mr. Novello may have been willing to accept my money, but I would have nothing to do with a man who used such language! I was, after all, a widow, a mother and the one person pledged to see that Metronome turned out clean pictures for the family trade. The replies of both Gertrude Stein and James Joyce were favorable, as far as I could tell, but as Letch said, "Jeest, baby, if they can't even write a sensible letter, how the hell can they write a whole script?" I agreed.

With so many pressing problems at the studio, with only an echoing empty house of memories to return to after a long, taxing day, I was beginning to lean more and more on dear Letch and on his sensible, down-to-earth judgment. Dudley du Pont was a pet, of course, but he was often too rarified

The busy executive

in his tastes and opinions to suit simple little me. I am a man's woman, and although I have achieved signal success in difficult fields—acting, producing, business, writing—did not want to be a bitter, dried-up career "gal."

Oh, I had a host of friends, to be sure. "Winnie" had opened up her new club, the Bar Sinister, a fashionable *boîte de nuit* on Sunset Boulevard. She had married "Al" ("The Violinist") Pizzicato as he lay riddled with bullet holes from one of those savage "gangland" shootings in which innocent bystanders, such as he, are sometimes the only victims. After his death, "Winnie" discovered that he was actually a Sicilian prince, but too democratic to use his title in a republic such as ours. "Winnie" was not and it was wonderful to have Princess Pizzicato (someone of my own class) to reminisce with. But I needed more than just an old girl-friend to make my life complete.

Lying sleeplessly in bed, I asked myself frankly: "Would darling Morris want to hold you forever?" The answer was No! I telephoned Letch Feeley that very night. The following morning I permitted Manny to inform the press that we were engaged.

Finally I was to know the glamour and the thrill of having a real church wedding with bridal attendants, ushers, pages, flower girls and all! I was even to be a June bride!

There was quite a bit of red tape and confusion with most of the nicer churches in the Los Angeles area. None of them seemed big enough for the sort of wedding I wanted, anyhow. Therefore I planned my own church wedding and built my own church on the back "lot" of Metronome. It was a perfect copy of the Cathedral of Notre Dame, only somewhat enlarged for the guests and camera crew.

I so wanted to have Baby-dear as my tiny maid of honor, but I decided that, to bring her all the way across the continent to be with her Mommy and then, right after the nuptial excitement, to have Mommy and her new "Daddy" dash off on an extended honeymoon, leaving her all alone in a strange environment, was psychologically unsound. "Better let sleeping dogs lie," I told myself, and chose "Winnie" instead. After all, I had known "Winnie" much longer. For bridesmaids I selected the twenty-four loveliest brunettes under contract to Metronome and I even brought Baby Betsy Kerr back as flower girl, as I knew no children. For Letch I chose two dozen of our leading actors and as best man, jovial Carstairs Bagley.

There was only one "fly in the amber": Morris had been dead for only seven months and I was still in mourning. Although, as I said earlier, Morris did not approve of me in black, I had to think of how things would look to the eager outside world were I to be married, so soon after his passing, in white. I discussed the problem with Dudley du Pont, whose taste I have always found infallible, and he came up with the perfect solution. "Sweetie-pie," he cried, "wouldn't it be divine to bill you as the Black Widow! Send out black invitations engraved in white. You wear black with your bridesmaids in tones of gray (which will photograph much better). In that way no one could possibly criticize." Clever Dudley! Describing this beautiful, beautiful event in *Vanity Fair,* my great friend and "booster," Alexander Woollcott, said: "No one in his

right mind could possibly describe Belle Poitrine's taste as even 'dubious.'"
Dudley's originality and sense of "rightness" had been vindicated. It was a glorious occasion. Our troth was solemnized by a sweet justice of the peace from
Van Nuys whom the wardrobe department had costumed in authentic copies
of the Archbishop of Canterbury's robes (originally made for Stuart Harris in
Oh Henry!). The cathedral was "S.R.O." as was the reception held in the exquisite gardens of Casa Torquemada. After cutting the mammoth black cake for
my guests, I tiptoed upstairs to my virginal little bedroom where the newsreel
"boys" took motion pictures of me changing into my black sequin going-away
dress. Then, through a shower of wild rice, Letch and I dashed for our car and
away, away, away!

It was farewell, house of sorrow! Farewell, "pesky" old studio! I was a
new little bride going off on a twelve-month honeymoon around the world
with a real, live prince charming. I was Mrs. Letch Feeley!

"Chums"

Helen Highwater

Gilbert Fleming

Pixie Portnoy

Endive

Carstairs

"Tex"

Mae Retch

Dudley du Pont

Vivienne Vixen

A BEL AIR HOUSEWIFE

1934-1940

IN LOOKING BACK OVER the turbulent years of my life I can now see, with the "wisdom of hindsight," that the turning point came when I allowed Letch Feeley to "rush" me into what was to be the longest, but the unhappiest, of all my marriages.

Oh, I felt that I was ecstatic at the time, that this was a true mating of beautiful bodies, pure souls and keen intellects. When I think of how our marriage must have looked to the average reader of "fan" magazines—the shopgirl, the typist, the farmhand, the shipping clerk; all of the Little People who worshipped the image of me—I can see a match of the sort on which dreams were made. And, pray, why not? I was at the peak of my popularity. I had youth, beauty, wealth, influence, power and fame. And I had just wed a "celluloid god"—the movie hero and matinée idol whose very name was a synonym for wit, charm, looks and virility. Letch and I had everything, or so it would seem. And so it did seem, for a time, to little me.

As with all people in the "public eye," there were naturally malicious, "back-biting" stories circulated about Letch and me by my enemies. They said, for example, that I was "old enough to be his mother." This, of course, is the sheerest nonsense! Although there were a few years' difference in our ages, the "gap" was in no way noteworthy. Letch was twenty-two at the time I married him—a mature, intelligent, well "set-up" young man who looked older than his years. I was but a tiny bit his senior. So much for that. Other gossipmongers spread stories, unflattering to both of us, to the effect that Letch married me for my money. That is too ridiculous. At the time of our wedding Letch was receiving slightly more than a quarter of a million dollars annually from the studio, plus a bonus of one hundred thousand for each picture he made with me. (He was cast in no others.) In those happy days, before the Government of the United States was seized by radicals, Socialists, Communists, "brain trusters" and other "riffraff," that amount was perfectly adequate for a young bachelor with simple tastes and no responsibilities. (As a wedding gift, I tore up Letch's old contract and wrote a new one, increasing his income to a point where he wouldn't—couldn't—feel like a "kept" man.) Ours was purely a "love match," but trouble soon started to brew, although in my bridal happiness, my golden hopes for a perfect future, I was perhaps unwilling to recognize it.

I believe my first inkling that Letch was not the most attentive of husbands occurred on the verdant campus of Radclyffe Hall in the rolling hills of Pennsylvania when, as a bride of two days, I took Letch to call on Baby-dear. Like any normal mother, I wanted to see my little girl, wanted her to meet her new father and wanted to explain to her why it would be impossible to have her spend her holidays at home, as Letch and I were bound for Europe and our honeymoon. I was cut to the quick when Baby-dear did not even recognize her own Mommy! But the worst was yet to come! The interview was not going well. Vivacious and interesting as I tried to be, there were long silences, embarrassing lulls in the conversation. When I turned to ask Letch if he did not agree that Baby-dear's hair should be slightly lightened, I saw to my dismay that his gaze was riveted on a group of older girls playing baseball in their brief "gym" suits. "Letch," I said more volubly, "I am speaking to you!"

"Huh?" Letch replied absently. "Excuse me. I gotta see a man abouta dog." He wandered off and was not seen again for hours until he happened to be discovered in the Upper School dormitories! Can you imagine the shame I felt for my child and myself? We had a frightful "set-to" in the Philadelphia Ritz that night, during which Letch destroyed several thousand dollars' worth of Louis XVI furniture.

In New York I "made up" with Letch by taking him to Abercrombie & Fitch and equipping him completely for all of his favorite outdoor sports. As he had never been to the "big city" before, I planned to show New York to him (and vice versa) with trips to the Metropolitan Museum, the Cloisters, the Statue of Liberty and so on. However, my husband's idea of culture in Manhattan began with the dinner show at the Casino de Paree and ended with the two o'clock floor show at the Paradise. Such refined favorites of mine as Armando's, the Central Park Casino, and the Coq Rouge bored Mr. Feeley. But he couldn't get enough of the unclad girls at the Palais Royal, the Hollywood, the Nudist Bar or similar vulgar places of "entertainment." It was a relief to board the *Normandie* and sail for France.

But, if anything, Paris was worse than New York. Letch cared nothing for the Louvre, the Opéra, the Comédie-Française, not while he had the Folies-Bergère, the Lido, the Moulin Rouge and heaven knows what other sordid spectacles, on either bank, to see. It got so that I dreaded to visit Alix, Vionnet and others *hautes couturières* for fear of what I might, or might not, find in our suite at the Meurice upon my return. We lingered in Paris long enough for me to choose from the fall collections. But when I became restive, Letch showed no desire to move on. The blow fell on Letch's twenty-third birthday (October 20, 1934) when, as a special treat, I took him to the opening night of Offenbach's lovely operetta, *La Créole*, starring my great favorite and the toast of Paris, Josephine Baker. Letch had been drinking quite heavily at Harry's Bar ("Just tell the driver 'Sank roo do noo.'" That was, unfortunately, all the French my husband spoke!) and dozed stertorously in his seat during most of the first act. I suppose he had expected a great star like Mlle. Baker to appear wearing nothing but a bunch of bananas. However, when he "came to," there she was on stage, wearing a sedate crinoline and singing in her own true soprano. Letch stood bolt upright. "What the hell is this," he shouted, "*Africa Speaks?* I can hear all the coon-shouters I want back home!" A riot was narrowly averted. We left Paris the next day.

Thus it went all over the world—a troop of girl bellringers in Zurich, a flamenco dancer in Seville, a female impersonator in Munich (*that* was a good joke on Mr. Feeley! Ha-ha!), a "belly" dancer in Cairo, a lady bath attendant in Tokyo. I sensed that Letch—a poor boy used to none of my advantages—would be better off at home, with a busy schedule of screen commitments to keep him out of "mischief."

Alone with me, Letch could be the dearest, sweetest, tenderest, most affectionate husband any girl could ask. But "turned loose" in the outside world, he just wasn't big enough to withstand the many temptations offered there. No question about it, "all play and no work made Letch a bad boy." I heaved a sigh as our taxi halted under the Moorish *porte cochère* of Casa Torquemada in the summer of 1935.

I was eager to resume my film career and even more anxious to find good rôles to keep my new husband occupied. Although he said he was in no hurry to return to the "lot," I told Endive Kissner to lose no time in "lining up" an impressive array of films for the two of us to do together. What a pity that only one of us was a dedicated performer! Had Letch cared less about "loafing," drinking and sailing we might, today, have been like the Lunts. As it was, Letch wandered off on his own every afternoon (while I was busily running Metronome) and many evenings as well.

Although Elisabeth Bergner and Marlene Dietrich had recently made abortive attempts at portraying the rôle, I was most interested in doing a biographical film on Catherine of Russia, with Letch as Potëmkin. After all, as Momma said saltily, what could a couple of *krauts* know about a Russian empress? Letch said he didn't want to get mixed up with a lot of Bolsheviks, but I gave orders to the studio to proceed at once.

As we still were not ready to "shoot" by December, I wrote to Baby-dear's school, with joy in my heart, asking to have my little precious sent home for Christmas. The holiday was a disaster. Letch met Baby-dear at the station. When she got to Casa Torquemada, she was quite sick and had to be put to bed. Mumps was the doctor's diagnosis! Letch came down with it three weeks later! And, if I do seem overly loyal to my own sex, I must say that my five-year-old daughter was a much more grown-up patient than my husband, although perhaps it is true that she suffered far less severely. To avoid contagion, I took a suite at the Beverly-Wilshire. Unfortunately, having mumps in common did little to strengthen the bond between Letch and Baby-dear. I was heartsick, but I realized that it was better for her to be back at school with people of her own age and mentality. She and Letch just didn't "hit it off."

Nor was Baby-dear the only reminder of Morris Buchsbaum that made Letch nervous and "moody." He seemed to resent the whole house where I had lived as another man's wife. At least he was in it as rarely as possible.

Hoping to please him and give him something that was "all his," I searched quietly around the Los Angeles area for a place where Letch might feel more at home. It was through Momma that I stumbled on just the right thing. Among Morris' personal papers was a mortgage to a most imposing French *château* in Bel Air, the exquisite home of a retired French inventor and his wife. M. Outré was now dead and his widow, owing to imprudent investments, penniless. Realizing that I was doing the poor old soul a favor by ridding her of a piece of real estate so costly to maintain, I quietly foreclosed and

offered her a very generous price for her furniture—all of which was very old. Naturally, as the French will, she haggled a great deal but, in the end, took my check and returned to France. (Without one word of gratitude, need I say?)

It was a terrible wrench to have to part with dear old Casa Torquemada, but Spanish was going out and I was able to get a fair offer for the house and grounds from a psychiatrist who wanted to establish an exclusive rest home in a quiet, residential neighborhood.

After renaming the new place Château Belletch and holding a two-week housewarming, I settled down and hoped that Letch would, too. But an unexpected turn of events at the studio occupied so much of my attention that I had little thought to devote to Letch Feeley. Franklin Delano Roosevelt and the New Deal had absolutely moved into Metronome Studios!

Needless to say, I was furious at this unparalleled intrusion upon free enterprise. How dared they demand to "snoop" in private financial records, disbursements, confidential contracts and agreements? "It is as though," I said on the historic three-hour, coast-to-coast radio broadcast which I bought (following Father Coughlin and pre-empting the Eddie Cantor, Manhattan

Merry-go-round and Major Bowes shows), "that Man in the White House, like some despot of yore, insisted on reading my diary, raiding my larder and ransacking my *lingerie!*" My impassioned plea for civil rights created a landslide of correspondence, and one sponsor even asked me to consider replacing the Eddie Cantor comedy hour on a permanent basis. But what quarter could a poor defenseless woman expect from a dictator who would even make so bold as to close all of the banks in our great nation? The savage barbarian hordes of red Russian Communism descended on the Athens that was mighty Metronome, sacking and despoiling with their Bolshevistic battle cry of "Soak the rich!" After an unspeakable siege, lasting the better part of two months, it was announced that the studio "owed" the government a tax debt in excess of eight million dollars while I, who had always remained aloof from such iniquitous practices as paying taxes on the salary I had earned and the little I legally inherited as Morris' helpless relict, was "stung" with a personal bill of such astronomical proportions as to "wipe out" all but a fraction

of my poor, hard-come-by savings. I was also publicly reprimanded, dragged through the mud by the radical press and made a figure of fun by such leftist publications as *The New Republic, The New Yorker, Time* and the *Christian Science Monitor.*

It was then that I availed myself of the rights of a citizen and declared the income tax unconstitutional. The litigation was costly and seemingly endless. I fought like a tigress but by the time I appealed my case to the Supreme Court (1937), Mr. Roosevelt and his "henchmen" had done their "dirty work" all too well, even going so far as to attempt to "pack" the highest tribunal in the land in order to defeat little me. Presidential coercion had succeeded not only in poisoning the courtiers, "toadies" and sycophants of the "bench" against me, but it had been so far-reaching as to discourage any lawyer in the nation from representing me! I was ready, like Portia, to present my own brief. But the Supreme Court wouldn't even *hear* my case! My plea was unanimously voted down and "thrown out." Again, my name was on all the front pages. I was, it seemed, *persona non grata* in every quarter, but not entirely without a staunch following of noted political thinkers and students of jurisprudence. As Charles Evans Hughes said, "Miss Poitrine's limitations as an actress are exceeded only by her logic as a litigant." Albert Einstein was quoted as saying: "The workings of the woman's mind amaze me." Henry Ford spoke of me as "utterly astounding." Heywood Broun wrote: "Belle Poitrine is the most original thinker since Caligula," and even F.D.R. had to concede that "if the rest of this nation showed the foresight and patriotism of Miss Poitrine, America would rapidly resemble ancient Babylon and Nineveh."

Not only were the court costs prohibitive, but I was subjected to crippling fines, in addition to usurious interest on the unpaid "debts" which the governmen claimed that Metronome and I owed—a severe financial blow. Nor, as Manny said, had the notoriety done my career "any good." My enemies were only too anxious to level against me such charges as "reactionary," "robber baroness," and even "traitor"! Traitor indeed! I point now with pride to the fact that, long ere the Committee on Un-American Activities, the Minute Women, the Economic Council and other such notable "watchdog" organizations were so much as heard of, I was Hollywood's leading bulwark against Communism, fighting single-handedly "creeping socialism" against such insuperable odds as the Fascio-Communist troops of the NRA, PWA, WPA, CCC and an army of more than twenty-two million mercenaries whom F.D.R. employed secretly, through the transparent ruse of regular "relief" checks.

Needless to say, my art suffered drastically during this turbulent period. Could it do otherwise? Even though I have always had a genius for "throwing myself" into every rôle and "playing it for all it's worth," no actress can be expected to do her best work when her fortune, her reputation, her livelihood, her home and her nation itself are all imperilled. Such sweeping distractions are hardly conducive to "Oscar"-winning performances. I tried my hardest, with little help, may I say, from my husband and leading man, but somehow the outside pressures were too severe.

Having (through *my* unflagging effort and devotion) achieved stardom, a fortune and a world-renowned wife at an age when most young men are casting their first vote, Letch proceeded to neglect them all. Never a "quick study," he now made no attempt to learn his "lines" and many a mile of film was wasted, many a scene—sometimes involving as many as a thousand fellow thespians—was taken thirty, forty, fifty times because Miss Poitrine's costar and "helpmate" had never learned his part. Each time Letch "went up" in his "lines," *I* was the one to be patient, helpful and apologetic while *he* indulged in outbursts of temperament, profanity and abuse, blaming others, going into "sulks" and, on more occasions than I care to count, storming off the "set" for the rest of the day. As for his finances, I was never privileged to know exactly how much money Letch had "salted away." It was I who paid for our little home, the food, the liquor, the servants—even Letch's bills at his tailor and the Los Angeles Athletic Club. Never once did he buy me a single gift, and for our third anniversary he gave me a dislocated jaw. (But that is another story.) As for his private monies, they were rapidly dissipated in drinking, gaming and carousing. More than once I was confronted by professional gamblers, "bookies," loan "sharks," gangsters, "thugs" and "finger men"—people of a class I did not even know existed—to repay my husband's staggering losses, "or else…" I shuddered to think that someone so dear to me could even associate with such a sinister *milieu*. And at three different times during our turbulent marriage strange girls, with the commonest of accents, telephoned to announce to me that Letch had sired their unborn children! Having the deepest of maternal instincts, my heart fairly bled when I thought of the darling pink and white "bundles from heaven" I would have proudly given my husband. "Ah, you're too old" was invariably his ungallant and untrue retort whenever I suggested "starting a family." Letch had made it abundantly clear that he did not care for the company of my own precious daughter. I now felt it wiser to keep Baby-dear in school and—during the summers—at a camp run by the Society of Friends all year around. Her presence only made Letch more distant and irritable and, in the hurry of buying Château Belletch, I had neglected to consider a room for Baby-dear, so there was no place to put her, anyhow. (I sometimes feel that God, in His infinite wisdom, *wants* us to have these inexplicable little lapses of memory. It almost always works out for the best.)

Yet I adored this man, Letch Feeley, why, I cannot say. With faint heart and a brave smile, I endured his long absences from Château Belletch, his coldness, his indifference, his slights and his abuse. The times I can recall when I was publicly humiliated by him—lovely dinner parties in our Trianon Suite where the collation was postponed and postponed and postponed, only to be served dry and overcooked at a table where the host's chair was vacant; a "splash party" at the new pool, which I had built in the hope of keeping Letch away from public beaches, when Letch and a certain Aquacutie stayed underwater together for the better part of an hour; a lovely Epiphany party at Errol Flynn's, on which sacred occasion Letch stole away with an unknown "starlet," leaving me "high and dry" to get home as best I could. These are but a sampling of the insults I endured. As Mrs. Letch Feeley, was it any wonder that I, once *the* social arbiter of Filmdom, was excluded from the smart entertainments given by the Astaires, the Coopers, the Gables, the Colmans, the Rathbones, the Taylors, the Thalbergs and such devout, closely knit families as the Barrymores and the Crosbys? As Letch's anti-social conduct increased, our invitations decreased and my heart was in my mouth whenever I played hostess at a fashionable "screenland" gathering.

Between 1935 and 1939 Letch and I made ten films together, each less successful, both artistically and commercially, than the one before it. Our last joint venture, *Sainted Lady,* a deeply religious film based on the life of Mother Cabrini, and timed so that its release date would coincide with the beatification of America's first saint in November, 1938, was a fiasco from start to finish. As I was playing Mother Cabrini, the picture was actually "all mine," with nearly every scene built around me. But in order to keep Letch in the public eye and out of trouble, I wrote in a part especially for him—that of a dashing ruffian who "sees the light" and is saved by the inspiring example of Mother Cabrini. And did he appreciate my efforts on his behalf? Did he trouble to memorize the very small part which I had "tailor-made" to his specifications, a rôle eventually cut down to three short speeches? Did he show the rest of the cast—numbering four thousand—the consideration of arriving at the studio punctually—or even at all? *He did not!* The "shooting" went on for eight months! Most of our working days were spent on the telephone calling "bookies," illegal gambling dens, a certain "residential club for young actresses,"

more than a hundred different bars or the steam room of the athletic club. Whenever he deigned to appear at the studio he was "hung over," uncooperative, rude and insulting. He made many tasteless, irreverent and *un*funny remarks, not only about me in the title rôle, but about religion in general. By the time the film was released we were three million dollars over-spent, war was imminent and the public apparently had forgotten all about Mother Cabrini. Thanks to Letch Feeley and the terrible strain he imposed on me, the notices were few and unfavorable. Only George Santayana seemed to understand and appreciate the film when he wrote: "Miss Poitrine has perpetrated the most eloquent argument for the Protestant faith yet unleashed by Hollywood." But it was small consolation.

In a rare fit of anger and spite, I "farmed out" my own husband to a small and most undistinguished studio to make one picture as a form of punishment. (An actor must have discipline.) The film was called *The Diet of Worms*, which I felt was just what Letch deserved. It turned out to be a life of Martin Luther, of all things! It was a disaster! In clothes, Letch simply did not project. He was laughed off the screen. At the same time, however, I availed myself of the services of that great English actor and master of make-up, Sir Gauntley Pratt, to do a "quickie" called *The Mystery of the Mad Marquess*, in which I played a young American girl who inherits a haunted castle on the English moors which is filled with secret passages and sliding panels and, unbeknownst to anyone, is still occupied by an eccentric maniac. It was a "potboiler" made on a "shoestring" and not the sort of film I like, as all I had to do was look blank and scream a great deal. My heart was not in it, but, oddly enough, it remains the most financially successful picture of my career. (I watched it on television late one night last week and it "stands up" remarkably well, even twenty years later.)

Letch had returned from his *débâcle* unrepentant and more badly behaved than before. I really loved that boy, and, in a feverish attempt to preserve our marriage and to try to revive the wonderful, wonderful person Letch had once been, I took my troubles to Momma, hoping that her earthy advice would help me.

"If I could only think of something at the studio, near me, to absorb his boundless energy," I said. "What is Letch interested in?"

"Bookies, booze and babes," Momma said bluntly.

Her reply stung me, but this was too important to let my hurt make any difference. "I can't turn the studio into a gambling hell or a saloon," I said.

"It might pay better if you did," Momma replied.

"But we have lovely stars—ladies whom I can trust. What about Helen Highwater?"

"That old lush?" Momma snorted.

"Or Pixie Portnoy?"

"A dike if I ever saw one. And I seen plenty."

"What about lovely Vivienne Vixen?"

"I'd hate to be hanging since she was forty," Momma said. "Letch don't want a mother, he wants a playmate—lots of 'em."

An idea struck me. "Maybe if we inaugurated something to encourage new talent—like the Wampus Baby Stars—and put Letch in charge."

"That would be like giving the Boy Scouts to Dudley du Pont," Momma said.

"But at least I'd know where to find Letch," I said.

"You'd know all right," Momma said.

"But *I* will select the girls," I said, knowing that my infallible instinct about people would not "let me down."

Thus Metronome inaugurated the Belletch Baby Starlets—twelve aspiring young actresses whom I'd chosen myself for beauty, talent and, I hoped, virtue. (Each was required to have letters of recommendation from her high school principal, pastor, former employer—if any—and a reputable business-

man from her home town.) Of the whole dozen, the most outstanding was a Mlle. Therese ("Tootsie") La Touche, who came armed with no less than a hundred letters! She was a pretty, winsome and gifted ballerina who was not without professional experience in that she had appeared with the Albertina Rasch Dancers in that lovely Friml operetta, *Madame Mazurka*, as a child prodigy (actually she was *much* older than she claimed). Momma took one look at "Tootsie" and said, "I smell trouble." But I was so hopeful of piecing together the shards of our marriage that I took a chance and started work on *Swan Song*, a life of Anna Pavlova, in which I was to play the title rôle, Letch was to play Nijinski and "Tootsie" was to be given the opportunity of a lifetime as Tatiana, my elder sister. What a mistake!

At first I was encouraged to see that Letch was always the first one on the "set," but I soon began to notice that he and "Tootsie" were spending more and more time in one another's company and that she was even inviting him into her dressing room! If there is anything I cannot endure, it is a woman who uses her sex as a means to ensnare a man! On camera "Tootsie" was unbearable, always doing "high kicks" and *arabesques* whenever I tried to speak my tragic lines and literally "dancing circles around me" in the few ballet episodes that were actually filmed. Her scenes with Letch were positively disgusting! Watching the "rushes," I could see that I had made a serious error in engaging this wanton little thing. Luckily, I was able—with some rewriting—to have "Tootsie's" part removed from the picture entirely, so that she ended up exactly where she belonged—on the cutting room floor! But, unfortunately, while performing a lovely *pas de deux* with Letch (who knew next to nothing of the dance), he dropped me and I sustained a severe sprained ankle. "Shooting" had to be discontinued and it was decided that the entire film had better be "scrapped." By selling the costumes to one of the many touring companies of the Ballet Russe de Monte Carlo, we were able to *recoup* some of our losses.

Incapacitated as I was, I retired to my *boudoir* at Château Belletch and whiled away my incarceration by taking singing lessons from the late Luisa Tetrazzini, in preparation for a musical film in the manner of those recently done by Grace Moore, Gladys Swarthout, Lily Pons, and Jeanette MacDonald. Nothing I could say or do—and least of all husbandly concern for a wife who might never dance again—could induce Letch to remain at home. I had no inkling of what was the matter *this* time. But my loyal friend, Dudley du Pont,

came to me one day, after I was quite weary from repeated performances of the "mad scene" from *Lucia di Lammermoor,* took both my hands in his and said, "Sweetie, I'm telling you this for your own good and because I think you should hear it first from a friend and not from Lolly or Hedda—although God knows why it isn't *all* over their columns. But his royal prettiness is at it again and this time with that two-bit hoofer, La Touche."

"Letch?" I said. "I can't believe it!"

"But it's true, my dear, too, too terribly true. He's rented a little *garçonnière* from this old boy-friend of mine down in Laguna Beach and what they do in that precious little house is too vomit-making for words." Private detectives proved Dudley to be one hundred per cent correct and investigation of "Tootsie's" flagrant past made it abundantly clear as to why so many businessmen had recommended her! I had suspected, from time to time, that Letch had been guilty of little dalliances, but this torrid *affaire* going on under my very nose, as it were, was the "last straw"! They did not even show the common decency to *pretend* that they were less than lovers! I could have divorced Letch then and there, but I did not. I had invested too much—in time, in emotion and in money—to "call it quits." Instead, I continued as the family "breadwinner" by commencing work on my musical *Wilma Tell*. Having been interested in both the stories of William Tell and Annie Oakley, I had combined them and turned them into a sweet operetta about a Swiss lady archer who saves all of Switzerland by shooting an apple from her lover's head. As F. Scott Fitzgerald once said of me, "Belle Poitrine has a genius for weeding out the inconsequentials and presenting them full blown on the screen." Heartsick over Letch, I had passed him by as my leading man for *Wilma Tell* in favor of one of the really great voices such as Nelson Eddy, Allan Jones or John Boles, none of whom happened to be available. Thus, while I toiled at the studio, Letch and "Tootsie" continued "carrying on"—sometimes right in Château Belletch!

Driving me home from the studio one evening, my chauffeur took a détour that led us past a large yacht showroom. In the window I saw a model of what I felt would be the perfect gift for Letch's twenty-eighth birthday—a pleasure yacht of moderate size complete with lounge, dining saloon, galley, four tiny bedrooms and two baths. It was more than I could afford but, knowing my husband's love of the sea, I hoped it might capture his fancy, if only momentarily. The salesman explained the mechanism of the motors to me

while I wrote out a large check and gave delivery instructions for my last gift to Letch—the *Belle de Mer*. It was, as the salesman said, "a trig little craft."

Conscious of Letch's heavy drinking during the past months, I became fearful that he might scratch the paint on the *Belle de Mer* or in some other way damage her and I did not want such a costly gift to go the way of the wrecked Cord roadster, the mislaid emerald shirt studs, the broken Capeheart record player of former, happier birthdays. For that reason, I telephoned my insurance broker and had the *Belle de Mer* fully insured and, while I had him on the "phone," reviewed my own policies, those I had taken out on Letch and on some of the younger Metronome stars.

Wanting to make this a truly memorable birthday celebration, I swallowed my pride and invited "Tootsie" La Touche to join Letch, Momma and me at the yacht club for luncheon on my dear husband's anniversary day.

As I said, the *Belle de Mer* was a "trig" vessel. Letch was so stunned when he saw it that all he could say was "Jeest!"

"Aren't you going to take us girls out for a sail, darling?" I asked.

"Sure thing," Letch said. "How about it, baby?" he asked Miss La Touche.

"Boy, oh boy, would I ever love to!" she said in that uncultivated, brassy fashion of hers. "Gee, on a *yacht*, Letchy!"

I had been aboard the *Belle de Mer* with Momma earlier that day, seeing that all of the appointments were exactly as I wanted them. But, when the time came to board for the "maiden voyage," I found myself suddenly indisposed with a severe *migraine*. "Oh, don't let me spoil your fun, Letch, *mon chéri*," I said sportingly. "You and Miss La Touche go ahead. Momma and I will just watch from the terrace of the yacht club."

"That's right," Momma said. "You youngsters go along and enjoy yourselves while you still can." We said *adieu* and ordered daiquiris while Letch and "Tootsie" boarded the *Belle de Mer*. He looked so young, so handsome, so virile, so full of life, in his white yachting cap, that it fairly made my heart leap. *She* looked very common.

From the terrace, I heard the powerful throb of the *Belle de Mer*'s motors and I waved my *mouchoir* a little sadly as that noble craft got under way.

"Poor tomcat," Momma said, or *something* like that. I wasn't sure.

"What did you say, Momma?" I asked. But I never heard her reply. The air was rent with an explosion that shattered my cocktail glass and broke every window in the yacht club. No sooner had the *Belle de Mer* reached the mouth of the yacht basin than it was blown to a thousand bits. There wasn't even enough left of it for the insurance investigators to examine. "Momma!" I cried. Then everything went black.

As there was nothing remaining of my poor, darling Letch and that lovely, talented young *danseuse* to bury, we held simple memorial services at the Chapel of the Avenging Angel the following morning. Although I was nearly prostrate with grief, I was surprised to see Momma climb into her red "Rolly-Polly" and drive off due south at an astonishing speed, rather than to return to Château Belletch or Metronome.

My fellow workers were amazed to see me, a widow of less than twenty-four hours, turn up on the *Wilma Tell* "set" directly after my dear husband's services. But, as I have always said, "the show must go on." Alas, it did not. While I was singing my big number, "Gemütlichkeit," I noticed that the Alps were moving. When I demanded an explanation, it was immediately offered by a rude bailiff. Metronome was in bankruptcy and the studios were being closed by order of the creditors! *Wilma Tell*, my greatest film, would never be seen.

My husband was gone, my studio was gone, even my dear mother was gone (to Mexico, I learned later). Nothing was left for little me but the insurance money. I faced the world alone again—bereft, bankrupt, beleaguered.

CHAPTER SIXTEEN

CALLED TO THE COLORS

1941-1945

The end of mighty Metronome · My need of a change · Finances · A girl's best
friend is her mother · Making the rounds as a star · I retire from motion pictures · War!
I do my bit · Momma becomes San Diego's most famous hostess · I win the Navy E!

THE *DÉMISE* OF MY MIGHTY METRONOME, following on the very heels of
my beloved husband's tragic death at sea and the disappearance of my dear
mother, came as a severe blow. With bailiffs all over the "lot," moving scenery,
cataloguing settings, costumes, "props"—even the desks, typewriters and
pencils in the offices!—I was helpless. I tried to put up a fight, for I am not a
woman who takes many things lying down. But it was useless. All of the legal
advisors I sought out said the same thing. Mighty Metronome, once the greatest film studio in the world, was bankrupt and in the hands of the receivers.
Momma, who had complete charge of the finances, who could answer all of
the questions as to the whereabouts of millions of dollars' worth of assets,
was nowhere to be found. I would have to give in gracefully to the venal
tradesmen and the socialistic government forces that willfully set about to
destroy the fountainhead of so much beauty. The studio, the theatres—
Buchsbaum's Baghdad in New York, the Bessarabian in Los Angeles, the Bac-
chanalia in Chicago, two dozen in all, each more lavish and imposing than the
last—beautiful Belleville in the desert (which I had planned to turn into an
Egyptian real-estate subdivision at a later date), even Château Belletch, and
its lovely antique French furniture, were impounded. All was lost save my

Luncheoning with "Roz"

poor wardrobe and the insurance money for Letch's precious life and the bonnie *Belle de Mer*. As for my jewels, they had simply "disappeared" when the "cutthroats" from the marshal's office came to wrench them from me.

Everything was gone save my contribution to Art. As Dudley du Pont and Carstairs Bagley said, while comforting me, "The greatest moments of your life are in the can." How true! Though everything might be gone, the unforgettable films I made had all been immortalized on celluloid and were there in neat rows of round tin cans to thrill the world for years to come. A screen actress' life *does* have its rewards!

Through my trusted friend and *confidante*, Endive Kissner, I learned that my adorable mother had gone, incognito, to Mexico, taking with her all of my jewels and the last few million dollars in the Metronome treasury for safekeeping. How like darling Momma! The jewels were later returned.

Physically, mentally and emotionally exhausted, there was nothing to keep me in Hollywood. So I availed myself of a month's complete rest at a private nursing home, run by a gifted surgeon of my acquaintance. When I returned everyone said that it was remarkable how much younger I looked. Certain catty actresses, who shall be nameless, were uncharitable enough to suggest that I had undergone cosmetic surgery, and one even came right out and asked if I had had my face "lifted"! What balderdash! I was much too young even to consider such a foolish and needless operation.

When I returned to the film colony, I engaged a small but attractive "bungalow" at the dear, dead Garden of Allah, my neighbors being F. Scott Fitzgerald and darling Robert ("Bob") Benchley. It was such fun to be back in a truly intellectual *milieu* once more, without the responsibilities of running a huge establishment like Château Belletch and the tremendous Metronome Studios. Although I was still in mourning for beloved Letch, I felt that the best way to forget my troubles would be to go back to work at another studio. Thus I began "making the rounds" again. But 1941 was not a very distinguished year in the annals of film-making. The parts that interested me, such as Regina in *The Little Foxes*, had all been given to lesser actresses owing to "pull" and studio "politics." As I had made it very clear that I would not accept "just anything," I was not annoyed by constant offers to consider inferior rôles. So respectful, in fact, were the producers and directors of my unique position in motion pictures that I was not called at all.

I was toying with the idea of appearing "in person" once again, in an entirely new concept of the beautiful Passion Play, when something happened

to change the entire course of my life and the history of our great nation—Pearl Harbor!

Ramon, a talented young Mexican actor, and I had returned to the Garden of Allah from attending church on that memorable Sunday. An exquisite dancer, Ramon turned on the wireless and the throbbing strains of "Orchids in the Moonlight," one of my favorite tangos, filled my drawing room. We had just commenced dancing when the music was interrupted by an earth-shaking announcement. For a moment I was too stunned to speak. Then I said, "Ramon, this can mean only one thing. America has joined the war!"

No time then for thinking about films or plays. On that day I retired from motion pictures. Every bit of my time would be devoted to the war effort. What red-blooded, patriotic American girl could shirk her duty at a moment like this?

By 1942 I was right in the thick of it, caring not for personal hardship or danger. Heedless of risk, I flew directly to Miami to entertain our boys in khaki. From there to Fort Benning, Georgia, the Stage Door Canteen in Manhattan, Fort Dix, New Jersey, and Lake Placid. Five performances in as many months! The pace was gruelling, my days and nights fraught with danger and discomfort, but no sacrifice was too great. Nor were personal appearances all I did. While "resting up"—if indeed it can be called relaxation—from my demanding routine, I was never too busy to pose for the all-important "pin-up" pictures to spur our boys on to conquest. Betty Grable, Lana Turner, Rita

With Peggy Gas(?) doing my bit

Hayworth—we all did it, but everyone said that there was something about *my* photographs that lifted "cheesecake" into a realm all its own. Not being affiliated with any motion picture studio, I had more than four million alluring "shots" printed at my own expense for distribution to our "G.I.'s" in all quarters of the globe. They were an enormous success.*

I was ready, willing and able to go overseas and to "do my bit," right in the muck and the mire, for our troops. However, an unofficial committee of

---

*A few hundred thousand of these 8″ \ 10″ "glossy" prints are still available. Interested readers can secure copies by sending $10.00 to cover cost of handling to: Belle Poitrine Enterprises. Belledame Farm. Cyclops, Connecticut.

right: In the thick of it!
With Hugh Martin in Miami.
below: Hors de combat

Army chaplains, of all faiths, sent me a very sweet letter stating that my appearance abroad "could very easily turn the tide of battle." I was extremely touched and, although I had become accustomed to the low whistles and the "wolf calls" of valiant boys too long absent from dainty feminine companionship, I did not wish my presence to be so inflammatory as to delay the total surrender of the Axis Powers by a single minute.

Meanwhile, my sweet Momma had returned from her long sojourn "South of the Border." Through Endive Kissner and other faithful old friends, I had heard from time to time of Momma's progress. My diamonds had long since been returned to me by Ramon, who had been Momma's constant tango partner at Acapulco. But now Momma had also heeded the call to arms and she, too, was right in the thick of the war effort.

Too elderly, perhaps, to take a job in an airplane factory or a defense plant, Momma had done the next best thing. She had leased a handsome house—large, perhaps, for a woman alone—quite near the San Diego Naval Base where almost overnight she had become that city's most famous hostess.

Wanting to do something for our boys, Momma had engaged the services of several very attractive young ladies and held a perpetual "open house" for America's jolly "Jack Tars." So thrilled was I in the knowledge that dear Momma was safe and sound in the United States once more that I hurried to be at her side. The house was lovely and Momma had "done it up" with her usual, individualistic taste—mirrors everywhere, luxurious tufted pink satin divans, polar bear rugs and oil paintings of voluptuous *Renoiresque* ladies. Her co-hostesses (Susan, Sheila, Jeanne, Jane and Eva) were all college girls of the highest type and there was nothing they wouldn't do to show our weary sailors a good time. From the roof of her house, Momma would watch the harbor through a telescope, and whenever a ship "pulled in to port," she would send Ramon down with her big old Rolls-Royce and what she laughingly called her "business cards." In less time than it takes to tell about, her house reverberated with the shouts and laughter of "Momma's Girls" and "Uncle Sam's Boys" enjoying themselves to the utmost.

I had meant only to spend a few hours with Momma, but so intrigued was I by the innocent revels, the sense of spontaneous gaiety in her salon that I stayed on and on and on, doing my patriotic best to keep Navy morale at an all-time high while fending off the spoilsports of the Shore Patrol.

Almost before I knew it, V-J Day was at hand. I felt almost wistful to think that these dashing boys would be returning as civilians to the farms and families that had spawned them. As for poor Momma, she burst into tears when peace was declared. There just *is* something about a uniform! However, it all seemed worthwhile on that unforgettable last night at Momma's house when a group of the "regulars"—boys who had been coming back and back and back to Momma's festive gatherings—presented me with the Navy "E." I knew then that I had given my all.

The world was at peace again. Without feeling selfish I could return to my career as a great actress, secure in the knowledge that I had been called to the colors once more and that I had not failed my country.

CHAPTER SEVENTEEN

BACK TO BROADWAY!

1946

I accept a rôle in musical comedy · A fearful shock · Magdalena Montezuma!
Billing problems · Professional jealousy · Ingratitude, thy name is Montezuma! · New Haven
Backstage rivalries · My show-stopping number · The Yale crew befriends me
Romance · Baby-dear · I bid *adieu* to the musical stage

IT IS INDEED AN ILL WIND that blows no one good (to paraphrase the late Thomas Tusser). Although World War II had brought its share of illness, death, unhappiness and inconvenience, it proved a tremendous "shot in the arm" for the living theatre. Were it not for the very existence of total war would such exquisite musical attractions as *Rosalinda, Up in Central Park, Follow the Girls, Song of Norway, Laughing Room Only, Firebrand of Florence* and *Hats Off to Ice* have been produced at all? I wonder.

It came as a most pleasant surprise to me when I was asked to appear in one of the loveliest and most elaborate of the postwar musical extravaganzas, quite by accident. En route from California to New York, I had several hours to "kill" between trains in Chicago. Naturally, I tried to telephone my dear old friend Colleen Moore, whose palatial residence in the "Windy City" I have often wanted to visit. However, the butler must have misunderstood my name when I called for, even though I telegraphed ahead of my impending arrival, Mrs. Hargrave (Colleen) was nowhere to be found. Therefore, I decided to "treat" myself to a good luncheon in the Pump Room. And who should be seated at the next table—also alone—but that wonderful old producer and

*"Goodie Godiva"—left to right: Deni Lamont,
Magdalena Montezuma and Sir Walter Mohair*

impresario Murray Minor Casebeer, lively as ever and still the possessor of a keen eye for a lovely damsel and a sensitive palate for a fine vintage! We fell into conversation and before long he was at my table, plying me with stingers, and telling me all about a lavish musical comedy he was about to produce— *Goodie Godiva,* an historical operetta and forerunner of such feasts for the eye and ear as *Lute Song, Candide,* and *Camelot.* As the afternoon wore on both of us became quite carried away, I with visions of returning to the boards in the title rôle of *Goodie Godiva,* and lovable old Murray with stingers. It was nearly dusk when I summoned the captain and two waiters to put our luncheons on Mr. Casebeer's bill and to assist him to his room. I very nearly missed my train, but I had in my purse a battered Pump Room menu with the information that I was to appear in *Goodie Godiva* scrawled on the back of it in Murray's own unsteady writing.

Always a conscientious actress and a meticulous stickler for accuracy, I did a great deal of research on that lovely English lady who saved the town of Coventry from her cruel husband's ruinous taxation by riding nude through the main street, adorned only by her flowing tresses. In the interests of my art, I signed up for riding lessons and cancelled my appointment for a "poodle cut" at Antoine's.

You can imagine my surprise, then, when I appeared at Murray Minor Casebeer's offices only to learn that he had no recollection of our discussion in Chicago! *His* surprise was even greater than mine when I produced written evidence of the meeting and of our agreement. Alas, he had not specified which rôle I was to enact in *Goodie Godiva* and it came as quite a blow to me to realize that the star of the show was to be not little me, but Magdalena Montezuma! How a common Spanish (?) nobody like Montezuma was to understand the emotions of an Anglo-Saxon noblewoman such as Lady Godiva (when I had *been* an English aristocrat!) was a moot point. I was given every opportunity to withdraw from the cast, but I was adamant. While I had given selflessly of my time and talents for the war effort, Señorita Montezuma had been busy "feathering her own nest" in Hollywood, even being so blatantly unpatriotic as to accept an Academy Award when our country was in peril. "No," I said to Murray, "I accepted this informal contract in good faith. A bargain is a bargain, and I shall appear in *Goodie Godiva* even if only as a 'walk on.'"

To be brutally frank, I was "skating on thin ice" financially. My income had been drastically reduced since the failure of Metronome Studios. Almost all of my war work, for the past five years, had been on a strictly volunteer basis. I had only a few dollars in the bank and my jewels (and many of them—nineteen bracelets, the fabulous Baughdie necklace and tiara, were pawned). I had tried to receive some aid from Baby-dear's ample trust fund but, naturally, her trustees, who had cash registers where their hearts should have been, would do nothing to help me. In addition, I had incurred many heavy obligations on the strength of appearing in *Goodie Godiva*. I had leased a suite in the Ritz-Carlton and gone into debt at the Wilma Shop, John-Frederick's, Gunther's and the French Bootery, for an actress must think of appearances at all times. I wanted the work and I needed the money. For that reason I would swallow my pride as regarded Magdalena Montezuma.

The company of *Goodie Godiva* was a sheer delight. In the rôle of Leofric, Earl of Mercia and Lord of Coventry, was that splendid English character actor, Sir Walter Mohair. Deni Lamont was perfect as that dancing "jackanapes," "Peeping Tom." Among the principals were such tried and true old "pros" as Blanche Silversides, Modessa Priddy, Shaun O'Brien, Sisi Sykes, Effie Pickerell, Warren Pease and Merrill Lynch. Even the horse was divine. Yes, everyone connected with *Goodie Godiva* was charming—*with one vivid exception*. That exception was the star, Magdalena Montezuma. On the first day of rehearsals, when I rushed up to embrace an old friend and fellow-performer, she side-stepped suddenly and I sustained a painful fall over an electric cable. Because she had had a fair measure of success in Hollywood when more patriotic thespians had set aside "mask and wig" to aid the war effort, it had all "gone to her head." How quick she was to forget the many kindnesses I had shown her in the old days when she was but a "flash in the pan" at the box office and *I* was married to the owner of mighty Metronome—how considerate I had been in releasing her from her contract, the trouble I had personally taken over her costumes and housing arrangements during the filming of *Nights on the Nile*. Was she appreciative? Indeed she was not!

To give just a few examples: Montezuma, in the rôle of Lady Godiva, had thirty different costumes designed for her by Gilbert Adrian. All were in brilliant colors or dainty pastels, shimmering metallic creations and gowns dazzling with bugle beads and sequins, elaborately trimmed with fur and feathers. I—a famous star—was given but one, ill-fitting black dress which had been made (but, understandably, never used) for a church pageant in Hackensack, New Jersey. That is what I call "petty"! My rôle, that of a common scold, was reasonably substantial when we began rehearsing, but every day Miss Montezuma arranged to have my part cut, cut, cut until I appeared in only two scenes—one with her, in which she saw to it that I delivered my few, paltry lines from way "upstage." Of the other scene—a real show-stopping "number" which I sang with "Peeping Tom"—more later. While Montezuma was reasonably gracious to the rest of the company, she never deigned to speak to me unless it was in the spirit of destructive criticism and even then all of her remarks were made through the director.

I stoically put up with such unseemly conduct like the true "trouper" I am. The critics and the audiences, I decided, would be the final judges of who was the *real* star of this offering. Instead of fighting fire with fire, I was as sweet and cooperative with the entire company—stars, principals, chorus "kids," "gypsies," stagehands, designers and musicians—as I could be. I even made a special point of bringing little surprises to the electricians, knowing full well that if they were "with" me, my "numbers" would be lighted to my greatest advantage.

After three agonizing weeks of rehearsal, we were ready to "try out." Our itinerary was to be New Haven, Boston, Washington, Philadelphia and then New York. I was tense with excitement.

Although I was financially on the brink of disaster, I felt that it was only proper that I take a suite in the Taft Hotel at New Haven. After all, quite a lot of people would be thronging to that city to witness my triumphal return to the theatre and it would hardly be proper to entertain them in a bedroom. Showing great foresight, I "booked" the largest suite in the hotel many weeks

in advance so that Miss Montezuma had to be satisfied with something far less elaborate. I went up to New Haven a day ahead of the rest of the company, laid in a generous supply of liquor for anyone who might care to call on me at the hotel, ordered the baskets of flowers to be handed up to me over the foot-lights, had a long talk with the theatre electrician and returned just in time to join the rest of the *Goodie Godiva* company at Grand Central Station for the trip to New Haven.

The story that ensues is not a very pleasant one, but it does go to show how the ego of a star can literally affect her reason. When I arrived at the the-atre on opening night, I noticed that on the electric sign outside the theatre the name of Magdalena Montezuma had not only been misspelled, but that it refused to light—at best flickering on and off intermittently. My own name, however, shone splendidly. Miss Montezuma, with "blood in her eye," was waiting in my dressing room when I arrived. No lady would understand—least of all repeat—the language Miss Montezuma used. Her accusations were too ridiculous to be treated with any seriousness at all. How, pray, could a helpless woman like little me have anything to do with something as tech-nical and complicated as an electric sign? Was it my fault if the electricians preferred someone as democratic and outgoing as Belle Poitrine to a cold, un-pleasant and conceited woman such as Magdalena Montezuma?

But that was only the beginning. Owing to some error—and these mis-takes will occur when a show is trying out—I was lighted in pink while the electrician who followed Magdalena with a spotlight had chosen green. For one whose complexion is as naturally sallow (not to say "muddy") as hers, the effect was most unfortunate. There was also a rather comical moment involving Montezuma's grand entrance by way of a door that refused to open and she "brought down the house" by coming in through a window. I could barely contain my laughter. And in the one scene which Magdalena and I played together, she was mysteriously enveloped in a curtain and narrowly escaped being struck by a falling sandbag. It was then that the lights all over the stage went out, save the flattering rose "follow-spot" that was focused on me. I was in a terrible quandary but, feeling that the play must be saved at all costs, I stepped right down to the darkened footlight trough and finished the scene alone. After all, "the show must go on!"

In the *entr'acte* Miss Montezuma again stormed into my miserable little dressing cubicle (the one *she* had assigned me) bringing with her Murray Minor Casebeer, the director, the stage manager, the master electrician, the master carpenter and several other contentious allies who could not even be fitted into my tiny quarters. The scene that ensued was too painful to record. Naturally, I denied all of her insane accusations (insane and insulting, as she had the gall to accuse me of being on terms of more than friendly intimacy with many of the stagehands and electricians) and I was finally forced to remind the many shouting people in my dressing room that the intermission had already lasted the better part of an hour.

But it was in the second act when Magdalena Montezuma showed her murderous and totally unprofessional qualities. During my big vocal number with "Peeping Tom," I was conscious at first of a certain uneasy inattention on the part of the audience, then of an uncomfortable wave of heat on the stage. I heard Mr. Lamont gasp and, out of the corner of my eye, I noticed that the long, tulle wimple attached to my unbecoming steeple headdress was on fire! Standing in the wings I saw Magdalena Montezuma with a Zippo lighter! At that moment a bucket of water was unceremoniously poured over my head by an assistant stage manager. Mine had been a show-stopping number in the truest sense of the word. The curtain was rung down, the fire department summoned and the theatre emptied. When I returned to my dressing room, my hair singed, soaked to the skin, Murray Casebeer handed me my notice and stated that my part would be written out of the show.

IT WAS WITH HEAVY HEART that I returned to the Taft Hotel and, by some caprice of instinct, drifted into the bar. At the table adjoining mine were three extremely personable young Yale men of the sort I could immediately "peg":

boys of the better class of American family. (I can always "spot" a gentleman.) They were discussing the disastrous opening of *Goodie Godiva* and I was somewhat cheered to hear one of them say: "The only decent thing in it was when that blonde caught fire." Feeling that these fine, clean-cut youngsters would be thrilled to meet a real star, I introduced myself. They seemed embarrassed at first, but I quickly put them at their ease. As I had a stylish suite upstairs, stocked with cases of those clever and economical Connecticut half-gallon bottles, I suggested that we repair to my rooms. The boys seemed more than willing.

So "starved" had I been for the company of "my sort" of men—my "Yalies," Bruce, "Larry" and "Jack"—that the time simply flew. Before anyone even bothered to glance at the clock, it was after ten the following morning and New Haven was in the grip of a furious snow storm! However, with three handsome *chevaliers* to do my bidding, we turned the whole thing into a "romp" and the boys were ever so sweet about "phoning" room service for "snacks" and ice. As I had engaged the suite for a week and because it was snowing, anyhow, I saw no reason to return, defeated, to Gotham where naught awaited me but the heartless "condolences" of theatre "friends" and dunning letters from my creditors. (Rather than being grateful that a star of my stature was adding lustre to a hotel whose days were numbered, the man-

agement of the Ritz-Carlton in New York was becoming increasingly "stuffy" about my mounting bill, which was really too trifling to bother paying, and I had already had a great deal of difficulty in removing certain valuable bits of wearing apparel from the premises.) So, by my innate courage, "guts" and good spirits, I was able to turn a defeat into a triumph. Yale men are noted for their chivalrous hospitality to "damsels in distress," and that certainly described little me during the bitter winter of 1946.

And—I may as well confess it—I had developed rather a *tendresse* for Bruce, one of my "Yalies." I quite "fell" for Bruce and vice versa. He came from a splendid old Boston family (the typical "rebel" who chooses Yale over Harvard), long established in a "gilt-edged" State Street banking firm, where Bruce, himself, was "slated" to step into a vice-presidency once he had graduated. The difference in our ages was too trivial to mention (he was very nearly at the quarter-century mark). After all, I had worked for so many years, did I not deserve a respite as a Beacon Hill bride?

While "Jack" and "Larry" returned to their classes, Bruce lingered on in my suite. I urged him not to "court" pneumonia by braving the elements of the Connecticut winter. After some slight indecision, he agreed. But at the end of the week when my bill was delivered, along with a Jeroboam of champagne, on a silver salver, I was amazed at its size. "Laying my cards on the table" with Bruce, I explained to him my embarrassment and I was distressed to learn that he was kept on a very close allowance.

I made several expensive and fruitless telephone calls to New York and to the "Coast." Helen Highwater was, unfortunately, in a rest home again. I tried several times to reach Dudley du Pont at his *chic* new decorating estab-

218

lishment on Rodéo Drive, but Felice, his assistant, said that Dudley was away on a "job" in Palm Springs and could not be reached by telephone. There was no one to turn to but my own daughter, Baby-dear. I placed a call to North Hall at Vassar College in Poughkeepsie, New York, and—after an interminable period of waiting—Baby-dear was summoned from the chemistry laboratory. I must say that she did not seem especially pleased to hear from a mother whose entire life had been spent in sacrifices for the sake of a beloved daughter, but only children (with the exception of "yours truly") are notoriously spoiled. This is undoubtedly my fault for being too doting a parent, and I accept the blame, my only excuse being that I loved my daughter perhaps "not wisely but too well."

Baby-dear appeared the following morning looking, I felt, quite "seedy" in a Peck & Peck suit, glasses and snow boots. I took her to task—which I felt was a mother's duty—for her somewhat "matronly" appearance, handed her our accrued hotel bill and borrowed just enough money to go out and have my hair and nails properly done. (They had, after all, been neglected for more than a week.) Upon my return I was stunned to find awaiting me in my suite only the receipted hotel bill, a return ticket to New York and a note saying that my own daughter had *eloped* with *Bruce!* In the words of Walter Hampden, "How sharper than a serpent's tooth it is to have a thankless child!" (More of my daughter's ill-starred *mésalliance* later.) The treasure to whom I had given my life, my love, my all had simply run off with a total stranger—attractive, I grant—whom she had known for an hour, without even consulting her own mother!

Heartsick and depressed, I returned to New York, checked my luggage in the station, and bravely faced the sneers of the Communist-dominated staff of the Ritz. Feeling, perhaps, that my future lay in musical comedy, despite the unkind blow dealt to me by Dame Chance in New Haven, I tried to interest a number of promising newcomers, such as Ethel Merman, Mary Martin, Nancy Walker, Carol Channing and Judy Holliday, in "testing their wings" as supporting players in a new operetta in whose starring rôle I would appear. You may not believe this, but none of them was even *vaguely* interested in playing "second fiddle" to an established star, and one of them was even quite *rude* and terminated our telephonic "get-together" with a burst of the most unprintable profanity! I sensed then that the spirit of "trouping," or "all for one and one for all" and of "starting from the bottom," was gone in the theatre. I bade *adieu* to the musical stage.

"Saint Joan"

"Private Lives"

"Romeo and Juliet"

AT A LOW EBB

1947-1950

HAVING SPENT MANY IDLE MONTHS in bustling Manhattan, trying vainly to secure a starring rôle suited to my special talents, I was desperate to do *anything!*

Sensing that the temper of the times was not one to approve of a star lolling in lassitude, bowed to and waited upon by liveried "flunkies," I had long absented my suite in the Ritz-Carlton in favor of a more modest apartment at the Hotel St. Vitus, much more conveniently located in West Forty-sixth Street. How right I was! Soon the dear old Ritz was to be no longer. It, and a more leisurely way of life, were to be "mowed" down by the advancing times. The world was changing and I would have to change with it.

Owing to many moments whiled away in a nearby radio-and-television repair shop, going to and fro interviews with theatrical managers, I became interested in the "magic box" that was television, "telly" or "T.V." Although such gifted comedians as Milton ("Uncle Miltie" or "Mr. T.V.") Berle had pioneered in this compelling new medium, I noticed that very few of the fair sex had been willing to lend their talents to the "picture tube." I have always had a throbbing interest in the new frontier, the exciting, the different. "Why not," I asked myself, "try to improve the level of television by volunteering to appear on a program of my own?" It was a challenge and, as I have said before, with me, the answer to the challenge is always "Yes!" I would call this stimulating hour *Belle Poitrine Thinks* and I would serve as "M.C."

I had envisaged my program as a sixty-minute show during which I would expound my views on fashion, politics, the arts and vital issues of the day. I would interview other celebrities and endeavor, in my own small way, to keep "Mr. and Mrs. John Q. Citizen" *au courant* with the exciting *haut monde* in which I was a focal figure. I thought of it as not only a stimulating and profitable way of life for me—breaking ground in a new art form—but as a public service. Jotting down some notes on the sort of observations I intended to make, I immediately set up appointments with the Columbia Broadcasting System and the National Broadcasting Company. Alas, I was to realize, to my sorrowful surprise, that these two great "Temples of Mammon" were neither willing nor able to cope with any idea as radical as *Belle Poitrine Thinks*. Instead of being welcomed by the important executives of these networks, who should have humbled themselves with gratitude for the gamble a performer of my stature was willing to make in an untried medium, I was relegated to underlings who were little more than "office boys." After countless cancelled appointments, after hundreds of costly telephone calls—each unceremoniously terminated because of faulty switchboard "service"—after having been given the "run-around" from office to office, studio to studio (where it often turned out that the "executive" I was to see was employed in the shipping room), C.B.S. and N.B.C. each said "Nay." It remained for me to discover a vital, young station visionary enough to "take a chance" on such an unusual new program.

Opportunity finally knocked in the form of WOE-TV, a small, experimental station located in Levittown, Long Island. Although no "time slot" was available when I first offered my services, the young man who was "chief cook and bottle-washer" (as he picturesquely described himself) took a definite "fancy" to little me and we spent many mutually advantageous evenings together discussing the future of "T.V." (the "idiot box" as he wittily referred to it). But there was little time left for "small talk." My finances were in shocking order. Everything I had once owned in the way of *bijoux* was pawned. When I tried to reach her for a bit of monetary assistance, Momma seemed to have been removed from the face of the earth and, as I had never learned Bruce's last name, it was impossible for me to locate my precious child, Baby-dear. The years of 1946 and 1947 had all but slipped by, without my having secured gainful employment.

But Opportunity appeared disguised as a disaster. During the great De-

cember blizzard of 1947, I received an unexpected telephone call in my bleak little room at the St. Vitus. It was WOE-TV. Would, they asked, I be able to rush right over to the Chinese Thrush Restaurant and "fill in" for their nightly television program? Their regular program, it developed, was a cage filled with extremely talented canaries that warbled to an electric organ accompaniment. These feathered songsters had been all but "mowed down" by the blizzard and the management of the restaurant had been unable to replace them. *Would* I? In less time than it takes to tell about, I had jumped into ski pants, stadium boots, a *décolleté* sequin blouse and a flattering "picture" hat and was fighting my way through the snowdrifts to the deserted restaurant.

Thus I began 1948 as a television star! The arrangement made between WOE-TV and Mr. Agropolis, *restaurateur* and genial "boniface" of the Chinese Thrush, was that I was to be "on trial" for thirteen weeks, appearing each night from ten until ten-fifteen in exchange for all the vegetarian chow mein I could eat. After this "tryout," my contract would be adjusted. My job was to lure interesting celebrities to this smart little *bistro* and, by holding casual and intimate conversations with them in front of the camera, make New Yorkers conscious of the existence of the Chinese Thrush and its exotic Oriental *cuisine*. Here *was* a challenge!

I began by subscribing to the Celebrity Service and inviting all of the interesting and distinguished guests I could think of. The results were rather disappointing. I had hoped for a "top-flight" gathering, "spangled" with names like Albert Schweitzer, Margaret Mead, Eleanor Roosevelt, Anthony Eden and Hamilton Fish Armstrong as well as the "Sardi's crowd." I am sorry to say that many of my old "pals" let me down badly. Nor were as many vivid theatrical personalities as I had hoped interested in appearing with me. (These, mind you, among actors who had once fought to be in my films when I was the "reigning queen" of mighty Metronome!) Another "wrench" was that the Chinese Thrush was located directly opposite the old Heartburn Theatre (recently renamed the Magdalena Montezuma!) where *Goodie Godiva*, the show in which *I* should have starred, was entering its second sell-out year. Darling old Sir Walter Mohair, who was still "packing them in" as Godiva's husband, assured me that he would have been happy to appear with me at the Chinese Thrush except that my program coincided exactly with his long soliloquy, "When My Lady Once Undresses, Save But for Her Raven Tresses." Of course I understood. As a consolation, "Wally" sent his understudy, who said many interesting things.

My loyal old school "chum," Princess "Winnie" Pizzicato, also volunteered to be interviewed while *en route* (she thought) to her *palazzo* in Sicily. Our little "chat" was going along ever so nicely when it was interrupted by two gentlemen from the F.B.I. who had long wanted to question "Winnie" about some of Prince "Al's" unlisted holdings. My deal old friend never forgave me, but the whole unfortunate incident was powerful proof of the deep penetration of "T.V." as a means of communication.

Dudley du Pont came onto my show one night while in New York and spoke stimulatingly about *décor*. It was a most controversial program and brought in a great deal of "fan" mail from viewers who wrote to say that they thought Bert Savoy was dead. It did, however, "hypo" Mr. Agropolis' business, for the very next evening the bar at the Chinese Thrush was thronged with young men. I was as "proud as Punch" and even spoke tentatively to Mr. Agropolis concerning the amount of my weekly salary after my "trial period" had been completed. I felt that, for all I had done for the restaurant, chow mein was an inadequate reward. Mr. Agropolis had to agree, for at the end of

My old boarding school "roomie," the former D. Winifred ("Winnie") Erskine, now Principessa Pizzicato of Beverly Hills, Acapulco and Palermo, Sicily

the week the Chinese Thrush was raided, many of its bright new *clientele* booked on charges of loitering. Before my contract was half fulfilled both the program and the restaurant were finished. Like Adrienne Ames, Constance Bennett, Wendy Barrie, Arlene Frances and so many other gifted actresses who squandered their talents as commentators before the unappreciative audiences of the "idiot box," I retired from the air waves. Clearly, television was not ready for little me. The Chinese Thrush was replaced by a *pizza* "joint" and *Belle Poitrine Thinks* by wrestling.

So depressed was I by my recent failures, by the absence of my loved ones, by the seeming cruelty and indifference of my fellow men that—yes, I confess it—I began to seek solace in the bottle. At first my drinking was purely "social"—a convivial glass shared with a gay acquaintance from the

Drinking more than is good for me!

past in some fashionable gathering place such as El Morocco, the Stork Club or Twenty-one. But when, owing to pressing commitments in other places, these old "pals" began to absent themselves, I discovered the quiet little bar of my hotel, the St. Vitus. Here a very palatable blended whiskey could be purchased for as little as twenty-five cents a "shot" and the bartender, "Jimmy," and I soon became fast friends.

Before I quite realized it, I was habitually "tipsy" hours before the "sun was over the yardarm" each day. I drank, I suppose, to forget the many hurts and slights I did not wish to remember. There were times when I resolutely vowed not to have a drink before noon, but "Jimmy," a most friendly and generous soul, often stopped in my room before opening the bar and he rarely arrived empty-handed.

"I've got to get hold of myself," I kept telling my reflection in the stained and cracked old mirror above my *chiffonier*. "Drinking this way is doing nothing for my face, my figure, my morale or my career." There had also been more than a few embarrassing "incidents" as a result of imbibing too heavily. On one occasion I sustained a severe fall on the stairs at Sardi's; late one afternoon I found myself without the "wherewithal" to pay for the twelve double martinis I had consumed at Tony's Trouville; and—horror or horrors—I was once asked to leave Schrafft's!

"If only I could find work," I confided to "Jimmy" one morning in my room. "I would be able to 'straighten out and fly right' in no time at all."

"Don't worry about it, baby," he said affectionately, filling my tooth mug to the brim with Imperial. It was easy to forget with an understanding companion like "Jimmy," but I knew that it was wrong and that this excessive drinking would get me nowhere.

Then, one afternoon, the chance to find redemption through good, hard work came my way. Resolutely quitting after my third drink, I had dressed carefully and was waiting for an interview at the newly formed producing "team" of Feuer & Martin. Earlier in the season I had lost the rôle of Blanche in *A Streetcar Named Desire* to Jessica Tandy, *Medea* to Judith Anderson and Catherine in *The Heiress* to Wendy Hiller simply because I had been unable to "pull myself together" and appear at the offices of various producers. Recently I had taken to arriving no later than five o'clock nearly every afternoon, ready to "read" for any part. Seated next to me was an attractive, sensitive-looking young man whom I felt sure I had seen before. We fell into conversation and he recalled to my memory that we had been seated together in the offices of

Rodgers & Hammerstein, John C. Wilson, Jed Harris, Leland Hayward, the Theatre Guild and many other top-ranking *impresarios*. Told that dear "Cy" Feuer could see no more people that day, my young neighbor and I departed and strolled to the nearby Raleigh Room where he offered me a cocktail.

His name, as I understood it, was LeGrande Barnwell, scion of a fine old South Carolina family of enormous wealth. Although LeGrande's blood was as blue as the flag of the Confederacy, he claimed—like little me—that he had "grease paint flowing in his veins," although his almost incomprehensible Southern accent had militated strongly against his being cast in any of the rôles he so longed to play. Discouraged, LeGrande, too, was drinking more than was good for him. Having, however, a burning ambition and unlimited funds, LeGrande was determined to succeed or die trying.

So engrossed did we become in our "theatre talk" that we forgot all about dining and went right on "chinning" until the bar closed and we were assisted out by a bus boy. From that evening onwards our plans materialized rapidly; utilizing LeGrande's considerable tobacco fortune, we would form our own "package" company and "barnstorm" the entire "straw hat" circuit doing the plays we both enjoyed most. I would serve as the star and big "ticket-selling" attraction and LeGrande, in the lesser rôle of my leading man, would gather invaluable experience. With a sizable advance on my salary, I was in a whirl of hairdresser's appointments, facials and fittings, leaving such details as minor actors, scenery and bookings to LeGrande.

When our "caravan" of "strolling players" was ready to "roll" on Decoration Day, we were an impressive convoy indeed! First came a station wagon filled with our six capable supporting players, then a truck containing our costumes, "props" and scenery and last, but not least, LeGrande and I in the *tonneau* of a splendid Chrysler limousine, driven by LeGrande's lovable old servitor, "Uncle" Cato. Our *répertoire* consisted of my friend Noël Coward's *Private Lives* (as a "peppy," sophisticated, up-to-the-minute comedy of manners), George Bernard Shaw's *Saint Joan* (as a modern "classic") and *Romeo and Juliet* (as our personal tribute to the immortal "Bard").

I had rather expected that we would visit the nicer summer theatres such as Westport, Dennis, Bar Harbor, Newport and East Hampton. But, owing to LeGrande's inefficiency and excessive drinking, our tour took us not to the important "show cases" usually visited by famous stars, but to unheard-of villages and hamlets for "split" weeks and "one-night stands" where we played in abandoned opera houses, disused cinemas, school auditoriums and church basements. Our audiences—whenever LeGrande was sufficiently sober to advertise a play far enough in advance for anyone to attend—were hopelessly provincial and ofttimes extremely rude, shouting indecent suggestions, and obscene responses, to some of the most exquisite passages written by Messrs. Shakespeare, Shaw and Coward. A witty, brittle comedy such as *Private Lives*, although I was at my most worldly in the rôle of Amanda, was totally wasted on these "bumpkins." And even so, Tallulah Bankhead and Donald Cook had covered much the same territory a season or so beforehand so that our production was always compared disadvantageously.

In the larger plays—*Saint Joan* and *Romeo and Juliet*—our little company had to be supplemented by strictly "local talent," and such bumbling amateur performances I have never witnessed—save, perhaps, that of my "leading man," LeGrande Barnwell!

While I entertained serious doubts as to LeGrande's histrionic ability during rehearsals in New York, I charitably "chalked it up" to "nerves" and hoped that he would do better when confronted by an audience. (Indeed, LeGrande could hardly do worse!) But after "running through" our repertory with him "on the road," I realized that he was hopeless. Try as I would to pass on to him the invaluable voice training and diction "pointers" I had received from Dame Florence Fleming, his Southern accent became thicker with every performance. One evening in Glockalooka Falls, Vermont, there was a power failure just as LeGrande came on as Elyot Chase, dapper "Man About Mayfair," in *Private Lives*. Speaking his first line in the pitch dark, he was greeted by a voice from the audience crying "What the hell is this, a minstrel show?" I had to laugh!

Nor did he even attempt to minimize his heavy drinking. In fact, as our tour progressed, his drunkenness seemed to become increasingly worse. Refused further service at a low "dive" in Moselle, Massachusetts, LeGrande wrecked the place in a fit of *pique* and was thrown into jail so that our company missed playing nearby Norton entirely. "Fuzzy" as to just which play we were performing one evening in Skowhegan, LeGrande stepped out onto the modern terrace setting of *Private Lives* dressed for *Saint Joan*. And, speaking of costumes—or their lack—I was astounded one night, in Pennsylvania, while waiting to appear on the balcony as Juliet, to hear a low snicker in the audience that increased in volume to hooting, catcalls and stamping. LeGrande, as my Romeo, had dressed ever so carefully, neglecting only to put on his tights! And one night, in Ohio, he was so intoxicated that he pulled the whole balcony loose, the result being that I suffered a painful and disfiguring black eye!

But physical pain was the least of my suffering. Imagine, if you will, my hideous embarrassment to appear as Joan of Arc in a derelict bowling alley in Aspidistra, Indiana, only to learn that Diana Barrymore was also playing Joan at the Elks' hall across the street! The humiliation! Even worse was when Miss Barrymore and I confronted one another in the local saloon, immediately following our joint portrayals of Jeanne d'Arc! And did LeGrande Barnwell (who, in his drunkenness had arranged the conflicting bookings to begin with) even lift a finger to help me? He did not! He had "passed out" into his drink as I was about to fling it at Miss Barrymore in self-defense.

Dear Momma had always said, "If you can't lick 'em, join 'em." After this degrading experience, I threw all pretense to the winds. Driving from one provincial backwash to the next, LeGrande and I always took along a thermos of whiskey sours, which we shared as amicably as possible. From then on I insisted on *two* thermos bottles. I joined him in his dressing room for drinks before, during and after every performance and even insisted on the use of real alcohol on stage. If *he* felt no obligation to his audiences, why should I? Thus the years of 1948 and 1949 passed by in a dense fog. How long our tour would have continued—*could* have continued—I cannot say. Everything ground to a halt when LeGrande was institutionalized in Missouri, leaving his brave little band of players stranded.

Happily, I had been able to save a great deal of my salary while on tour with LeGrande. And, as he had never been in any condition to deal with such details as withholding taxes and so on, it was all free and clear. I also took possession of the cars, the truck, the costumes and scenery, just for safekeeping until their rightful owner would be declared responsible to reclaim them. With all of this equipment, and six professional actors "on my hands," it seemed only right that I should put it to good use.

For some time I had been thinking about an original play somewhat similar to *Shanghai Gesture* in feeling, but entirely different in treatment. It was called *Hong Kong Hideaway* and I felt certain that, with little me in the starring rôle, it would be an enormous "hit" and re-establish me as an actress to be "reckoned with" almost overnight. But the project was beset by troubles. Even though I had written *Hong Kong Hideaway* myself, I had terrible trouble remembering my "lines." I was plagued with alternate chills and fevers and I suffered intense *migraine* headaches every morning. Too nervous to come

into New York with the play immediately, I decided that we would open out of town and work eastward. Always having been a keen student of sociology, I decided that "Middleton, U.S.A." (Muncie, Indiana) would be the ideal place to hold the world *première* of my play and "iron out" any "wrinkles" before moving on. I was in an extreme state of "nerves" on the day of the opening and, in order to calm myself, indulged perhaps more heavily than I should have. (Bear in mind, please, that I was near both physical and emotional collapse.) "Break a leg!" (the traditional theatrical good luck wish) one of my fellow thespians said to me as I made my unsure way to the "wings" on opening night. "Thank you," I mumbled. I have only the dimmest recollection of the curtain going up on that ill-fated evening in Muncie and I do not recall at all its being lowered. All I remember is awakening several days later, strapped to a hospital bed. A doctor standing over me kept shaking his head and muttering "Delirium tremens—one of the worst cases I've ever seen. That *and* a broken leg." A long dramatic criticism-cum-news story in the Muncie *Evening Post*, which I was only able to read several weeks later, described my play, my performance and the tragic fall I took into the orchestra pit.

It was a shattered and defeated woman who returned, ignominiously, to New York at the end of 1950.

ʃING FOR YOUR ʃUPPER!

1952

My long illness, aggravated by drink · From bad to worse · Eugene · A near-fatal
accident · The Women's Detention Home · "Billie" Divine · "Billie" takes me in
A supper club *diseuse* · A fearful shock · All's well that ends well

OF THE NEXT SEGMENT OF MY LIFE, the less written the better. Suffice it
to say that I existed—certainly one could not employ the term "lived"—
through it somehow.

Returning to New York, I thought only of finding a dark, lonely "hole"
and crawling into it. Although I had some money left, I felt no desire for the
niceties of such hostelries as the St. Regis, Hampshire House, the Plaza, the
Ambassador—any of the addresses which were almost as much a part of me
as my name. Instead, I moved from one wretched hovel to another, not caring
about my looks or my surroundings. I rarely dressed, almost never left whatever room I was living in. I was usually able to get on friendly enough terms
with a bell boy—usually one who was very young or very old—so that he
would bring me an occasional sandwich, a bowl of soup and a bottle.

I was sick with an illness no doctor could cure and I wanted only enough
liquor to stifle the pain until the Great Casting Director would call little me to
the Celestial Set.

From time to time I found the energy to move myself and my belongings
to a still cheaper hotel, more sordid than the last had been. In the ultimate of
these—a miserable establishment on West Twenty-ninth Street called, I be-

Down and out

lieve, the Tarantula Arms—I planned to end my days alone and unknown. It was small, dirty and impersonal, which suited me perfectly. It was finally Eugene who was able to rouse a spark of life in the empty shell that had once been Belle Poitrine.

Eugene was the only bell boy employed in the hotel. In addition to carrying what little baggage went in or out of the place, he also ran the elevator and the switchboard. He was a sweet "kid" of about sixteen, forever reading *Photoplay, Variety, Theatre Arts*—any show "biz" magazine he could get his hands on.

Carrying my one bag to the dingy little air shaft "cubby-hole" that had been assigned to me, Eugene scrutinized my face quizzically and said, "Pardon me, lady, but ain't you Belle Poitrine, the old-time movie actorine?"

"I might be," I said listlessly, too ill and *distrait* to care even for flattery.

"Gee, my Mom she thought you were great. No Sarah Bernhardt, maybe, but awful pretty and good for a lot of laughs."

"Did she?" I said, sinking wearily to the bed.

"You bet. I seen you on TV and my Mom used to catch your pictures at the Buchsbaum Babylonia. That's up in the Bronx. It's a supermarket now. She used to get you and free china for a dime. That was, if you got there before six-thirty when the prices changed."

"That's nice," I said.

"One thing my Mom always says about you," Eugene went on, "if it wasn't for you she wunt of got a lot of laughs and dinner service for sixty persons. She's only got a dinette but the plates—they're the Bird of Paradise pattern—are real handy for leftovers in the Kelvinator. That's a gas-type refrigerator, I guess you know."

Handing him a dollar bill I said, "Please run out and get me a pint of muscatel—Four Star brand. Keep the change."

"Aw, I wunt never do that, Miss Poitrine. The change is more'n the booze."

"Take whatever you like, then," I said. I was ill with fatigue.

"I wunt take nothing if you could maybe gimme your autograph. Gee! Would Mom ever die, though. She was always crazy about you blonde comics. Carole Lombard, Thelma Todd, you, Lyda Roberti. You ever know anya them?"

"Intimately," I said. "They're all dead. And so am I."

"An' there was Marion Davies and Mae West and Una Merkel . . ."

"My bottle, please," I whispered.

Eugene, who cared

"Mom an' me, we watch Eve Arden and Lucille Ball and like that on T.V., but we don't get the laughs out of them we got outta you old-timers. Gee, will she ever be excited when I tell her you're stayin' here."

When he came back, bringing exact change, I tried to sign my name on a slip of paper for him, but my hand shook so that I could hardly read my own writing. "I'll try again tomorrow," I told him. After drinking off half the bottle, I went to sleep for a long, long time.

The next afternoon I was feeling like death, the last of my muscatel had spilled onto the grimy coverlet. It was then that I heard a tap at my door. It was the bell boy, Eugene. He had gone out, on his own volition, and purchased a fresh pint of Four Star. In addition, he brought me a pot roast sandwich from his home in the Bronx. He reiterated how amused his "Mom" had been by my *Nights on the Nile*. I thanked him, paid him for the Four Star and requested that he deliver another bottle the following afternoon.

It got so that every day Eugene would stop in for a cozy "chat," sometimes bringing me some delicacy from his "Mom's" fragrant kitchen, perhaps a "movie" magazine or a copy of *Confidential*—we were both avid readers.

He also undertook to run such errands for me as cashing my modest

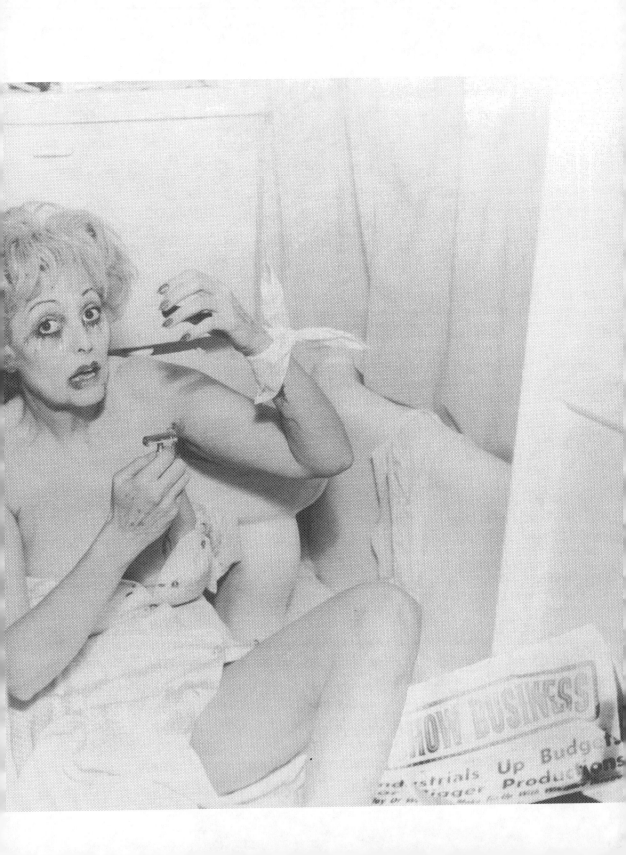

checks at the nearby liquor store, fetching aspirin or cigarettes from the druggist. One day he even brought me a lipstick and a bottle of nail varnish that had been on sale at the pharmacy. (I had quite forsworn artifice, not caring any longer how I looked.) "Try some of this, Miss Poitrine," Eugene said. "I bet it'd look swell on you." And it did!

Bit by bit, Eugene began luring me back to life. Hair sprays, combs and brushes, astringents and nourishing creams would mysteriously appear in my tiny bathroom. Although I cared nothing for a beauty I felt had long since vanished, I did try to "arrange" my face and *coiffure* if only to please the young admirer who had purchased the "beauty aids."

On Christmas Eugene even arrived with a gaily wrapped box. It contained a *négligée* from an inexpensive *lingerie* shop on Broadway! I was moved almost to tears. I felt that I must do something to repay this loyal and selfless lad. "What time do you go off duty, Eugene?" I asked casually.

"Four o'clock, Miss Poitrine. Same as always."

"Is your, uh, 'Mom' expecting you right home?" I inquired.

"Oh, no. Mom an' me we celebrate *our* Christmas the night before on accounta I gotta work days, see? So today she goes out to see my married sister that lives in Massapequa. She owns her own home."

"Then why don't you and I have our own private little celebration, as soon as you get off?" I slipped a five-dollar bill into his hand. "See if you can't pick up a fifth of rye from someplace. I mean, after all, it's Christmas."

Eugene looked almost handsome standing there in his ill-fitting maroon livery. There's just something about a man in uniform!

I "got myself together" as best I could, put on the new *deshabille* my "swain" had purchased, rinsed out two bathroom glasses and draped pink Kleenex over the stained lampshade. It lent a soft, subtle, flattering glow to my quarters and to little me. I then "polished off" the pint of muscatel all at once, knowing that "relief" was on the way.

I had not long to wait. Shortly after four there was a rapping at my door and Eugene entered with a fifth of Imperial and two bottles of ginger ale. He was wearing a sateen jacket with the name of his bowling group—the "Tremont Tigers"—embroidered on the back and a necktie with the likeness of "Lassie" painted on it by hand. The eyes, he confided, "lit up" in the dark. Always the perfect hostess, no matter how bedeviled by Fate, I indicated to him a place on the bed where he might sit and poured out two "highballs."

The warm, strong drink "hit" me much faster and much harder than I had expected. And, as I later learned, Eugene was quite unaccustomed to drink, coming from a family background which, though appreciative of the arts, was in many ways extremely strait-laced.

"Merry Christmas, Eugene," I said and emptied my glass.

One of my last recollections was a sentimental one. I thought of how many, many men in my life Eugene reminded me of. He had—or so it seemed at the time—the shy gentleness of my beloved Fred, the dash of George Jerome Musgrove, the tense, animal vitality of Letch, the suave good manners of Bruce, and the devil-may-care grandeur of LeGrande.

"You know, you could be very attractive," I said. "Let's have another."

"Let's," Eugene said.

The next thing I knew it was twelve hours later. I was lying on the bathroom floor in a pool of blood—*my* blood! Two officers of the law, and an extremely ill-bred policewoman, were shaking me roughly. There was the hotel manager saying something about "running a decent place" and the frustrated old spinster who occupied the room beneath mine repeating, needlessly, that it might have been "a blessing" had a "wanton woman" such as I been "allowed to die." A reporter and a cameraman kept firing questions at me and another woman—a real fury—kept shouting accusations in my ear.

When my wounded wrist was bound up and the flow of blood stemmed, I was yanked rudely to my feet and thrust out into my poor little bedroom. I saw Eugene, his clothing wildly dishevelled, being very ill into a wastebasket. The "fury" kept caressing him and then dashing back to shriek imprecations into my ear.

"Please," I said, mustering what dignity I could, "leave my room, all of you."

"You're comin' with us, Delilah," the policewoman said crudely.

The next thing I knew I was on Tenth Street, in Greenwich Village, being incarcerated at the Women's Detention Home! Eugene, supported by the voluble "fury" who still screamed hysterically, was with me. The woman turned out to be none other than his famous "Mom." The charge on which I was "booked" was one so vile, so vicious, so vituperative that I can barely bring myself to repeat it—"*contributing to the delinquency of a minor!*"

SOME TIME LATER, my wrist grudgingly seen to by an unsympathetic nurse, I was given an ill-fitting uniform and thrown into a cell. In the gray dawn and, weak from shock and loss of blood, I could not focus very well. I knew that

my room

X

The Women's Detention Home

there was another occupant in my cell, but I was in no "mood" for social in-
tercourse. Exhausted and shivering with the cold, I flung myself onto an un-
yielding cot. I was aware only that some other person had placed a blanket
over me and "tucked me in." Then I fell into a deep, agonized slumber from
which I hoped I would never awake.

But awaken I did the following day when the unfeeling wardress came
around to inspect our cells. I was shaken awake and cursed at.

"Why ain't you up? Made yer bed? Doncha know the regulations?"

"No. She don't," a deep voice said. "She just came in last night."

"Well, show her the ropes," the wardress said and marched out.

I glanced at the person who shared my cell with me. She was handsome,
rather than pretty—or she could have been, with a few cosmetics, something
done to her short, coarse hair and, of course, a more becoming frock than the
uniform she was wearing. "Hi, kid," she said bluntly. " 'Billie,' 'Billie' Divine.
Put 'er there."

Wanly, I extended my hand and breathed my name.

"What the hell!" she said. "Whaddaya know. Belle Poitrine. Why, I used to have a real crush on you. Saw all your movies, had three scrapbooks filled with your pictures. And to think..."

And to think, indeed! To think that I, Belle Poitrine, once the idol of America, had come to this. Why couldn't I simply have died?

My roommate, Miss "Billie" Divine, who had visited the Women's Detention Home on two previous occasions, described the routine of the institution, gave me valuable "tips" on some of the personalities on the staff and explained the reason for her present visit. She had, it seems, been having a quiet drink with a woman friend in a Greenwich Village bar popular with working girls when, for no reason at all, the "paddy wagon" had been summoned and the establishment emptied. And we speak of Civil Liberties! "Billie," however, had been blameless and expected to be given her freedom momentarily.

Surreptitiously "Billie" extracted a reeking old cigar "butt" from her bedding, lighted it and puffed clouds of smoke out of the high, barred window. Although I have always loved the smell of a fine cigar, this one made me a little ill. I wanted a drink desperately, but something told me that it would be foolish to order one.

"Billie" spoke quite frankly about her "checkered" career. A woman of nearly forty, she had grown up in the midst of the depression. She had come to New York, moved into a tiny flat in the "Village" and had turned her hand to all sorts of things. She had been a waitress, a clerk in a bookshop, had worked for a female veterinarian and had even driven a truck! She had become an *artistes'* representative, dealing exclusively in the field of entertainers. As her clients, she now "handled" three young actresses, a soprano, a ballerina and a small all-girl band. She said, tentatively, once or twice, that she would be delighted to "handle" little me, as well. But in my bleak desolation, I fully expected to die in that prison cell—rather hoped that I would, in fact!

Late in the afternoon, however, a "reprieve"—of sorts—arrived. It was a letter from Eugene (one I shall always treasure) and I quote it here:

Dear Miss Poitrine,

I sure feel terrible and suppose you are the same.

I brought your suitcase to the jail because the hotel don't want you to come back there when you get out. I have been discharged. That is o.k. as I want to go back to high school.

The inclosed clippings sure prove that your still a "headliner." Page 16 in the Daily News and p. 8 in the Mirror. It isn't true that you was going to cut your wrist. You were shaving under your arms and the razor slipped. Accidents will happen.

Also Mom is not going to bring those charges against you. She was excited is all. I finally was able to explain to her what could there be between you and I. Me just a kid bellhop and you a lovely lady even older than Mom. She understands now but made me promise never to drink another drop.

Your friend,
Eugene.

I was terribly, terribly touched. There *are* some good people in the world, after all!

A few minutes later I was given my bag and released, at the same time "Billie" Divine was set free. I paused for a moment on the wintry street, not knowing exactly which way to turn. The thought of another cold, impersonal, cheap hotel; of being all alone again; of having no one to turn to. I wondered what the temperature of the river was at that time of year.

"Uh, listen, kid," she said hesitantly, "if you've got no place to bunk... well, my apartment's not very far from here. It's got a woodburning fireplace. Maybe we could have a drink together and kind of talk over your maybe thinking of going back into show biz?"

I paused for a moment while "Billie" stood there eagerly gazing at me. In her slacks, *béret* and trench coat she did have a certain style. She was strong and resilient whereas I... "Very well," I said, "but just for a day or two. I wouldn't dream of imposing."

"Good for you, kid," she said. "First let me buy some decent cigars."

At last, after so many years of fear and loneliness, I had someone to lean on.

I was dismayed, at first, to glimpse the exterior of "Billie's" residence. It was a "grim," scaling old loft building that made some of the "dumps" I had recently occupied look like the Beverly Hills Hotel, by comparison! But, once

243

having been helped up the steep, dark stairway, I was most pleasantly surprised by "Billie's" apartment.

It contained a large combination living room-and-office, tastefully furnished in extremely modern furniture, most of which "Billie" had designed and made with her own two hands! There was a large, sunny bedroom in tweed and leather (all hand-tooled by "Billie") and a modern kitchen and bath, which "Billie" had created from the most "primitive" beginnings by being her own electrician, carpenter, mason and plumber! In the middle of the flat was a large room which housed "Billie's" work bench, her lathe, tools and the scrap metal and blowtorch she used in her sculpture as well as a complete little "gym." "Billie"—a great one for physical fitness—exercised strenuously every day with bar bells, punching bag, rowing machine and electric "bike." (Some days later I expressed a half-hearted wish to regain what had truly been an amazing figure. Although I had been only "lukewarm," "Billie" was *adamant*. She made me "work out" for hours in her "gym" and then pummelled me on the massage table until I begged for mercy.) Also in the apartment were two female boxer bulldogs whose facial resemblance to their owner was often laughable.

"Billie" lighted the fire, poured drinks and grilled spareribs on the scarlet coals, but I don't believe that I ever got around to eating. I closed my eyes and when I opened them it was morning. I had been undressed and put to bed, only to be aroused from my slumbers by the vision of "Billie," in a Charvet dressing gown, appearing with a hearty breakfast of steak, potatoes and "flapjacks."

I knew that I could not impose for too long on the generous hospitality of this unusual woman and felt that I should move on to yet another dreary hotel. But, each time I suggested it, "Billie" would "invent" an errand or some light household task as a "delaying action." She had already put me on the "1-2-3 System" of drink reduction. (One drink before luncheon, two before dinner and three during the evening.) Although "Billie" drank considerably more herself, I found that after a few weeks, six drinks a day seemed plenty for someone of my delicate constitution. She kept me so busy exercising in the "gym" or posing for her Statues (the torso, "Earth Mother," won Honorable Mention in the Washington Square Art Exhibit that year) that I had little time to brood or feel sorry for myself.

Although I never met any of her clients, she seemed to be an efficient and forceful artists' representative and I was impressed to observe how a girl like "Billie," with very little formal education, could handle nightclub owners, producers and the like over the telephone. After each conversation, "Billie" would slam down the receiver, puff furiously at her "stogie" and growl, "Men! How I hate 'em!"

She was so very masculine herself that I could never understand this. I have always revelled in the company of males, enjoying to the utmost their sense of "give-and-take." "Billie," I decided, must have been terribly hurt by some boy back in her childhood to feel as she did.

Nor was life with "Billie" always "rosy." She was possessive and jealous by nature and would go into "fits" of blind fury over nothing—such as the time she caught me joking with the old gentleman who ran the delicatessen, inquiring after the dry cleaner's wife (who suffered with dropsy) or simply being civil to the "counter man" at the Jefferson Diner. She indulged in public "scenes" and once she even struck me! When the shoe was on the other foot, however, that was a different matter entirely! Many was the night I stayed at home alone, with the liquor under lock and key, not knowing where "Billie" was or when she would return. Her invariable excuse was always "business" with a "client." But about *my* feelings she seemed to care little.

Yet "Billie" had so many endearing qualities that I could forgive her a few little faults. As I have always said, "Nobody is perfect!" And it was through dear, kind-hearted, generous "Billie"—rather inadvertently—that the whole course of my life changed radically.

"Billie" had installed her own "hi-fi" and she had a great collection of female vocalists—Hildegarde, Marlene Dietrich, Greta Keller, Spivy, Mabel Mercer and dozens of other supper club *chanteuses*. Every night she was at home we would have a little "concert" and then "Billie" would discuss the possibilities of my making a "comeback" as a fashionable night club singer.

I had but little heart for such a notion. My confidence had been too terribly shattered by the many cruel blows I had been dealt since the war. On the other hand, I realized that I could not go on living on "Billie's" bounty indefinitely so there seemed to be no question about doing as my benefactor suggested. It was either "sing for your supper" or starve.

With my health and my looks more or less restored, I began working up a *repertoire* that would be suited to what remained of my voice. (Once the possessor of a sweet, true coloratura, hardship and the passing years had left my voice with a "husky" quality, not unattractive to hear, but difficult to "fit" with melody.) Eventually I settled on "I Love Life," "Stout-Hearted Men," "The

Song of the Open Road" and "Ole Man River." "Billie" was very firm in "veto-ing" these selections. "Men," she said, "are so depraved that when they go to a night club they want a lot of 'sex' for their money. Since you're supposed to be a movie queen, make those cheap bastards think of all that phony Hollywood glamour! Now get busy!"

Cut to the quick, I did a lot of research, bought a great deal of sheet music, changed a few notes to fit my range and, after much "trial and error," created a program entirely built around "Music from the Movies." I began with Janet Gaynor's "If I Had a Talking Picture of You." Then I went into Gloria Swanson's "Love, Your Magic Spell Is Everywhere," Marlene's "Falling in Love Again," Pola's haunting "Paradise" (from *A Woman Commands*) and, finally, my own "Hooray, Hooray for the Scarlet A," which I had first sung in *The Scarlet Letter*. As an encore, if called upon to grant one, I planned to sing Musetta's "Waltz" from Puccini's lovely *La Bohème*. "Billie" said, albeit grudgingly, that she "supposed" my *repertoire* "would do" and ordered me back into the steam cabinet.

I had rather imagined that I would make my supper club *début* at the Plaza, the Pierre, the St. Regis, the Waldorf—in all of which I had been an honored guest—or, if not in one of the great hotels, at a place famed for the *chicté* of its entertainment such as Versailles or the Blue Angel. When I suggested these, "Billie" only scoffed. "You'll be lucky if you can get a booking in the Minetta Tavern," she said.

After tense days of waiting, of listening to "Billie's" telephone conversations, an opportunity presented itself. It was not in New York, but "Billie" assured me that it was a very smart *rendezvous* for the "horsey" set in the country. Located in Hohokus, New Jersey, it was an *intime* establishment, of the French persuasion, called Le Baiser de Mort. "Billie" gave me some money—a "piddling" amount—told me to go out and buy a new brassière, a decent dress, get my hair done and "lay off the liquor until opening night."

Some of her instructions were easier to follow than others. At Klein's, "On the Square," I was able to purchase a sleek one-piece foundation garment which did the utmost for my figure. In a Madison Avenue "re-sale" shop, I secured a handsome brocade ball gown said once to have been in the personal wardrobe of the fabulous Mrs. Byron Foy. It did not fit perfectly, but, as I was gifted with the needle, I knew that I could alter it into a "custom-made" creation in a "jiffy." The Trifles and Treasures Thrift Shop offered up a very passable "bunny" cape (which I made more "authentic" with the addition of some used ermine tails) and a pair of "opera length" kid gloves that were hardly soiled at all.

I rather regretted the ministrations of the "beauty school" student who had attempted a "perm" and a strawberry blond "rinse." If only, I thought, staunch Endive Kissner could be overseeing my *coiffure* and if loved ones, such as Momma and Baby-dear, could be at my side to "root" for little me through this ordeal! But for the brusque "Billie," who tended to "pooh-pooh" my many qualms, I again had to "go it alone."

Of all "Billie's" instructions, the hardest to obey was "lay off the liquor." I had, by now, completely overcome my dependence on the "glass crutch" and was perfectly satisfied with my six drinks a day—on Sundays even less! But to face a challenge such as Le Baiser de Mort and to find the liquor cabinet locked *and* padlocked was, indeed, a blow. "Billie" continued drinking in my presence, but no amount of begging would induce her to share a drop with me and she kept me so short of money—doling out exactly what I would need each day for subway fare, demanding a careful accounting of each penny spent and even taking over my meager bank account!—that I could not even afford a glass of beer. My nerves were terribly frayed.

The night of my opening was raw, damp and penetrating. "Billie" had consumed an entire steak by herself, telling me that it was bad to eat before a performance and that I would be fed something "between shows." Driving through the cold New Jersey night in "Billie's" old "rattletrap" of a Chevrolet, I developed the "shakes" and shivered uncontrollably. "Shut up and sit still, dopey" was all the comfort I received from my manageress, Miss Divine.

In my *naïveté* I had pictured Le Baiser de Mort as a *chic* country supper club, along the lines of "Bill" Miller's old Riviera at the Jersey end of the George Washington Bridge. I was aghast, however, when "Billie" braked the car and turned into a dark, nearly deserted parking lot. Le Baiser de Mort was nothing more or less than a barnlike roadhouse set down in a tawdry neon "oasis" of "discount" houses, garages, garden furniture stores and cheap clothing shops, literally "in the middle of nowhere"! I had been given "star billing," but then I was the only attraction, save for a discordant six-piece dance "band." My heart sank as I was rudely ushered to my dressing room. It was a crude tar paper "lean-to," mercilessly exposed to the elements and containing a rickety bentwood chair and a disgusting dressing table pitted with cigarette burns.

"Nervous?" my friend "Billie" growled.

"Terrified and freezing to death," I said through chattering teeth. "Do you think I could have a drink?"

"I know you couldn't. Now fix your fat face and stop looking so glum. I went to a lot of trouble to get you this booking." That was all the help and comfort I received from *her*!

Somehow or another I got through the nine o'clock show. The place was practically empty and my audience—three or four tables of two, some "teenagers" who couldn't have been old enough to attend my last film, a family wedding anniversary party of some sort and a very drunken, lone gentleman—was polite, if little more.

"How was I?" I asked "Billie," hopefully, on returning to the dressing room.

"Fair," she admitted. "I ordered you a sandwich and some tea. Just stay here and keep cool"—hah!—"I'll be back to catch the midnight show when this joint really starts jumping."

"You're not going to leave me here!" I cried.

"I gotta tool over to a dump in Passaic an' catch the Everleigh Sisters." (A very vulgar "comedy team" which "Billie" also represented.) "I'll be back. Didn't I *say* I'd be back?" With that she was gone.

I was served with a "pasteboard" sandwich, garnished with limp lettuce, a radish rose and a sweet pickle (the only edible thing on the plate) and a pot of tepid tea. My nerves were so "shot" that I felt I'd give my soul for a drink. Having to relieve myself, I made my way to the ladies' room. Le Baiser de Mort was beginning to fill up and, as I passed a table, I heard someone say, "Belle Poitrine? I thought she was dead." I wished that it were true.

But in the toilet I spied a crumpled five-dollar bill on the floor! At first I couldn't believe my eyes. It represented the largest amount of money I had had for my "very own" since the day I first moved in with "Billie." I tucked it furtively into the bodice of my gown and headed straight for the bar. I had to have a drink—just one—to soothe my nerves. I ordered vodka and hot water, feeling that it would warm me and leave no "telltale" odor. The only other occupant of the bar was the drunken man who had been seated alone during the nine o'clock show.

"Service is so bad here I have to sit at the bar to keep the supplies coming through on time," he said thickly. He was quite elderly and seemed far too well dressed for a place such as Le Baiser de Mort.

"Really?" I said pleasantly, sipping my drink. I felt its blessed warmth coursing through my system.

"Care to join me in another?" he asked.

"Oh, no, thank you . . ." I began, but it was too late. He had already signalled the bartender for a "round."

"You were great tonight," he said. "It took me a long way back."

"Thank you," I murmured.

"Why, I remember you, with Charles King and Anita Page, in *The Broadway Melody*."

"I beg your pardon?" I asked, mystified.

"And before that. You and William S. Hart in *The Aryan* and even in *Intolerance*. I was a young man then—in the prime of life—and so were you, Bessie."

Good heavens! This man was confusing me with Bessie Love—an actress who had been well known in pictures before I even attained stardom!

With that, I ordered another drink. Anything to give me courage to face this cold, unfeeling, short-memoried audience in the midnight show.

But I never kept my "midnight *rendezvous*." I awoke from a long, troubled, terrifying nightmare in which I was running, running, running with "Billie" chasing after me cracking a long whip. The sun was blazing into my eyes. Squinting against the glare, I made out the form of a large, elderly man standing over me. He was wearing underwear and I was clad in nothing.

"Who are you?" I asked. He looked vaguely familiar.

"A. K. Frobisher of 270 Park Avenue and Southampton," he replied. "Who are *you*?"

"I *think* I am Belle Poitrine. But *where* are we?"

"I'll try to find out," Mr. Frobisher said. With both hands—which were shaking worse than my own—he picked up the telephone and made a few direct inquiries. When he rang off, he was so shaken that he had to sit down on the edge of the bed. He was ashen and seemed unable to speak.

"What did they say?" I demanded. "I've got a midnight show and..."

"We are in the Lovers' Lane Motel in Elkton, Maryland. Today is Thursday, November twentieth, and we have been here ever since four o'clock last Saturday morning when we were married by the justice of the peace across the road." Saying that, Mr. Frobisher fainted dead away. So did I.

CHAPTER TWENTY

I FIND GOD IN
SOUTHAMPTON

1953 - 1954

Getting acquainted · Separate honeymoons · Marriage in the "Autumn of Life"
Our cottage on the dunes · A Southampton socialite · Momma moves in · "Billie's" visit
Hurricane warnings · Mr. Frobisher's strange disappearance · I find God in Southampton

LIKE INTELLIGENT, MATURE, CIVILIZED PEOPLE, Mr. Frobisher and I decided to sit down calmly and "face the facts." Over a revivifying bottle of domestic champagne, served by the management of the Lovers' Lane Motel, we decided that neither of us had made *too* bad a bargain. We had got ourselves into this situation and now we would face it bravely for as long as seemed possible.

Mr. Frobisher told me that he was "pushing" seventy and retired from his own prosperous brokerage firm. He was a childless widower who enjoyed travel, warm climates and—perhaps too much so—the pleasures of the bottle. Seeing his bulging alligator wallet, his Patek Philippe watch, his Jaguar sedan and the fine Upmann cigars he favored, I was relieved to know that my husband was, at least, a man of means. While admitting that he had known younger ladies, Mr. Frobisher said chivalrously that he, too, might have done worse.

I was pleased to see the snug apartment he kept in The Marguery. From there I telephoned "Billie" to inform her of my happiness. After a torrent of abuse—employing language that would not be used by a "dock walloper"—she hung up on me! As there was no answer when I called back repeatedly, I

Mrs. A. K. Frobisher—the new me! 1953

could only assume that she had pulled the telephone out of the wall—a favorite method of "Billie's" for showing displeasure.

Ordering a shaker of martinis to be sent up to our apartment, I explained to Mr. Frobisher that my luggage had been irretrievably lost and that I would be needing some new clothes. Say what one will about Mr. Frobisher's unfortunate drinking, he was generous to a fault. The very next day—my ball gown hastily tucked up to "street length"—I made an eight-hour "assault" on Bergdorf Goodman and returned feeling half-way decently clad. While modeling my *trousseau* for my "bridegroom," the fifty-nine-cent strand of plastic "pearls" I had been wearing broke, scattering beads all over our drawing room. Mr. Frobisher gallantly bent down to gather them up for me, but I was sud-

denly struck with a better idea. Removing the thick stack of pawn tickets from my purse, I suggested that, in *lieu* of buying me a wedding ring, Mr. Frobisher might better get the Baughdie Diamonds out of "hock." He seemed a little stunned at the total cost but, after a "pony" or two of *cognac*, he was willing. My husband, after all, was not "getting any younger" nor could he "take it with him." Better, then, to "make hay while the sun shines."

Save for his dependence on the bottle, Mr. Frobisher was quite a sweet old gentleman and I know that he counted himself lucky in picking little me from the "garden of love." There was a bit of unpleasantness about my being listed in the New York Social Register but, as I said comfortingly to my husband, what can inclusion in such a volume mean to one whose name has graced the pages of *Burke's Peerage*?

As our "honeymoon" had consisted of only a few days, which neither of us could remember, in a common Maryland motel, and as Mr. Frobisher was so fond of travel, I suggested that we go off to Europe on *separate* honeymoons, have a few minor—but necessary—treatments, and then surprise one another in Paris in the spring. Mr. Frobisher was dubious at first, but later that night he had to admit the wisdom of my idea. Having been bedded down in the guest room of his flat (his snoring disturbed my rest to such an extent that I felt it better for us not to share the master bedroom), he had dozed off, dropping his lighted cigar onto the carpet. I was very nearly a widow again and, had Mr. Frobisher's butler not discovered the conflagration in the very "nick of time," The Marguery might have saved much time and litigation in trying to empty its premises of residential tenants. Thoroughly "scared," Mr. Frobisher agreed to try a sanitorium for "problem" drinkers in Switzerland.

Early in 1953 we set off—he to a clinic at Bern and I to a gifted and resourceful physician near Lucern. Once my bandages were removed, I was speechless with surprise and gratification at what a few weeks' complete rest and relaxation—plus the teensiest bit of assistance from Dr. Umlaut—could do for a girl's face, figure and morale. Tiny little lines (undiscernable to anyone except me, but, nevertheless, there) had vanished. My chin, throat, upper arms and bust had taken on a firmness they had not had since my coming-out year. My teeth were pearl-like in their whiteness and even my hair seemed more golden than ever before.

I telephoned "Daddy" (my "pet" name for Mr. Frobisher) every night, but his progress seemed far less spectacular. After a time the director of his clinic asked me to come in for an interview. Mr. Frobisher, he said, was proving a "hopeless" case, somehow managing to secure beer, "schnapps," wine or even rubbing alcohol, despite the constant surveillance of the clinic's staff. From Mr. Frobisher's "case history," the psychiatrist said, it appeared that he had only gone on periodic "binges" until his marriage to me. Since then his drinking had become habitual. The best "cure" for "Daddy," he stated, would be an immediate annulment! I was outraged!

"How dare you," I shouted, "try to put asunder a deeply spiritual sacrament like our marriage? No wonder the Swiss are always right in the middle of a war!" Without further ado, I removed "Daddy" from that melancholy prison and took him directly to the Crillon in Paris. The love and devotion of an adoring wife, I felt, could work greater miracles than the cold, clinical approach of a lot of money-mad foreigners.

Borrowing a "leaf" from "Billie's" book, I decided to adapt the "1-2-3" system to one more generously tailored to Mr. Frobisher's needs. Carefully figuring his age, income, constitution and life-expectancy, I placed "Daddy" on my own "1-to-7" formula. I gave him one drink upon awakening, two with breakfast, three before luncheon, four with the midday repast, five at cocktails, six with dinner and seven during the evening. He responded splendidly, making almost no trouble at all, and his gratitude was indeed touching.

True, my life with "Daddy" wasn't all "jam." While he remained happily in his bedroom most of the time, there were isolated instances of his "cutting loose" and creating disturbances. During my shopping tour of Paris he did the most embarrassing things, and right in the middle of such world-famous shrines as Shéhérazade, the Pré Catalan and Christian Dior's! But most of the time he was docile and, with my "new look," my jewels and ravishing new wardrobe, I was never at a loss for an attentive "cavalier" to "squire" me about the "City of Light." But, after "Daddy's" unusually trying conduct with a blouse buyer from Cleveland in the Crillon bar, I decided that "East, West, home's best." Mr. Frobisher would undoubtedly spend a pleasanter summer in Southampton where he was known, loved and understood. However, I took advantage of one of his mellower moments to remind him of my unflagging devotion, pointing out that no matter how young he felt, "we all have to go sometime" and that he had better get his will in order.

Our little cottage on the dunes was *sweet*! No other word for it. "Daddy's" former wife, a spotless martyr named Eleanor, had showed both taste and restraint in arranging its appointments. Wanting to leave the house more or less as a monument to that unhappy woman's memory, I had Dudley du Pont flown to the east coast to "do over" only an even dozen of the rooms and to install a convenient bar next to "Daddy's" bed.

It was a happy summer for both of us and I was the absolute social "wow" among the younger men of that gay resort, leaving many a "deb" angrily tapping her foot while I was "danced off my feet" at the galas and coming-out parties of the "little season." Only a few isolated "instances" marred our joy that summer: "Daddy" was asked to resign from the National Golf Links after an unfortunate accident in the bar; he very nearly drowned at the Southampton Bathing Corporation over Fourth of July weekend; and we were barred forever from Henderson House. Otherwise we were just like Darby and Joan.

As our little Park Avenue *pied-à-terre* had never quite "risen from the ashes," I took advantage of "Daddy's" inordinate love of travel, and left Dudley behind to "give it the works," while we spent the fall and winter visiting Sea Island, Aiken, Palm Beach, Cuba, Nassau, Jamaica, Vera Cruz, Acapulco, Palm Springs, Tucson and Aspen—staying in some of these famed "watering places" for as long as a fortnight before "Daddy" would "break loose" and we would be asked to leave. By this time the results of the Belle Poitrine Frobisher 1-to-7 System had received such "word-of-mouth" publicity that an article on our marriage appeared in *Confidential.* Twenty-four hours after the magazine "hit the stands," the receptionist at The Marguery "rang" our apartment and, with disbelief in his voice, announced that "A woman who claims to be your mother is here." It was Momma! After so many years of hardship and deprivation—not knowing whether my beloved mother was dead or alive—I cannot accurately describe the emotions I felt at having her appear at our little place on Park Avenue, bag and baggage!

"Families," Momma said, "should stick together," and her visit was to be an indefinite one. However, Momma was not without her uses. She was one of the few people in the world who could literally "drink" Mr. Frobisher "under the table." Another was "Billie." At long last she was gracious enough to show some gratitude for all that I had done for her and came crawling back begging my forgiveness. The coarse young women whose dubious talents she had tried to sell to stage, screen, television and night clubs had all deserted her. She was "broke" and most definitely "at liberty." Thus, our little *ménage* had doubled in size when we set off for our second Southampton summer.

But somehow the 1954 season was not as serene as our nuptial summer had been. While Southampton society had welcomed little me to its bosom, recognizing me as "one of its own kind," it was not so simple to win acceptance for Momma and "Billie." Full of picturesque, "salty" characters as it may have been, Momma's personality was just a wee bit too picturesque and "salty" for many of the Southampton *grandes dames.* As for "Billie," it was openly bruited about the Southampton Club that she was better suited to Fire Island than to the "Hamptons." Try as I would to outfit her in simple, becoming frocks from the Southampton branches of Saks, Bendel's or Peck & Peck, "Billie" stuck doggedly to what she called her "own style" of dress. I nearly perished of mortification during the tennis matches when the late Mrs. Livingston Livingston stared long and hard at "Billie" and then said, "A *woman*? I thought it was Big Bill Tilden!"

Nor had adversity, nor the fact that she was living on my charity, served to soften "Billie's" bluster, her bravado, her fits of jealousy or her terrible temper. She referred to my dear husband quite openly as the "old lush," the "rum pot," the "old soak" and other epithets far from flattering. She no longer seemed to resent the fact that I belonged to "Daddy," but her antipathy to my many gentlemen admirers was marked and voluble. In a fit of jealousy she twisted Dudley du Pont's arm quite painfully. She created a "scene" over me and a young lifeguard, in whose career I was casually interested, that caused us all to be evicted from "Herb" McCarthy's Bowden Square Restaurant. And one evening, when I had driven quietly to the Hedges in Easthampton for a *tête-à-tête* dinner with a "juvenile" from the John Drew Playhouse, "Billie" marched in—a perfect "sight" in Bermuda shorts, lumberjack's shirt and dirty "sneakers"—and all but wrecked that lovely eating place. There can be no doubt about it, "Billie" was rapidly becoming *persona non grata* throughout Suffolk County.

So "high-strung" and nervous had the presence of Momma and "Billie" made me that I looked forward, eagerly, to Labor Day when "Daddy" and I could return to town and disperse our "house guests" to the "four winds."

Odd that I mention "winds," for during the last week of August the fine weather that had prevailed during that hectic summer began to change. There were gray, cloudy days, rain, waves and breezes of a velocity that made it impossible to refer to them as "gentle zephyrs."

"Looks like a 'twister' might be comin'," Momma said, glancing out to the sea one morning. "Why don't we blow this dump?"

I should have heeded my mother's wise advice, but, instead, I said, "Oh,

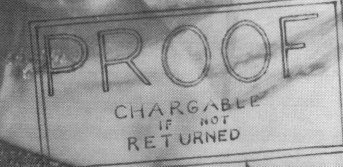

"Billie"—just a beachcomber

Momma, don't be silly! Besides, I'm giving a lawn party on Labor Day to 'wind
up' the season."

"No skin off my ass," Momma said philosophically.

But, as the day progressed, the weather grew worse and worse. Storm
warnings were posted, every few minutes the radio issued dire bulletins of the
impending hurricane—until a power failure caused all of the lights to go off
and the wireless to be silenced. By nightfall the gale was at the height of its
fury. The four of us had congregated in the "rumpus" room where, by candlelight, we were "roughing it" on a cold repast of pâté, Fritos, left-over ham,

fruit, cheese and burgundy. Pushing back from the poker table, "Billie" declared that our humble meal hadn't been "half bad." Then she added, "Now for a good cigar. How about it, Rummy?" (By which she referred to my dear, gentle husband.) The search was on—the ghostly figures of "Billie" and Mr. Frobisher, outlined in flickering candlelight, "combing" the house for cigars. Every humidor was empty.

"Well," my friend "Billie" said, getting into her old trench coat. "I guess there's nothing for it but to drive to the village for a box of stogies."

"Don't be ridiculous," I said. "You can't take a car out in weather like this. The roads are awash. You couldn't make it to the gate."

"Well, then let's 'hoof it.' Are you game, Lushmore?" (Again she addressed poor Mr. Frobisher.)

"I forbid it!" I said firmly. "Are you insane? Here, help yourself to my Virginia Rounds," proffering my gold cigarette case. "I have a whole carton upstairs."

"Those sissy 'butts'? I'd rather smoke cornsilk," Miss Divine scoffed. "Come on, Boozeboy, we could be there and back while we're 'yakking.'"

My protests did no good. Before I could stop them, the terrace doors banged open, furious winds bellying the curtains. "Come back!" I screamed, but my voice was lost in the gale. The last I saw of him, poor "Daddy" was lurching down to the beach with "Billie."

"Billie's" story, as she told it to the Coast Guard, the police, the coroner and the *Park Avenue Social Review* the following day, was that she had let go of Mr. Frobisher's arm for just a moment and the next thing she knew he had been swept out to sea. Three days later my poor husband was washed up on Jones Beach—the only fatality in all of Southampton.

The lovely Labor Day lawn party I had planned was automatically transformed into a funeral for "Daddy," attended by Southampton society and both Easthampton branches of A.A. It was a calm, placid, sunny day—our gardens looking as though naught but balmy breezes and gentle rains had ever ruffled their serene beauty. "Lead Us Not into Temptation" was the theme of the clergyman's eloquent eulogy to Mr. Frobisher and, as I stood there, soothed by his resonant articulation and reassuring words, a far Greater Voice came to me from the general direction of Montauk Point. "Belle," I heard It say, "what is done is done and what must be must be. Accept your fate and know that everything will be all right." At that moment, a shaft of sunlight penetrated a

Sur la plage—Southampton

fleecy cloud, sending its radiance down upon little me—and *only* upon me—among the hundreds standing with bowed heads on my lawn. From the "rumpus" room the "hi-fi" struck up the exquisite chords of "Nearer My God to Thee."

"Yes," I breathed. "*Yes!* At last I have found *Him!* I have found God in Southampton!" He had singled me out as one of His favored children and, in this hour of despair, He had come to me in the garden and spoken to me. Despite the years of turmoil and hardship, in spite of my terrible sorrow, I knew now that God had found little me—and vice versa, of course—that from now on everything would be all right!

The rest of the details of that day are hazy but I am told that I wore a beatific smile of radiance all the way to the cemetery and at the cocktail party that followed. So ecstatic was I, with my newfound peace and tranquillity, that I positively beamed through the reading of the will which I had helped "Daddy" write. And when a delegation of Southampton's oldest and most influential citizens came to me and offered to buy up Mr. Frobisher's estate for double its value if Momma and "Billie" and I would prefer to move away from this house and this community of so many memories, I accepted their proposition without reservation. "This," I said, "must be His will and I bow to it. When may I expect your certified check?"

Southampton, fabulous playground of the gilded rich, you may have robbed me of my beloved husband, but you gave me something even better in his place—you gave me faith!

CHAPTER TWENTY-ONE

FRANKLY FORTY

1960

Pastorale · The "golden years" on my Connecticut farm · Surrounded by my
loved ones · "Lance" Leopard, my protégé · "Billie" · My affairs in order
once and for all · My philosophy of Life · Down the sunset trail

MY COURSE IS RUN, MY RACE IS WON! At forty—and why try to "kid" anyone about anything as silly as age?—I have found peace and contentment
here at Belledame Farm in dear, sleepy little Cyclops, Connecticut, the highest
point in the state, where New York and Massachusetts meet the "Nutmeg
State" in the rolling foothills of Bear Mountain. My house, once a sweet stone
tithe barn, built in the seventeenth century, is commonly referred to as "one of
the seven wonders of the state." It was added to by the late Frank Lloyd
Wright (under my supervision) and—after the untimely passing of that master builder and great visionary—finally finished by local artisans according to
my own plans. It is a bit of tradition, a bit of modern and a bit of pure "fantasy." On Sundays and on summer weekends the road between Cyclops and
Salisbury is clogged with cars and "rubberneck" buses filled with sightseers
who just can't "believe" Belledame Farm. (See plan.)

 I have everything a woman wants—security, quietude and the warm
comforting companionship of my loved ones. My darling Momma is with me

*Four generations of "Belles"—Momma (Lulubelle);
Little Me (Maybelle); Baby-dear (Isabelle); and tiny
"Presh" (Christabelle), 1960*

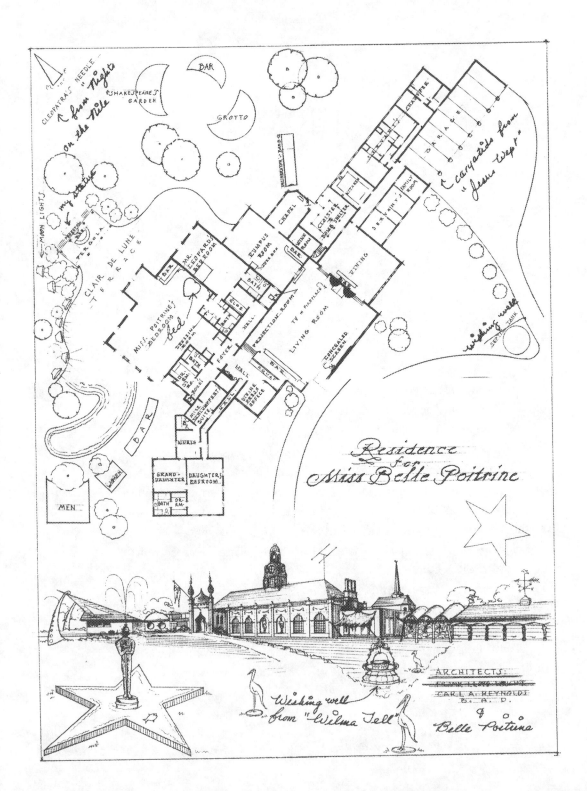

CLEOPATRA'S NEEDLE
"from *Tights*"
On the Nile
SHAKESPEARE'S GARDEN

BAR

GROTTO

MOON LIGHTS
"my *Ditty*"

CLAIR DE LUNE TERRACE

PERGOLA

Caryatids from
"*Jesus Wept*"

MISS POITRINE'S BEDROOM
bed

DRESSING ROOM
BATH
CLOS.

MR. LEOPARD'S BEDROOM

RUMPUS ROOM

CHAPEL

CLOISTER
SOME SUITE

SERVANTS

GARAGE

GARAGE

KITCHEN

FAMILY ROOM

DINING

PROJECTION ROOM

TV "FIREPLACE"

LIVING ROOM

CONCEALED SCREEN

BAR

FOYER

HALL

GUEST

MISS SCHLUMPFERT SUITE

NURSE

SEPT. TANK

wishing well

MEN

WOMEN

GRAND-DAUGHTER

DAUGHTER'S BEDROOM

BATH

DR. RM. 2

Residence
for
Miss Belle Poitrine

Wishing well
from "Wilma Tell"

ARCHITECTS:
CARL A. REYNOLDS
B.A.D.
&
Belle Poitrine

still, a wonderful little old lady bustling about her own, spacious self-contained apartment here at Belledame Farm. Momma comes and goes as she pleases—little "jaunts" to Miami, Atlantic City, Las Vegas, wherever whim and Momma's delightful sense of mischief dictate—but I always know that, sooner or later, she'll be right back here with *me*! Momma turned *eighty-five* just last month. What a celebration we all had! Of course no one will believe her true age. She's so pretty and gay and youthful that she's more like a girl of sixteen than a great-grandmother in the eighth decade of her rich, full life.

And did I "let the cat out of the bag" by mentioning that Momma was a great-granny? Perhaps I did, but this is the best of all—*I am now a grandmother!* And at my age!

Yes, finally, Baby-dear came home to her Mommy with her sweet little daughter, Christabelle, although we all call her "Presh" (short for "Precious"). And so, after the many, many, many years that circumstances separated me from my own darling daughter, I now have my own little girl and *her* little girl right here with me at Belledame Farm. Baby-dear's marriage to Bruce did not, I am sorry to say, work out well. Baby-dear was perhaps too intellectual, Bruce too fun-loving. Who is to say? My own feeling is that Bruce needed a more mature woman to channel his high spirits and animal energies. As is only right and proper, Baby-dear has custody of little "Presh." For who can guide an innocent little girl past the reefs and shoals in the "Sea of Life" better than a devoted and understanding mother? However, "Presh" spends every August with her "Papa" at Watch Hill, and Belledame Farm is a silent and strange place during that long, long month without the clatter of her little feet, the laughter of her shrill, piping little voice.

And we still have our "head of the house" in blunt, good-natured "Billie" Divine. Dear old "Billie," my faithful friend and constant companion. She has "stuck" to me like "glue" ever since Mr. Frobisher's untimely passing. And how I have come to depend upon her! Having no head for financial matters, little by little I have placed the entire burden of handling Mr. Frobisher's considerable estate on "Billie's" broad shoulders. She has done her work well and, through clever "manipulations" and transactions on the "market"—deals so complicated that even hearing about them makes my poor head spin!—dear old "Billie" has increased the value of my "portfolio" by more than double since Mr. Frobisher's will was probated. What would I do without her? Gradually she has simply taken over all of the onerous responsibilities connected with administering the estate. I simply gave her "power of attorney" and told her to "do her damnedest"!

And recently we have even acquired a very young, very personable and—*I* think—very talented "man around the house." For what five females would want to live in a "harem" devoid of male companionship? This gifted youngster is named "Lance" Leopard. He describes himself as "sixteen going on seventeen" and as liking to "fool around with singin'." I can, perhaps, go a bit further to "fill you in" on the facts. "Lance" is tall, personable, extremely well built, a bit shy and the unconscious possessor of a truly golden singing voice. I first "bumped into" him at a record store in Salisbury, "mooning" over the "discs" of Elvis Presley, Fabian, "Bobby" Darin, Paul Anka and other very youthful "pop" singers. In *my* estimation, "Lance" Leopard has them all "beat a mile" and has a voice we will all be hearing some day soon.

But what hope has a sixteen-year-old orphan boy of being discovered in these tranquil northern hills? I sensed, immediately, that what "Lance" needed was the experienced guidance and advice of an older professional—one who had "been through the mill" of the entertainment business herself. And so, without quite knowing it at the time, I acquired a *protégé* whose career I can mould and develop. For the past six months "Lance" has lived here at Belledame Farm where I can look after him properly. His room adjoins mine so that any hour of the day or night he can come to me with his problems, his ideas, his desires or just drop in to "chin" with an understanding "pal." I try to give him all the benefit of my long and varied career. We have elocution lessons (his accent and diction, once appalling, have come along beautifully—almost to emulate mine), exercises in grace and poise, and plenty of practice in "putting over" a popular tune. Every day I am reminded more and more of that long-ago and far-away time when I found a young "nobody" named Letch Feeley and turned him into a star overnight.

"Billie" is, of course, very scornful of "Lance" and his "rusty pipes," as she calls them. She refers to eager, earnest, young "Lance" as that "hillbilly jail bait" and is barely civil to the poor, motherless boy. Her overpowering jealousy is something I'm afraid she simply never will outgrow.

I am still besieged with offers to return to the stage, make another film, record some of the songs I made famous and even to have a weekly television hour of my own. I am often tempted, but I steadfastly refuse. I have retired

With "Lance" Leopard, my protégé—youth will be served!

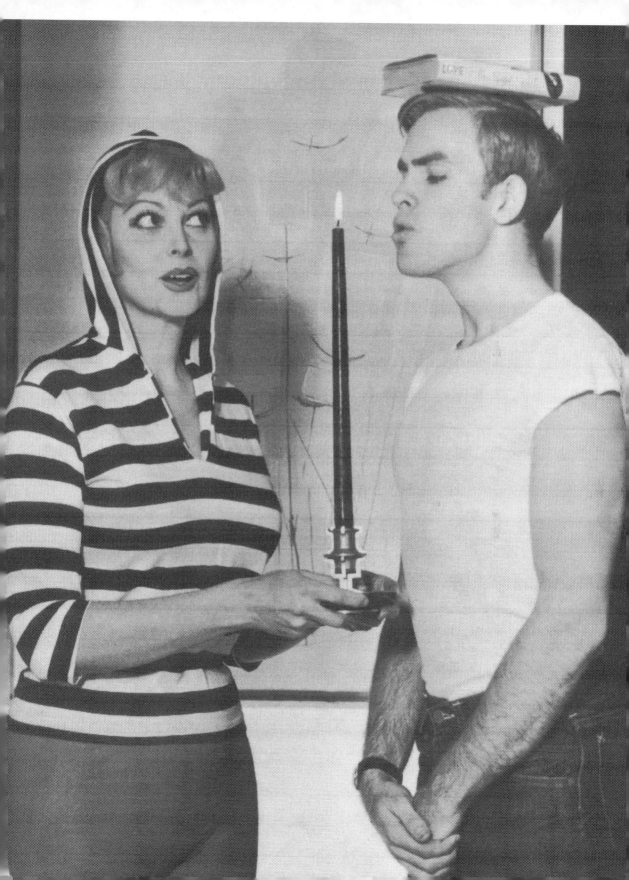

from the "hurly-burly" and have found contentment here in high hills with my little family, my work and my God. As mischievous "Connie" Talmadge once said, "Leave them while you're looking good."

The deep and unswerving faith that found me in a moment of bereavement and desolation has never once left me. It has become my comfort, my friend, my guiding light through life's darkest moments. From it I have developed a true philosophy of life.

If anyone were to ask me my rules for a happy, rich and successful *modus vivendi*—and people often do—I think I would offer these few "pointers" for leading a truly beautiful life:

1. Do unto others as you would have them do unto you. Nothing is accomplished by being spiteful and vengeful. If you set others the example of your truly Christian conduct, they will quickly follow suit.

2. No matter what others say about you, always think and speak kindly about them. For example, I have it on good authority that Magdalena Montezuma is spreading it around town that I still drink to excess. This is patently *un*true! But far be it from me to tell you how much that Spic lush can "guzzle" at a single sitting! By holding good thoughts about her, she cannot wound me with her vicious lies.

3. Never be greedy or "grabby." If you give in gracefully on the little things, the big things of life will naturally come your way.

4. Be scrupulously truthful with others and with yourself. No lie—even a little "white" one—can go long undetected. The truth will inevitably come to the surface so, as I have always done, respect it from the very beginning. It is bad enough to try to "kid" others, but to deceive one's self is the equivalent of suicide or self-mutilation. "T. T. T." ("Tell The Truth") should be everyone's motto.

5. Be a ruthless critic. Not of others (charity, love and understanding should be the "keynote" there), but with yourself. Always ask "Where have I failed?" and answer with brutal honesty. I realize now that, when certain of my films were not "boffo," the fault lay not with others, but with little me. They were ofttimes ten or fifteen years "ahead of themselves," too intellectual for both public and critics. In refusing to lower my standards, the blame was exclusively mine.

6. Think not of material rewards but of *spiritual* gains. Costly possessions such as furs, jewels, fine raiment and lavish surroundings are nice to have, but they are nothing compared with "peace of soul." Through living my

entire life on a higher spiritual plane than most, I have achieved both. A rare and rewarding accomplishment.

7. Always keep faith—faith in others (and they will not let you down—as a rule), faith in yourself and faith in Him. When all has looked darkest in my life, I simply turned to Him and He saw little me through to ultimate victory.

With these simple rules, religiously adhered to, no one can fail. This is the advice which I give freely and gladly to all who seek it. Take it with my blessings!*

Mine has been a good life. I revel now in its rewards. Last week dear "Billie" made a complete inventory of all my "holdings." I was most pleasantly surprised at her final tabulation. At her insistence I have drawn and signed my last will and testament. I am at peace with the world, at peace with myself and at peace with my Lord. My house is in order.

What a funny expression that one is! If you could see my house at almost any time, "disorderly" would be the only adjective. At the moment "Lance" Leopard is in the shower singing "Polecat Kitty Dontcha Make a Monkey Outa Me" (one of his quaint "country" ballads). Baby-dear is in the library rereading *The Anatomy of Melancholy*. I tell her that she doesn't get out enough, that life will pass her by while she sits with her "nose in a book" ruining her lovely eyes. Precious "Presh" is in the big bar practicing on her clarinet, the high, pure strains of "Flow Gently Sweet Afton" penetrating every nook and cranny of the house. Momma, I suppose, is seated at her fire, a hot toddy warming her brittle old bones and going over her "papers," albums and scrapbooks.

It snowed very heavily last night and the high hills and mountains surrounding this peaceful valley look like a lovely Christmas card by "Grandma" Moses. My senses tingle just to see it! Sheer Drop Cliff—one of our favorite walks—is a veritable "mountain of glass" today.

"Billie" has just come in and suggested a bracing hike into the hills. I am of two minds about going. It is bitterly cold and ever so slippery underfoot. The shadows are lengthening, for the days are growing shorter. It would be very nearly dusk by the time I got into what "Presh" calls "Granny's snow-suit" and hiking booties. But "Billie" has been acting so odd and "moody" for the

---

*A more detailed analysis of my philosophy of life, entitled *He and Me* (98 pages) by Belle Poitrine with an introduction by "Billie" Divine, bound in genuine simulated leatherette, is available from the Divine Press, Belledame Farm, Cyclops, Connecticut, at $5.00, postpaid. Please specify color (eggshell, turquoise, lime, scarlet or shocking pink).

past week or so that I suppose I'd better go along with her, if only to "keep peace" in the family. Besides, the air will do me good.

Yes, my course is run, my race is won. My little book is finished. Now to drink the hot buttered rum "Billie" has just prepared and then off to the hills! The answer to the challenge is always Yes! My life has been one long beautiful adventure. Who knows what the future holds in store?

THE END

Belledame Farm
Cyclops, Connecticut
December 13, 1960

Miss Jeri Archer, who appears throughout this book not only as Belle Poitrine, but also as four generations of herself—Momma, Baby-dear and little "Presh"—is a lady of many talents as well as many faces.

As a dramatic and musical comedy actress she made her debut on Broadway in a role created especially for her by George Abbott, Betty Comden and Adolph Green—that of Mitzi Green's sidekick in the musical *Billion Dollar Baby*. She was featured with Bert Lahr and Jean Parker in the Broadway revival of *Burlesque* and caused something of an international furor when she appeared as "Britannia," the famous nude, in Sir Laurence Olivier's New York production of John Osborne's play *The Entertainer*.

Television audiences have seen her on *Playhouse 90* productions, *The United States Steel Hour*, Phil Silvers' *Sergeant Bilko* series, *Nightbeat* and many, many others.

The owner of even more voices than faces, she has played—like Belle Poitrine herself—Cleopatra, a mother superior, a juvenile delinquent, a night club singer and dozens of other roles (including male ones) on such beloved old radio thrillers as *Gangbusters, Counterspy, Top Secret Files, Treasury Agent* and others and was last heard—but, needless to say, not seen—as the dulcet voice of an angel food cake on a television commercial touting a margarine.

She has been the same size—39-25-35—since reaching the age of twelve (some of the costumes which she designed and made at that tender age appear in the pages of *Little Me*), so that her career as a model has been long and profitable with no end in view. She has modeled everything from bikinis to ballgowns for painters, photographers, the mass market manufacturers and the exclusive one-of-a-kind collections. As a cover girl she has run the gamut of magazines from frosty sirens gazing disdainfully from high-fashion journals to the folksy housewife on the front of the *Saturday Evening Post*. In addition she has taught modeling, cast and directed the shooting of pictures for magazines and catalogues and performed in seven of the annual Society of Illustrators' Shows. She has also designed dresses and hats for some of New York's biggest garment manufacturers as well as for some of its most awe-inspiring custom shops.

Undoubtedly born with squirrel blood in her veins, she has never knowingly thrown away a stitch of clothing and is the harassed owner of a wardrobe—bursting closets, bulging trunks, bags of fur and feathers, oil drums overflowing with hats—of twentieth-century clothes rivalled only by the costume collections of the Metropolitan Museum of Art, the Brooklyn Museum and the late Collyer brothers (who are now out of the running and don't really count). Nearly half the coats, suits, hats, dresses, movie and stage costumes worn by Belle Poitrine in this book have sprung full-blown from the Archer Archives of Outlandish Outfits.

ACKNOWLEDGMENTS

The author and the photographer would like to thank a great many people for a great many things.

For the generous loan of old clothes, new clothes, hats, props, jewels and furs, our gratitude goes to Mrs. E. P. Adam, Miss Kaye Ballard, Mr. Kurt Bieber, Mr. A. L. Brandon, Dr. and Mrs. William G. Cahan, Miss Peggy Cass, Mr. and Mrs. Francis Dobo, Mr. Robert Fryer, the Generosity Thrift Shop, Miss Dody Goodman, Carol Irwin Hollister, Mr. Sterling Jensen, the Manhattan Hardware, Miss Alice Pearce, Mr. Walter Pistole, Miss Rosalind Russell, Mr. Martin Scheider, Mrs. Curtis Walsh and Miss Vivian Weaver. And our special thanks go to Mr. Robert Riley and the staff of the Design Laboratory of the Brooklyn Museum, who offered not only their valuable time and advice, but who turned over their priceless collection of authentic period costumes to this frivolous venture.

For wigs, beards and hair styles we are indebted to Mr. Wally Mohr and to Ryan-Davis Hair Culture.

We would also like to thank the luckless owners of many splendid houses, apartments and studios—Mr. Alexander Bender, Mr. Hervey Jolin, Mr. and Mrs. Floyd Jefferson, Mr. Franklin H. Kissner, the New York City Center, Mr. Shaun O'Brien, the Plaza Hotel, Mr. Carl Reynolds, Mrs. Edward Tanner, Voisin Restaurant, and Mr. H. D. Vursell—who stood by with grim smiles while their furniture was scratched, their carpets soiled and their fuses blown. Typographical pyrotechnics were seen to by the horrified Dorris Huth.

And most of all we would like to thank our cast of 100, most of them busy actors and dancers who missed meals and sleep, dashed across town in full war paint between matinee and evening performances and even sacrificed that time most sacred to the members of Equity—Sunday morning—just for the fun of appearing in this book. We love you all.

Printed in the United States
by Baker & Taylor Publisher Services